THORSON'S BAY

4

THORSON'S BAY

Elmer T. Adrian

VANTAGE PRESS
New York

This is a work of fiction. Any similarity between
the characters appearing herein and any real persons,
living or dead, is purely coincidental.

FIRST EDITION

Copyright © 2001 by Elmer T. Adrian

Published by Vantage Press, Inc.
516 West 34th Street, New York, New York 10001

Manufactured in the United States of America
ISBN: 0-533-13559-1

Library of Congress Catalog Card No.: 00-91326

0 9 8 7 6 5 4 3 2 1

THORSON'S BAY

1

The Shoot

Zeb Hawkins held both hands high as the din of many voices simmered and gradually ceased, like a teakettle when taken from the stove. In the ensuing silence, Matt Berglund listened to the slapping of waves against the other side of a long narrow point that formed Thorson's Bay.

Boats and canoes lined the water's edge on the village side of the bay. The few houses clustered close to the general store. From where he sat on the warehouse wharf, Matt could see the smoke of the wood-burner that would soon come roaring down the track close by. The warehouse also served as the town meeting hall and community center, and tonight there would be a dance on its rough-hewn board floor.

From all around the bay area, the assorted boats and canoes brought settlers, Indians, and lumbermen who would be the participants and audience for this event. Emerging from this crowd was Zeb Hawkins, the local handyman, who served as general referee.

Matt had known Zeb for as long as he could remember. There wasn't a home in the area that didn't welcome Zeb into their family circle. Even today, the tots edged into his path to get a quick squeeze and one of the big smiles that spread across his ample black face.

Matt noticed Zeb as he looked down the line of contestants for the swim competition. One of the ten was female, an Indian girl dressed in a loose fitting swim garment that covered her from neck to ankles. The men wore chopped-off dungarees, except for Matt, who sported the suit from his swimming team days at seminary. Matt wondered why a petite young woman would dare to compete with all these men who were rough and well-muscled from the physical rigors of outdoor life.

"Swim to the raft and return to the wharf," Zeb briefed the swimmers, indicating the raft approximately a hundred yards out in the bay. "May the best man..." Zeb looked at the Indian girl, "er, the best swimmer win. On your mark! Get set! Go!"

Matt hit the water with all the forward lateral thrust he could muster. He swam powerfully, the result of hours and hours of practice. He held the lead, but as he turned at the raft another swimmer turned a split second later. It was the Indian girl. Matt tried to increase his speed but lost his rhythm. In doing so, he could see she was pulling even with him, so he settled down and concentrated on getting the most out of every stroke. A hundred feet from the wharf, Matt gave it all he had. He knew he had never swum faster. Barreling into the wharf, he looked up at Zeb confidently. He must have won, but Zeb looked at Matt then down the line at the Indian girl.

"It's a tie!" Zeb declared.

Matt climbed onto the wharf and ran over to help his cowinner out of the water. Just then, a boat, making erratic headway too close to the wharf, swung into what was surely a collision course with the girl. Taking in the situation with a gasp, Matt lunged the last few feet toward her and, with no time for finesse, in a single down-sweeping motion, grabbed her under the arms and swung her up, out of the water. Almost simultaneously, the boat crashed against the wharf. As stunned as the onlookers, the rower picked himself up from the bottom of the boat and pushed away, without even stopping to assess possible damage or to make an apology.

"You can put me down now," Matt's captive demanded. Still somewhat stupefied by the swift succession of events, Matt stared at her. She was much lighter skinned than he had noticed at first. Even with her hair pulled tightly back and plastered to her head by water, she was quite pretty. "You can put me down now, thank you," she repeated, smiling at Matt. He realized with some surprise that he was still holding her, her feet dangling above the wharf.

"Oh, excuse me." Matt colored slightly. "Guess I was just enjoying the view. You're some swimmer! If you didn't have to wear all those trappings, you'd have really beaten me. Anyway, congratulations!"

The crowd was rapidly closing in around them. The Indian girl looked with some apprehension at them and then turned back to Matt.

"I do thank you, but I'm getting out of here." Matt watched her lithe springy stride as she went over to a group of her people.

"What happened?" a voice boomed above the others.

"Oh, nothing really. It's all over," Matt answered, but he wasn't so sure that was the truth.

This gala occasion, still called, "the shoot," was an annual event. At first, men from all over the bay area gathered to test their marksmanship. Through the years, other skills had been added to the competition. Now there were ten contests anyone could enter with the payment of a dollar entrance fee.

Matt couldn't remember when Mike Doran hadn't been the all-events champ, but this year, Mike found the going rougher. He was being challenged by young Jim Beaver, an Indian who worked as a tree topper in one of Doran's lumber crews. Jim, at six feet eight, was straight-standing and beautifully muscled. Matt, only an inch shorter, was broader and heavier, but he still provided the others with stiff competition.

When Jim barely nosed out Matt in the foot race, the two young behemoths responded in mutual admiration and became friends immediately. Little did they realize that it was to become one of the most fulfilling, yet one of the most painful, relationships either had known.

The tree climb was a favorite of the spectators. A bell was hung near the top of a pine tree, some hundred fifty feet above the ground, and whoever rang it in the shortest time was the winner. Many hopefuls rang the bell this year, men who spent their days among the big pines, but Doran sprinted up that tree fifteen seconds faster than his closest rival. Well over six feet and broad shouldered, he moved his big frame with catlike quickness. One look at his powerful arms and the expanse of his chest erased any doubt why he had been the champion. Red hair curled in ringlets at the back of his large neck, the vibrant color speaking well of the vitality of Mike Doran, even at forty. Along with the tree climb, Mike had won the shoot and the logrolling and had placed well enough in the other events to pick up points.

Besides the foot race, in which he had edged out Matt, Jim Beaver claimed top honors in the ax throw and archery events. Matt finished first in the canoe race and had full credit as co-winner of the swim. Matt and Jim had accumulated points in other events, and now Matt was about to try his luck at wood chopping. As he slid his hands up and down the ax handle waiting for the event to get underway, he felt a little foolish thinking he could beat Doran. Mike had always won this one, but Matt had spent much time clearing the land and cutting firewood. The big ax in his hands was a familiar tool, honed to a fine edge with his father's advice. Thinking of the long rows of firewood stacked beside their house, Mr. Berglund's eyes met Matt's, and he gave him a grin of encouragement.

This event had been narrowed to three finalists, Matt, Mike, and another lumberman. At Zeb's signal, each man brought his ax down into the log before him. As the chips began to fly, the lumbermen shouted encouragement to their favorites. Matt's cheering section was smaller and more subdued because of their conviction that no one could beat Doran. That is, with the exception of pretty Maude Thorson. Maude was jumping up and down, her clenched fist keeping time in cheerleader fashion as she yelled, "Come on, Matt! Come on, Matt!"

Matt was doing well. In fact, he was almost through his log. Beads of sweat covered his forehead as he bore down harder and harder, expecting the familiar victory yell from Mike's corner. As if choreographed, the three men's final swing hit the centers of their respective logs. The logs separated and fell apart, three arms went up and the roar of the crowd escalated. Matt's supporters went wild as the decision went to him, based on split-second timing.

Zeb Hawkins picked up the tally sheets from the judges and raised his hand for silence.

"Ladies and gentlemen, we have a three-way tie for the events so far. Berglund, Beaver, and Doran each have fifteen points. The winner of the last event will break the tie and become the grand champion."

Matt knew what the next event was. Directly in front of the onlookers was a ring sixteen feet in diameter. Posts were imbedded in the ground at intervals with a strong log-railing on top of the posts four and a half feet above the ground. The object of the contest was to eliminate the opponent by throwing him outside the circle, either over or under the railing. Matt felt a wave of discouragement tighten his muscles. Who could beat Doran? Some even called this "Doran's arena."

By the call of a coin, Jim and Mike were first in the circle. Matt's heart pounded as he watched the other two contestants. As Jim held out his hand, probing for a hold, Mike caught it, closed in, grabbed him around the waist and lifted him off his feet. Before Jim knew what was happening, Mike had dumped him over the railing. There was pandemonium in the lumbermen's section. The men's morale had been boosted by a few bottles of whiskey, and there was no containing their boisterous appreciation of their champ. Mike looked toward his crew and pumped his fist in acceptance of their spirited approval.

Matt felt anything but confident as he vaulted into the ring. Again, Zeb gave the signal, and the two giants moved toward each other. Matt was suddenly cool. He knew his only hope was to try to stay away from Mike and look for an advantage. Mike was eager to close in. Matt found the quick-moving Irishman hard to elude. Twice Mike almost had him in his grasp, but he wrenched away and escaped. This brought signs of impatience from Mike, and Matt could hear his own backers yelling for more contact.

"Come on, Matt! Go get him, Matt!" they yelled.

Mike finally stopped in the center of the ring and grinned at Matt.

"We don't seem to be getting anywhere."

Matt took a step forward, and Mike lunged. Matt veered aside just as Mike grabbed for him, leaving Mike down on his hands and knees almost outside the railing. Roaring as he got up, the angered, frustrated Mike came at Matt with his arms wide apart. Bent low, young Matt rammed his shoulder into Mike, hip high, then came up fast. Mike was catapulted over the railing, bellowing as he sailed through the air. He hit the earth heavily, ten feet beyond the ring, and lay there pounding the ground in disbelief.

Prizes were awarded on the basis of one dollar a point, and Matt made several trips to the judges stand to receive his winnings. Between trips, he sat with Maude Thorson, who smiled proudly at him each time he looked at her. There was no doubt that he enjoyed the thrill of victory and the adulation of this beautiful woman.

"You and your pa are eating supper with us tonight," she informed Matt. "It's been arranged."

"I'll be awfully hungry. Your mother will be sorry, because I haven't eaten much all day."

Matt remembered the first time Maude had extended an invitation to supper. It was at the graveyard, when his mother was buried. He was seven. It seemed that from then on, he and his dad had been involved in most of her family's activities. Matt had carried her books as they walked home from school together. Theirs had been a comfortable, friendly relationship. Still, he wasn't unaware of the affection and admiration they felt for each other, and he had an idea that they would always be together, though he wasn't in a hurry to change things right now. The future looked good to him, but misty and vague.

Just then, Matt and Star White Otter, the Indian girl, were called to receive their joint prize for the swimming event. She now wore a simple store-bought dress. Matt again congratulated her. This time she looked at him squarely and smiled with open friendliness. His casual interest perked up, and he found himself staring into lovely brown eyes that stunned and held him as though he were in a vise. Her hair was hanging loosely now in thick soft waves that outlined her oval face.

"Good-bye," she stated firmly enough to break the awkward spell between them. His eyes followed her as she walked back to her family and friends. He felt shock waves of attraction that might not be entirely one-sided. Matt was still a little shaken when he returned to Maude, and she was well aware of this.

"Just who is she?" Matt asked.

"Chief White Otter's daughter. She's quite a lady," answered Maude. "I'll tell you what I know about her."

5

Their eyes met. Matt saw a pretty young woman saying in unspoken words that she was his girl. He did like Maude a lot. He squeezed her hand but dropped it hastily. In the back of his mind, he wondered if this was a case of a bird-in-the-hand.

"Some other time, maybe."

There was a special ceremony to honor the All-Events champion. Zeb recounted what transpired during the day, then turned to Matt.

"Ladies and gentlemen," Zeb's voice boomed ceremoniously, "I present to you our new grand champion, Matt Berglund."

Loud cheering came from all but the lumbermen. Mike bounded out of his group and grabbed Matt's hand.

"I'll see you next year."

His voice contained no sign of resentment. This was a cue for the lumbermen's section to join in a deafening roar of applause. Matt's admiration for the tough gladiator grew.

Maude's dad, the storekeeper, had shipped in a crate of lemons, and free lemonade was appreciated by all, with the exception of those who were imbibing stronger potions. The woodburner gave rides up the track for a couple of miles, then returned by backing down. The railroad company had donated the engine and one flatcar lined with benches and a railing around it for safety.

"Finish your drink," Matt nudged Maude. "We're going for a ride."

They sat on a bench in the rear of the flatcar. A short toot, a belch of smoke, and they were on their way through pine and swampy areas. The engine stopped on a bridge that extended over a small bayou, where the engineer lowered a hose into the water and began pumping water into the tanks for the boiler. Everyone seemed fascinated by this procedure. The children particularly were entranced when the firebox door was opened and short logs were thrown into the blazing interior. Flames leaped out and sparks flew high into the air. An occasional breeze carried the acrid smoke back over the passengers, but the attitude of celebration overcame any momentary unpleasantness.

As they continued over an uneven stretch of track, the flatcar lurched, throwing Maude onto Matt's Lap. Maude looked up more in enjoyment than surprise at their close contact, and Matt impulsively kissed her upturned mouth. He felt a heady quickening of his pulse and let his lips linger on hers until she drew away slowly and soberly. Forcing a lightness she didn't feel into her voice, she laughed.

"My goodness! You are hungry."

Matt grinned.

"Would you believe it if I told you I had forgotten about food for the moment?"

2

The Dance

Maude stepped out of the tub and reached for the towel. She hurried to her bedroom, still toweling. The euphoria of Matt's first kiss was still with her.

She had met him at the train when he came home from seminary. Then he had picked her up so that her eyes were even with his and looked at her as though he wanted to swallow her. The hug had been warm and extended, but somehow it seemed to be just part of the manifestation of their high spirits, generated by his homecoming. Nevertheless, today he had kissed her!

She stopped in front of the mirror and surveyed herself from head to toe. The swimsuit Matt wore earlier that day revealed his muscular perfection. As she studied her own body, she wondered if her proportions would be pleasing to him. Her parents had sent her to an all girls' college, where, along with the regular curriculum, she had learned some of the social graces. She excelled in dance routines in her physical education class, was winner in a beauty pageant, and enjoyed the other attentions that her physical attributes afforded. Now she looked at the reflection of her firm, pointed breasts, flat slim waist, curving hip lines and long, lithe, tapered legs less from vanity than a deep concern that Matt would be as attracted to her as she was to him. Shaking out the long blond hair, still damp around her shoulders, she stared back at the mirrored image with wide-set blue eyes and a smile of hopefulness mingled with confidence.

It's purely conjecture, but in some experimental cells of God's choosing, perhaps He does some selective nudging to bring out an improved variety of the human species. Thorson's Bay seemed to be an Eden, a test plot, if you will, free of the corruptive influences to which similar communities had been subjected. Here the blend of strong, highly motivated parents produced offspring of nearly perfect bodies and minds. Maude Thorson and Matt Berglund were surely two of the choicest beings raised in that community.

Maude had been nurtured with love and example that resulted in more than perfection of features and proportions. A sweet and sensitive nature, along with the drive to express those characteristics, was evidenced in her caring for the sick, sitting with the children of the surrounding area, listening to troubles with a sympathetic ear, and, with her dad's sanction, providing food for those with empty larders. When she helped her father in the store, Mr. Thorson was aware that people often came by just to absorb some of Maude's sunshine.

Matt had also been raised in the positive atmosphere of Thorson's Bay. His physical proportions would have made him a standout in any group. As a seminary student, teachers had credited him with an unusual sharpness of mind, stability of character, and an approach to life that was unspoiled and unfettered by bias and prejudice. To his frontier friends, he was a man's man. To Maude, he was her man.

Maude wasn't so naive that she was unaware of the advantages of being attractive. By contrast, June, her roommate and close friend at college, was ignored by men because of her plainness. Sometimes young men from a neighboring school were invited in for a dance. Seeking to rescue her roommate from the wallflower role, Maude asked one of her partners to dance with June.

"I will if you put a sack over her head," he had laughed. Hurt by the young man's rudeness and feeling defensive of her friend, Maude refused him the next time he asked her to dance. When he appeared crestfallen, she wondered if she had done the right thing. After all, it is natural for both sexes to be attracted to handsome people.

Although she participated in the social activities, she dated no one at college. She loved Matt, and although glad to be attractive to the opposite sex, Matt was her world. She hoped and prayed that world would never crumble.

She took from the closet the dress that she would wear to the dance that night, a filmy blue organza her mother had helped her make. As she looked in the mirror, approval and sudden emotion overwhelmed her.

"Oh, Mom! I hope Matt likes it!"

Her mother smiled, then hugged her quickly before Maude could notice the moisture in her eyes.

"If that doesn't melt him, nothing will."

"l love him so much," Maude said, suddenly serious. "I guess I always thought we'd go through life together, but now I'm not sure he loves me that way. I know we're good friends, but that's no longer enough for me."

"Somehow you're going to have to gently let him know that. That dress should shake him up a bit," replied her mother.

Kitchen work was yet to be done, so Maude laid her new dress on the bed and slipped an everyday dress over her undergarments. Everything must be in perfect order for the dinner.

To Matt, the dinner was a complete success. He felt at home with the Thorsons. Maude's mother was a good cook. The corn on the cob was at its peak of tenderness, and the rooster that had crowed that morning was now supine and tasty-looking on the platter. The giblet gravy and the new potatoes received his special attention. Young green peas couldn't be ignored either. He was hungry from the natural appetite of youth and good health, as well as the added stimulus from the day's physical exertion. He was expected to ask for seconds, at least, and he did his part flawlessly. As he was feeling the need to decline further helpings, Maude's mother spoke up.

"Maude, it's time for that pie you made for Matt."

"Oh, Mom! I wasn't going to tell him I made it," Maude protested. Her heightened color as her eyes met Matt's stirred a warm feeling inside him, and he surveyed both the thick chocolate pie topped with equally thick meringue and the girl serving it with equal pleasure.

Despite the earlier onslaught of food, Matt found room for pie. Chocolate was his favorite, and this was pie at its best. Scarcely had he finished his last bite when Maude came back from the kitchen with another piece. As she leaned over his shoulder to put the plate before him, her face was close to his. He had a sudden urge to kiss her again, but now everyone was watching, so he turned his attention back to the pie.

Later, Matt's dad looked out the window at the western sky. The setting sun was partly hidden by clouds.

"Matt! You'll want to bring your canoe up onto the shore and tie it down. I've a hunch we're in for some foul weather tonight. You might suggest the others do the same."

While Matt followed his father's suggestion, Maude changed into her party dress. She met him at the door and what he saw gave him a titillating shock. In honest admiration, he noted the lowered neckline, which emphasized the rounded fullness beneath. His eyes followed the contours of her dress right down to her slim ankles and back up to her searching eyes of a deep blue that matched the intensity of the fabric's color. Suddenly, Matt saw Maude as a woman, a formidable adversary making a direct assault on his intentions. He thrilled at the challenge, feeling the natural reluctance of the male animal to submit to full captivity, yet knowing his escape routes were diminishing as he devoured Maude's loveliness.

"Wow! I hope I still have the honor of escorting the prettiest lady in these parts to the dance." Laughing together, the pair started down the road toward the warehouse, the eyes of approving parents following them.

Noise in bedlam proportions greeted Matt and Maude as they entered the warehouse. Children were in abundance, since their parents wanted to watch or participate in the night's festivities. Popcorn and candy were provided for the young and the not so young. Mothers sat on the benches along the sides and leaned against the hewn log tables. Older men clustered in conversation groups, while the young bucks with puberty just behind them eyed the females for partners for the first dance. Zeb Hawkins had been drafted, as usual, to furnish the music.

Perhaps it was this divine nudging that brought Zeb to Thorson's Bay, to add his virulence and strength of character in unique ways to this test plot of exceptional persons. Zeb was a large, muscular African, and his aura of friendship drew young and old like a magnet. Matt had known Zeb since childhood. In his own mind, Zeb hadn't changed over the years, although he was sure that he must be about the same age as his dad. Zeb was the community handyman, available for emergencies of various kinds all around the bay, day or night. More than that, some of the pieces of furniture he had made were works of art, and he could handle ax and saw as well as any lumberman. His yeoman work habits and consistent cheerfulness were contagious.

As the adults admired and respected Zeb, the children adored him. They loved the stories he pantomimed. Zeb had a special name for Matt. As a toddler, Matt would climb on Zeb's lap to give him a big bear hug. Zeb never stopped calling him "Cub." Matt would have felt denied now if he used any other name. "Hi, Cub," Zeb's hearty voice would call out, and they both knew the hug was implied. If Adam Berglund wondered where his son was, he had only to look for Zeb. Out of this mutually fulfilling relationship, Matt tried by osmosis to pattern his own outlook on life after the big black man's.

Newcomers to the area soon learned of Zeb's prodigious strength and wondered why he didn't enter the shoot as a contestant. It just wouldn't have seemed right though, not to have Zeb in charge of the event. He enjoyed the role of general referee and gave no indication of any desire to compete. Indeed, if there was the slightest dissatisfaction on Zeb's part about his place in the community, no one was aware of it, least of all Zeb himself.

11

3

The Storm

Little was known about Zeb Hawkins's life previous to his arrival in Thorson's Bay, except that he came from the South with Mr. Jackson about the time the war between the states broke out. Sam Jackson bought a house on the bay, enlarged it, and furnished it well. He lived a quiet life in the north woods community, largely because of his poor health. It was rumored that Jackson had freed his slaves and brought Zeb with him, not in a master-servant relationship, but as a friend and companion. The young black man took care of him until he died during the second winter there, leaving the house and his ample holdings to Zeb. Zeb's wants were simple, and he never touched the money, earning enough for his needs by being that extra hand almost everyone needed at times.

Due to Sam Jackson's influence, a side of Zeb as musician and scholar emerged. The bay citizens admired his skills in these areas as much as his physical proficiency. Zeb played the violin well, playing classical, ballad, or popular tunes. Tonight he would play popular music unless there were special requests for Mozart during the intermission. In spite of the apparent simplicity of the people, such requests were not uncommon. Zeb opened the evening's festivities with a lively polka on his accordion.

Immediately, the floor filled with energetic, though not sophisticated, swinging, swaying, and boot stomping. Matt and Maude joined the merriment. Maude was easy to dance with, and Matt knew he was no match for her capabilities. Zeb laid the accordion aside and stroked his violin for the next dance, a quadrille. Mike Doran was ready for this dance, looking fresh and clean shaven and showing no trace of ill-will over his defeat earlier in the day. He danced well, and the ladies loved dancing with him because he made them look even better than they were. Mike moved his big frame with unusual smoothness, his great strength controlled as he indicated the next step to his partners with gentle but subtle pressure.

During a tag dance, Mike tapped Matt's shoulder and floated away with Maude. Gradually the other dancers moved aside to watch this couple, and Zeb switched to a waltz. Maude and Mike responded with the poetry of long, sweeping strides and hesitations. They separated, danced side by side, until Maude turned in to make a circling-backward bend as Mike held her waist. They whirled all around the open area of the dance floor, the flare of Maude's dress skimming the bystanders and giving a provocative glimpse of her underpinnings. Matt watched with a sort of possessive pride. The dance ended, and the big lumberman brought Maude back to where Matt was waiting. Mike was smiling as he placed Maude's hand in Matt's, but there was a strange look in his eyes.

"I hope you know how lucky you are," he said, and turned and walked away quickly.

"Oh, that was fun!" Maude said a bit breathlessly. "He didn't learn to dance like that cutting trees. I'll bet he could tell some stories."

A great clap of thunder overrode the other noises. Then, as if announced by the thunder, the wind roared its presence, increasing in intensity until it shook the building. Surprised into silence, the crowd stood as if frozen in place. Even the children stopped their play, anxiety paling their small faces.

Doran's voice boomed out in the temporary hush, "Everyone over against the wall. You men get the tables over here and get the women and children under them." Mothers grabbed their children and herded them toward the wall. In wordless haste, the men moved the heavy log tables to one side and crouched under them with their families.

Impelled by the savage wind that buffeted the frame building, the whole shift of activity was achieved in a few moments. Two or three men blew out the kerosene lamps to avoid possible fire if they overturned in the scramble. Here and there a child whimpered in fear. Low voices of parents were thin in their own panic. The north woods had known storms in season, but something more sensed than known from external signs warned that this one was going to be especially severe.

Through the small windows, sharp flashes of lightning showed the grotesque gyrations of tree limbs.

As yet, the rain was minimal, but the wind seemed to keep accelerating, tearing at the sides of the warehouse with maniacal force, as if trying to penetrate the weathered slab boards to get at the huddled humans inside. Eyes, half-blinded by darkness interspersed with the cruel strokes of lightning, could make out the heaving of the roof. The adults crouched still lower, shielding children with their own bodies.

Simultaneous with a blinding flash close at hand came the splintering of a tree. As it fell, it scraped the west end of the building, like a

13

giant hand clawing and grasping for help. In that same flash, Matt saw a small child toddling toward the center of the room. Disengaging himself from Maude, Matt lunged in the direction the child had taken. Just as he grabbed Susie Dahl, he saw a shadow of someone else also reaching for the child. Bent protectively over Susie as he headed back toward the wall, he felt the rush of the wind as the roof tore open above him. Through the almost deafening crash of rafters, he heard Mrs. Dahl's anguished, "Oh, God!" Then a piece of timber bounced off his back, causing him to stumble and nearly throw the screaming child into the arms of her hysterical mother.

Like a tired beast, the wind subsided, but the rain came in torrents. Part of the roof had fallen at an angle against the wall and beckoned them to take advantage of its shelter. After checking to determine the soundness of its position, most of the group, who had assembled in such high spirits, were now subdued by the force of the elements. They began making their way to the partial covering. Matt thought suddenly of the shadow who had gone after Susie.

"How about a roll call to make sure everybody's safe?" he suggested.

Over the pounding of the rain, the families checked on each other calling out in triumph.

"Nelsons all here!"

"Sandbergs okay!" The rest of the families called out in a similar manner.

Everyone was accounted for but Mike Doran. Using the lightning flashes that continued every few seconds, Matt made his way to the fallen roof section. As he ran his hands lightly over the soaked shingles, cold rainwater ran down his arms and inside his shirt sleeves. Suddenly his knee struck an object. It was a man's boot. He sucked in his breath with a mixture of foreboding and hope and felt the leg, stiff and still, pinned under the fallen timbers.

As if on signal, Zeb was at Matt's side, and the two men worked without speaking to lift away the heavy beam and pull Mike free. Someone lit one of the lamps, never questioning the providence that had kept its wick dry enough to produce a wavering bit of light. The lamp was held close as Zeb put his ear to Doran's chest.

"He's alive," Zeb pronounced. His hand on Mike's came away with smears of Irish blood. Underneath the thick mop of hair was an egg-sized bump. Freed from the restriction of the beam, Mike's breath began to come in irregular gasps. As it became stronger, the tension in the room eased, but the big man's form still lay unmoving on the damp floor.

14

"Bring him to our house," Maude offered. "We'll take care of him until we can get a doctor here." It was common knowledge that it would take a couple of days to get one.

Just then, Mike groaned and flexed his fingers without opening his eyes. He lifted one leg experimentally, grimaced, and sat up. Turning to grin at Maude, he staggered to his feet.

"Sorry to refuse your hospitality, ma'am, but I've got plans of my own." As he stood, the lamplight made his shadow firm and dark against the rain-streaked wall. "I've been hit harder than this with a peavey. Now that we don't need a hospital, how about those of you who live close taking your kids to get them bedded down for the night, assuming you still have homes."

The rain had slackened to a light drizzle, and the rest of the group emerged from their temporary shelter. Small children clung to their parents, apprehension still heavy around them. At Mike's words, most of the other children moved toward Zeb.

"Aw, come on," he grinned, "I can't handle all of you."

4

Doran

Most of the lumbermen, including Doran, used what was left of the warehouse for their sleeping quarters that night. Mike awakened to the clamor of his companions with a throbbing in his head. Stepping into his boots, which was all that he had removed for sleeping, he heard the toot of the logging train coming north. The men scrambled out into the sunshine that belied the storm of the previous night, and the train slowed for them to board the empty flatcars. There would be no breakfast that morning. When they arrived at the logging area, it would be time to start the working day, and the most that could be hoped for was a cup of black coffee, swallowed so fast it burned the throat.

Except for a few muttered complaints, it was a subdued group. Some had headaches from their imbibing during the events of the shoot. Mike's head cleared somewhat out in the open air, and his thoughts went back to the day before, particularly to Star. He had secretly rooted for her in the swim. She had tied that young blond fellow who had later outmaneuvered him. Mike felt no rancor by his own defeat; indeed, there had been only friendliness and mutual admiration between them as he shook hands with Matt, but Star had center stage in his mind.

Star was now the same age her mother had been when Mike first saw and fell in love with her. While not a carbon copy of her mother, Marie, she was as beautiful. Mike had run away from his third year law school to try to sort out his future, leaving behind a promising niche in his father's law firm. The skills he had learned while on the boxing, rifle, and rowing teams at college served him in good stead in his life as a frontier lumberman. He met Marie when he competed in the shoot as he claimed the championship the first time in an unbroken series of victories. Marie, as the chosen queen of that event, pinned the medal on him. The result was a lightning-like cataclysm. From that moment, the vibrancy of their beings reached out to each other—Mike Doran, the scholar turned adventurer, who found excitement and fulfillment

16

in the rugged outdoor life, and Marie, half Indian and half white, whose life was involved with both the conflict and compromise of the two cultures.

When LeBlanc, Marie's fur trader father, became aware of the girl's interest in Mike, he forbade them to see each other. Doran immediately went to LeBlanc and asked permission to marry Marie. While LeBlanc was sympathetic to the young couple's feelings, he was adamant that a promise long ago must be kept. Marie had been promised to Chief White Otter.

LeBlanc's promise, which was to prove so fateful to Marie and Mike, had been made partly because White Otter had saved his life during a blizzard when he had been frozen beyond his ability to struggle on. Also, very practically, such a marriage would cement LeBlanc's relationship with the tribe and keep the fur trade coming his way. It was a blend of a matter of honor and the more tangible effect on LeBlanc's income that held LeBlanc firm on his word.

"I can't go back on my promise," he told Doran. "You must leave. It wouldn't be fair to Marie or you, and it wouldn't be wise for you to stay here."

The days were bleak with the cold barrenness of winter. Dreams Mike and Marie had built together crumbled around him, closing out the freedom of spirit he had found in these north woods. Eventually, he returned to his parent's home, where he was welcomed as a prodigal son, but the hurt of losing Marie shadowed all his days and nights. Waking and sleeping, the bitter sweetness of their last hours together filled his mind and made concentration on the task at hand impossible. At the first call for volunteers, Doran enlisted to fight against the South. Despite his daring, which at times was almost suicidal, he came through battle after battle unscathed.

He had been in combat for more than a year, when a letter from Marie caught up with him.

My dearest,

I have thought about it for a long time and finally decided you would want to know. Our baby has arrived. Yes, our baby, yours and mine! Her name is Star. She has dark brown hair, but sometimes I can detect a reddish tint. Everyone thinks she is the result of my marriage to White Otter, but I know and you know she's yours, and because of that I'm almost happy. White Otter is good to me and not too demanding, and I try to be a good wife to him.

But, oh, Mike, although it has to be from a distance, I want you to love your daughter and know she is the fulfillment of our love for each other that can never be blotted out. Please know I wouldn't have missed

those short days we had together for all the eternities there are. Do not write to me.
 I am forever yours,
 Marie

Doran kept the letter, badly worn now from folding and refolding as he reread it. After the war, he returned to the general vicinity north of Thorson's Bay, wanting to feel some closeness to Marie and to the daughter he dared not claim. The lumber camp where he worked was farther north. When one of the Indians on his crew died, Mike attended the funeral at the Mission. As Father O'Brien talked, Doran saw Marie a few rows away with a little girl, fairer skinned than her mother. His gaze was fastened on them, when Marie turned just enough to meet his eyes. In that second, he knew that neither time nor distance had changed anything between them. Marie's color rose slightly, noticeable to a close observer, even with her lovely, olive-toned skin. Bending over her daughter to conceal her confusion, she patted the little girl's hair, and Star's winsome face turned toward her mother.

Although he had never talked with either of them, it was the sporadic opportunities to see Marie and Star that kept him going. Through bits of local conversation, he knew that Star was especially bright and gifted. As he watched the girl grow, his love both for her and for her mother increased until there were times he felt it must burst his chest.

In the rough simplicity of logging life, there were many opportunities for transient alliances with the women that followed the camps or inhabited the villages, but always before him was the image of Marie and, now, of Star. In his refraining from some of the pastimes of his fellow workers, Doran gained a reputation for aloofness. This added to the strength of his position as production boss of the Monarch lumber operations. He was a strict disciplinarian, demanding and receiving maximum results from his crews, respected because of his fairness and as a man to be trusted in time of trouble.

When Star was fifteen, Doran opened a bank account in the city. Money could be drawn from it only by Father O'Brien, whom he had taken into his confidence. No one else was to know the source of the money that was to provide Star's further education. He was filled with pride and joy to learn that Star had attended a prestigious school in the East, graduated with honors, and had chosen to return to teach at Father O'Brien's Mission school.

Just once he had spoken to Star. Jim Beaver, one of the foremen, had invited Star to come with him to see the lumbering operations. When Jim was called aside to care for a company problem, Doran saw

Star wandering the woods by herself, discovering wild flowers and wading in a little stream that flowed nearby. Doran followed her every movement, fighting the desire to identify himself.

Suddenly, Mike realized he wasn't the only one who was watching the girl. Rube Finney, one of the workman, who boasted about his prowess with women, came out of the trees and grabbed her roughly around the waist. Caught off guard, but struggling instinctively, Star bit his hand, rammed her knee into his groin, and broke loose. Finney, in shocked pain, hesitated a moment and then ran after her. Doran felt admiration for his daughter's response to Finney, but with a rage that cut his own reaction time in half, he overtook Finney, grabbed him, raised him over his head and flung him against a tree stump. Finney slumped to the ground. In that moment, Doran didn't care whether Finney was alive or dead; his concern was for Star.

"Are you all right?" he asked her anxiously. She nodded and, as soon as she could catch her breath, began thanking Doran for coming to her rescue. Doran could not trust himself to be silent any longer. He turned on his heel and strode toward the work crews, watching to see that Finney had preceded him.

When the heat of the moment had passed, Doran reflected that this was the first time he had known of Jim Beaver's special interest in Star. Well, she could do a lot worse. Jim was a good lumberman, loved the woods, and had a natural respect for living things, which was part of his upbringing. Besides, he was an admirable specimen of manhood, as good for Star as anyone he knew.

As the train reached the lumbering area, Mike's thoughts shifted back to the reality of the present. He hopped off the flatcar.

"Okay, men, let's get with it."

5

Eva

The logging train slowed, and Adam Berglund, Matt's father, stepped off one of the empty flatcars as they neared two log structures close by the tracks. This was one of his fishing stations. Fish were cleaned as they were caught, boxed in ice, and shipped to the city the same day on the returning afternoon log train. The fishing station was also the home of Ed Swedberg, his wife Aly, daughter Gretchen, and son Karl. Ed and Karl were on the lake now, emptying and replacing fish traps.

"Hello, Mr. Berglund," Gretchen called out.

"Hi, Gretchen." Then as her mother appeared at the door, "Aly, do you need anything from the store when I come back in a few days?"

"Here's a list," Aly pulled a scrap of paper from her apron pocket. "Sure hope they have the raisins this time."

"We'll give it another try." Adam pocketed the list and went over to check the supply in the ice house. Satisfied that there was enough ice to last the rest of the season, he closed the heavy wooden door, locking in the cold vapors that rose from the big blocks of ice cut from the frozen lake during the past winter.

Two milking goats nibbled on lush grass and underbrush in a small enclosure behind the ice house. *Goat's milk is what keeps the Swedbergs healthy,* thought Adam, as he headed toward the lake.

Across the lake were the Youngbears, an Indian family who ran a line of fish traps for him and brought their catch to the Swedbergs for shipment. Six stations along a thirty-mile shoreline kept Adam busy. He liked to make frequent contacts with the people who worked for him. According to the going standards, he paid his workers well. In turn, he was liked and respected. Picking up the oars as he climbed into one of his boats, he headed across the lake to the Youngbears.

Rowing was therapy to Adam. It gave him time to think and to remember. Twenty-two years ago, he had homesteaded a hundred sixty acres of lakeshore land just a quarter-mile down from Thorson's Bay. He had been twenty-one then, ambitious and full of zest for living. He cleared some land and built a two-room house. Working for others in the bay area, he accumulated enough money to furnish his home com-

20

fortably. Hans Yocum ran a saw mill on the edge of town, and through his dealings with Hans, Adam met his daughter Emily. She was pretty and available, and he was lonesome for association with persons his own age. Despite Emily's strict sense of propriety, their romance progressed. Adam asked her to marry him, and she accepted with her father's blessing.

He was often puzzled that she would evade him when he made the most innocent approach. In one of their more romantic moments, he dared to remark that he was looking forward to sharing the same bed with her and asked her how she felt about that.

"When we're married," she replied primly, "I'll do my best to keep you happy in every way."

Her words and manner threw a chill over his enthusiasm. That feeling of coldness and rejection would come over him many times in the months and years ahead. Not until after the wedding would she consent to even visit his house. With mounting anticipation, he watched as she inspected each room in turn, his feeling of pride in his self-made home infiltrated with doubts as she offered no comment about the little touches he had added for her coming. Suddenly the little bowl of wild flowers looked like silly weeds. The new ribbons which held back the curtains were harsh and out of place. Adam tried to push back his disappointment and pulled her into his embrace. Shrugging him away, she put a step or two between them.

"There's too much to be done around here for that."

And so it continued. The few times they made love, she made him feel he had wronged her. Once when he felt their moment of intimacy had been more successful, she quickly stripped him of any lingering glow.

"My grandmother warned me that all men are beasts."

It became clear that she was launching her own crusade against the animal instinct in man. Yet she continued to be a puzzle to him. She seemed to deliberately parade around the house in scant clothing revealing a figure that became more voluptuous and enticing than when they were first married. When she let down the thick braids to wash her long golden hair, shaking it loose around her white shoulders, Adam nearly went crazy with longing. But Emily's policy seemed to be audience without overtures. He tried desperately to break through her shield again and again.

"Is that all you think about?" she asked him frigidly. Adam had to admit that he did think about it a lot.

Pregnancy came soon, and Emily shut the door entirely. Adam resigned himself to the role of unwilling celibacy. Within the year, Matt was born, and Adam delighted in the unfolding of that little personality. He was allowed to change the baby and to watch the intimate relationship of mother and son at feeding time. It was obvious that Emily considered the boy solely a product of her own efforts, and any time Adam had with him was something in the nature of a loan grudgingly given. Her affection was now bestowed exclusively on little Matt. Adam was shunted into the pattern of provider and handyman. While he grabbed at every opportunity to enjoy his son, Adam felt more bewildered and unfulfilled each day.

Then the war between the states, our Civil War, began to impact even the somewhat isolated north country. When a call for volunteers came, Adam enlisted in the Engineering Corps to build bridges and roads for moving war equipment, supplies, and personnel. Emily took the news of his enlistment with dry eyes, and Adam knew she would get along well without him. She was active in the church, admired in the community, neat and industrious, and a good mother. The painful thing was leaving behind the little boy, who was just beginning to walk and say a few words.

Adam wasn't leaving Emily entirely alone. Zeb was already part of the family. In fact, Zeb could come in and take Matt out of his crib, bounce around the room, and sing songs his own mother had sung to him. Adam couldn't have gotten away with such pampering. He would have received a "don't disturb him" retort from Emily.

Years before, when Sam Jackson had come to this bay, Adam had helped Zeb add two more rooms to the already largest home there. It was there they discovered each other's capabilities as master craftsmen in the fitting and finishing of wood. They became close friends. Sam Jackson saw the solid oak in Adam's character and gave him some good advice on investing. So did Zeb. By the time he joined up, his finances were such that Emily should have no problems. He knew that Zeb would happily be there to take care of Matt when Emily needed a break and often just to enjoy the "cub."

Adam attained the rank of major in eighteen months because of his expertise, ingenuity, and ability to handle men. After a period of constant engagement with the enemy, they encamped on the outskirts of a town that had been hastily evacuated by the Confederate army. The Union soldiers were given a few days for rest and regrouping and the procurement of supplies. Adam set up his headquarters in an empty law office.

Once that was accomplished, he decided he needed a belt for his uniform. There was a business-as-usual attitude about the town in spite of the recent occupation, and Adam found a variety store in the same block. He entered the store, proceeded to the belt rack, selected one, and took it the counter, where a young lady was busy taking inventory. When she looked up, they stared at each other as though in shock. It was like two streams converging, blending into one.

The wordless trance continued until an older lady came and stood beside Adam.

"May I help you?" she asked.

The spell was broken. The young lady and Adam laughed. The trill of her laughter lay like a balm on Adam's heart.

"Oh, Mother, I think I can handle this."

Her mother backed away and began to tidy up a stack of trousers as Adam found his voice.

"I'm a married man," he said awkwardly, not knowing why he felt compelled to offer this information to a complete stranger.

"I'm engaged to a young man in the Confederate army," she replied.

"My name is Adam Berglund."

"My name is Eva Atwood."

"Can I talk to you alone?"

"I'll be through in half an hour."

Adam purchased the belt, and Eva watched him go out the door. She thrilled at the tall muscular trimness evident in that uniform. Suddenly, she needed her father, but he had been killed in action six months earlier. He had been her confidant and advisor until the war had changed everything, including her future. Her singing voice had been recognized beyond local acclaim, but the war had blotted out all thoughts of further training. She was now needed to help in the store to eke out a living for herself and her mother. As the door closed behind Adam, Eva's mother came over to her with a questioning look.

"Mother," asked Eva, "is it possible to fall in love in an instant so completely and surely that there can be no doubt that it has happened?"

"It happened that way between your father and me. It was our greatest hope that you'd find someone who would give you what we had."

"I've found him," said Eva, "but he's married and I'm engaged. I never felt anything like this with Bob. I wasn't anxious to get engaged, but it seemed to be the thing to do because he was joining up."

"He is certainly a fine looking gentleman," said her mother. "I guess I'm supposed to hate him because he's a Union soldier, but I don't, even before I knew what was happening between you two."

"Well, it's not quite over yet," said Eva. "He's going to walk me home."

As Adam waited, his mind refused to dwell on anything but Eva. Her voice, her smile, and, somehow he knew, her love had opened up a world of unbelievable fulfillment that preempted all else.

When Eva came out of the store, she smiled and put her arm in his as though it was something they had done often. Adam saw the sun highlighting the waves in her beautiful auburn hair. Her step was lithe and springy, and her fitted garment couldn't hide the perfection beneath.

"My home isn't far away," he heard her say. "My mother's close behind us, and the neighbors are wondering why I'm with a Union officer, so I can't show you how I feel outwardly, but I think you know."

"I wanted to hear you say that, and I want you to know that what has happened between us is more than I ever imagined life could offer, and if this is really the end, these few moments will add meaning and enrichment to whatever lies ahead."

Eva stopped at a gate.

"I told mother about what happened to us," she said, as they waited for her mother to come to them.

"Mother, I want you to meet Adam Berglund. I know we have fallen in love. Adam, this is my mother, Mrs. James Atwood. Dad was killed in action six months ago."

Mrs. Atwood looked at Adam and read the honest sorrow in his expression. Simultaneously, they reached to hug each other.

"I'm glad and sad. You two have what many never find."

Tears started down her cheeks as she turned and went into her house. Eva came close to Adam. Her fingers touched his face as though she were trying to remember every contour and expression. There were tears on both faces.

"God keep you safe." She turned and fled into the house.

The next morning, Adam was making requisitions for supplies when a sudden premonition came to him that Eva was in trouble. He wasted no time. He strapped on his service revolver, grabbed a rifle, and ran to the store. As he came near, he heard angry screams he knew came from Mrs. Atwood. He slammed through the door and saw one soldier grappling with Eva. Her blouse had been torn, exposing a breast. Two other soldiers were trying to stifle her mother's voice. Eva, partially choked, was sagging to the floor. Adam rammed his rifle butt into the rapist's jaw. The sound of crunched teeth could be heard as the soldier fell backwards to the floor. Adam turned his revolver on the two holding her mother.

"One false move and you're dead. Drag your buddy back to your company commander and try to explain what happened. *On the double!*"

The two soldiers helped their dazed and wounded buddy to his feet and left. Adam didn't look toward Eva. To gaze upon her exposed disarray would be very low.

"There will be a guard on duty here as long as we are around. War makes animals out of some of our men. They feel they may die tomorrow and consequently cast aside all moral restraint."

Eva came to him wearing a robe her mother had taken from a rack.

"I prayed for you to come. Our love must be such that it denies separation."

"You're right," Adam agreed. "There was no doubt in my mind that you called for me. I hope I'll be able to respond if you ever really need me again."

Eva put her arms around Adam and looked up.

"Kiss me just once."

Adam kissed her. He wanted to forget the rules and smother her with abandon, but he honored the seeming sacredness of the moment. Tears mingled as their lips melted together in ecstasy and sorrow. As though a signal had sounded, they both drew back.

"We won't say good-bye." Tears flooded Eva's eyes. "Let's say, 'until our tomorrow.'"

Adam looked at Eva through the pouring deluge of his tears.

"Until our tomorrow." He quickly turned and left.

Hardly a day had passed in those twenty years of separation that Adam hadn't relived those few moments with Eva. At times he felt still strong interplay of their love with such certainty that he knew the door of love was still open. He also felt sure that God had engineered their meeting for reasons not yet explained.

Appomattox finally came after three and a half years of courage and cowardice, nobility and debauchery, defeat and victory, rape, pillaging, and killing, with North and South equally due both praise and blame. In the mustering out, Adam received a quarter-section of land next to the one he already owned and came home to Thorson's Bay.

Matthew was five now. He looked at Adam with the reserve and mistrust he might accord a stranger. Although Emily kissed him when they met at the station, before they had gotten to the house, she had begun listing all the jobs that needed to be done. Adam knew nothing had changed. His role was still breadwinner and handyman and nothing more.

For all her strength and tirelessness, a year and a half later, Emily caught a cold that grew progressively worse. By the time the doctor arrived, she was delirious with fever. The doctor diagnosed it pneumonia and said he could do nothing to pull her through. In the long hours of the night, Adam sat by her side with the light just high enough that he could catch any changes in the woman who lay on the bed. She was still young and quite pretty, though the illness had taken its toll. Even as she waged the inward struggle against her illness, Adam felt a surge of the old attraction he had held for her the day they met at Hans Yocum's mill.

As he replaced the cool damp cloth on her hot brow, a lucid moment occurred, and Emily reached weakly for his hand. He leaned close to catch her words.

"I know . . . I haven't been a good wife. I know, Adam, and I'm going to try from now on." Two hours later, she died. No other words came from her lips.

Emily had wanted Matt to be a minister. That idea had been drilled into him until the time she died. Now, over a decade and a half later, Matt was in his last year at the seminary, and Adam wondered if that was what Matt really wanted to do. In the years following Emily's death, there had been opportunities, even the necessity, for closeness between Adam and his son. Nevertheless, there were still those times when he felt that Emily's influence on Matt's thinking was too strong, as though her will over him had transcended the grave. Maybe, he thought, that influence and Zeb's was bringing out the best in Matt.

Approaching the other shore, Adam could see the wigwam of Youngbear back among the trees. Youngbear's squaw waved a greeting as Adam drew close. Her little boy toddled down to the water's edge, awaiting the usual piece of candy. Youngbear and their sixteen-year-old daughter were out running the trap lines.

"I brought some cough medicine," Adam said and tossed a small bottle to the squaw who grabbed it eagerly, tucking it into a fold of the nondescript outer garment she was wearing.

"Thanks, Mr. Berglund. He got bad cough."

Adam suspected they would finish the bottle of cough medicine before the night was well along.

"Tell Youngbear to change the traps to another spot tomorrow. We don't want to catch too many in one place." He knew it would be done, even without his admonition, because the Indians seemed to be natural conservationists.

As he rowed back to the Swedberg side of the lake, Adam's thoughts were of the lumbering operations farther north. Recently, he had ridden the logging train to the end of the line, where the timber was being cut. He had been shocked at the decimation. From the lake, all that could be seen were stumps and piles of brush waiting to be burned. Even the war hadn't denuded vast expanses so completely. In a few years, the lumbering would move nearer the now quiet and scenic Thorson's Bay. It was like an inexorable glacier, leveling all in its path, leaving barrenness behind. Something needed to be done to stop this total cropping of timber, but what and how? Adam didn't know. Then the irony of it struck him. Some of his fish were feeding the destroyers.

6

Star

As the close of his seminary training came nearer, Matt found that he was more and more disturbed by thoughts that recurred. His grade average was high. In fact, though Matt hadn't been aware of the letter, Dean Caldwell had written to his dad that Matt was again at the top of his class academically. "More than that," he wrote, "we who are his teachers recognize in him a keenness of judgment and a spirit of integrity that are exceptional. His discernment and insight are well beyond his years and experience. I know we share with you the hope that he finds a way to fulfill his total capacity for serving."

Adam glowed with a fatherly pride as he read the dean's letter. He had shared it with Zeb. He would need to wait until Matt came home and the mood between them was such that he could really let his son know how he felt. Conditioned by years of restraint, still conscious of Emily's shadow, Adam was cautious about showing his open affection for Matt.

On his part, Matt rebelled against the capsuled dogmatic emphasis of the seminary's teaching. In little groups, the students argued their differences. He finally asked for an appointment with the dean to air his feelings.

"I have a problem with parts of the Old Testament," he told the dean. "I think God would have explained creation more believably to the analytical mind He gave to us." Matt liked to think of it as man's revelation of his God in his long searching for God. He winced at the killing of babies of the Exodus, but another thought seemed to ring true, which was that God has to work with what He has to bring us to His revealing of Himself in the New Testament.

"The kind of people I want to work with," said Matt, "have problems and troubles that need positive and immediate attention. Many will find little comfort in ritual and sermonizing until some solutions to their everyday problems are found. I am unable to accept some of the prescribed attitudes taught here. I believe God is more concerned with results and that He will overlook a lot if one is really trying to make a better world. I feel," he continued, warming to his subject, "that our church people are often fed a religiosity that depicts God as a bigoted, selfish deity, instead of the all inclusive, loving, caring, and forgiving God that comes through in the New Testament. They are steeped in twisted emphasis and sectarian prejudice. God must be sickened by our devious attempts to declare His simple message."

"Would you be surprised if I told you I think much of what you have said is true," responded the dean. "I encourage you to keep your mind open and keep listening for what God seems to be saying to you. Remember, change comes slowly. Some feel if we don't offer those palliatives, others will steal our members. Many of your classmates will be content to marry and bury and preach in the same old patterns. Maybe you can be one who makes a real difference in the communities you serve. I'm all for you! If you want to reshape lives more than listen to your own pipe organ, more power to you! Let's see what happens."

Matt felt only a little better when he left the dean's office. There was still the heavy feeling, the uncertainty of his direction. His mind went back over the years, trying to trace the pattern that had brought him this far. As far back as his memory could reach he recalled sitting beside his mother in church. Her voice echoed in his ears now.

"Some day, you'll be there, Matthew. You'll be a leader in the church."

Almost as though an exterior force was controlling him, Matt had gone into the seminary program. For the most part, he had found the curriculum interesting. He enjoyed the informal debates with other theology students, which challenged him to articulate his own beliefs. In the background, there was always the feeling that this wasn't the real world, this enclave in which he had hidden himself for three years.

"There are those who mouth the scriptures without inner conviction. The Church wants honesty," the dean had said. Was he, Matt, being totally honest if his calling to the ministry was put on like an outer garment, rather than coming from the strength of his faith?

And how did his father feel about it? Matt had never discussed his decision to study for the ministry with his father. In fact, he mused, he hadn't entered into many serious discussions with him. There were times when a special closeness seemed to bond them together, but often when they reached out for each other, there was a drawing away. Matt admired and respected his father as a man of fairness and integrity. He knew that Adam made it a matter of principle to keep his word and that he was highly regarded by those in his employ, but there was often a door not quite open, an invisible wall that separated them. In the final analysis, it was Zeb who had been his other father figure from the very first. Zeb's honesty of faith and their love for each other made Matt want to reach for his potential, so he wouldn't be a disappointment to Zeb. Matt knew that, as yet, his inner conviction wasn't strong enough to really call his own. It was more like wearing a garment of faith, but not feeling qualified to be worthy of the demands of its calling.

The bitter January wind whipped his pant legs and tugged at his coat as Matt crossed the campus in long strides back to his room. Thorson's Bay would be piled high with snow. The Youngbears, Swedbergs, and others would be ice fishing. The icehouses would be filling with blocks cut from the lake for next summer's use. Matt quickened his pace, eager for release of tension brought about by lack of physical activity. It would be good to get back home, to train and compete in another shoot, to put all his energies into something that gave satisfaction, even if only momentarily.

In the spring, as the ice was breaking up in the lake country, Matt received his degree. Appointment to a church would come soon. He had asked for a parish in one of the northern lake country communities.

Home looked good to Matt. On Sunday, Pastor Wiggins, the minister of the church at Thorson's Bay, introduced him as a fellow member of the cloth, and they all congratulated him at the close of the service. Even among people he had grown up with, he was embarrassed at all the attention. So far, he was a dry run. Sure, he had prepared sermons in seminary and delivered them for the criticism of his classmates and professors. But sermonizing wasn't the whole of being a pastor, and some of the other aspects of the profession scared him. How could he baptize people? Would it be just an act or would he have a sense of the positive presence of God working through him? Even for preaching, he wasn't sure he had any live ammunition. Right now he just wanted to be at home in the lake country with its open confrontations of man and nature. Primarily a man of action, Matt was glad to have the studying behind him. It was time to get back in tune with the world he knew and loved.

"I'm going to get in my canoe and paddle until I feel like coming back," he told his father the second day home.

Back on the lake, Matt felt the weight lift from his shoulders. Now, the present moment was sufficient. Paddling the canoe swiftly and effortlessly, he was keenly alert to his surroundings. Although the sun bore down directly on him, the heat of it was tempered by the breeze that ruffled the lake surface. In the quiet bay, the pines on the banks were reflected and clouds like cotton balls were mirrored. Here and there a patch of water lilies formed a floating carpet.

A mother duck proudly led her brood through a reedy point. Suddenly there was a loud splash and a quick scattering of the ducklings.

The mother duck quacked them back into line and Matt wondered if she knew one of them had been food for a northern pike. Gulls flew close to the canoe, swooping with unerring accuracy to scoop up small fish. He watched the appearing and disappearing of the loon, so gracefully agile in the water. A porcupine swimming purposefully across the lake almost bumped into his canoe. Matt breathed the pine-scented air and listened to the cawing crows, realizing how much all this meant to him.

His thoughts turned suddenly to Maude, sweet, fresh, blond, and pretty. Everyone liked her. She would be the ideal preacher's wife. He wondered about being married to her. That first night, how would they react to each other? It wasn't as if he had been raised in an incubator. Those bull sessions with his fellow fledglings for the ministry weren't prayer meetings. Stuart Monroe was one of the group who, according to his teachers, had the proper qualifications for a minister—good grades, an excellent voice, and natural charisma. He was also a womanizer and a braggart. He often marked the letter X on the blackboard in Old Testament class. That meant he had a willing sex partner the preceding night. Sometimes he marked an O and acted like a frustrated male as he returned to his desk. Matt held him in low esteem, but he had to admit that sometimes he listened with interest to some of the detailed accounts of this behind-the-barn education.

One of Matt's friends came to confide a close call. Albert had dated an excitingly amorous young lady from a sorority of another college. After he had taken her to see a play, she had invited him to her home. Her parents had retired and he was receptive to her kisses. Soon she invited him down beside her on the carpet.

"Don't keep me waiting, Albert," she said.

Suddenly he knew he was one of a series of sex companions, and his fire went out. In revulsion, he left, sickened at the thought that his lovely date was a whore.

Stuart Monroe, who answered to "Stu" and, in closed groups, to "Stud," knew Matt's moral concepts.

"You don't know what you're missing," Stu said.

Matt hated it when Stu's persuasive power converted others. At the time, Matt had hoped the professors would have unearthed that abrasive flaw in Stuart's character, but they applauded his flawless contributions to the daily class sessions.

Matt suddenly realized he had forgotten about Maude in his replay of Stud Monroe. He knew he didn't want a wife that had been a community plaything, and he had no trouble with the fact that Maude deserved no less from her man.

A small speck in the distance caught his attention. The uneven shoreline caused it to be out of sight, and then it appeared again. He veered to the shore where a tall pine towered above the others. This would be a good excuse, he thought, to get in some tree-climbing experience and to check the unfamiliar object on the lake. He pulled his canoe out of sight into some undergrowth. The tree he had picked was just behind a small sandy beach.

Matt went up the tree, using the gorilla-like method of Doran's and was pleased with the time it took to get to the top. He chose his perch and felt a giddy exhilaration as the tree swayed in the cooling breeze. Looking far up the lake, he could make out the outline of a canoe with two people in it. He decided they were Indian women in brightly colored clothing, mostly red.

As they came closer, one of the women pointed toward the shoreline in Matt's direction and immediately turned the canoe. Soon he heard voices and laughter, and in a few minutes, they beached the canoe directly below his vantage point. In a flash they began to take off their clothing, giggling and talking in some incomprehensible dialect. Matt was petrified. He wanted to shout a warning, but his momentary hesitation was too long. The two were stripped to the skin and heading for the water.

After deciding that silence was the best policy, Matt made up his mind to enjoy the show. Then he realized that he was looking at Star, his co-winner of the swim of last summer. Both of the girls were well formed, not at all like some of the dumpy, stolid specimens that he had learned to identify as the Indian female. The other girl's skin was coppery brown, but he paid little attention to her. He watched Star as she swam toward the center of the lake. He noticed the sun catching a reddish tint in the sheen of her brown hair. She turned, churning the water in a beautiful rhythmic pattern as she approached the beach. She was using the same swimming stroke that he used, and he had never seen it executed more perfectly. Star came out of the water and with a graceful pirouette, sat down on the sand, tossing her hair around to shake the excess water from it. She was breathing fast from the exercise of swimming, which further emphasized the fullness of her breasts. Matt couldn't rid himself of the feeling that this was a shoddy thing to do. He remembered the Scripture, "If thine eye offend thee, pluck it out." One thing was certain, he was not about to impair his eyesight, but he wondered how Pastor Wiggins would have handled a situation like this. He squirmed to find a new position for his cramped posterior.

Crack! The limb he sat on gave way, and he began his crazy descent, grabbing at the limb below him which tore violently out of his grasp, tossing him in a gyrating fashion to bounce his torso off another limb. His head hit a larger limb, and Matt felt the world explode with a sudden numbing pain, saw a blurred picture of the ground coming to meet him, and then, oblivion.

When Matt regained consciousness, he heard voices of two people talking in a strange language. As his memory came back, he knew it was the voices of the two Indian girls. One was applying a cool, damp cloth to his aching head. He wondered which one. Suddenly she spoke in English.

"I don't know why I'm doing this for you, you yellow-haired coyote. I should have just let you lie here. What a miserable human being you must be."

Matt detected no bitterness in the soft voice. He had the feeling this was the way she would talk to a stray kitten. He was afraid to open his eyes for fear the girls were still naked, so he kept them shut and began to talk.

"Will you please hold your judgment until you hear my side of the story? I was up in that tree long before I knew who was in that canoe. You tell me how I could have known that two ladies would decide to come here and undress before I could holler. You sure got out of those clothes fast. What would you have done if you were me? This is my first experience as a Peeping Tom, and I am turning in my suit. Nothing will top this."

Matt opened his eyes and found himself almost unnerved by the directness of the returning gaze of his brown-eyed nurse. They looked at each other for a moment, and seeing unmistakable signs of mirth in her expression, Matt broke into a grin, then a laugh. They both laughed, and her companion joined in at the sudden release of tension. They stopped to catch their breath, only to hear the echoes coming back from across the lake, which started them laughing again. As they tapered off, Star was still wiping the gash on his forehead. Matt looked searchingly at her. She was even more lovely at close inspection. Her shapeliness was still evident in the calico dress, but he was studying her face, the perfection of which was highlighted with her hauntingly beautiful eyes. He lay there in a state of happy shock, and knew he had to break the spell.

"I guess you remember me. I live down the Lake a ways. You know I'm telling the truth. Believe me, you're a very beautiful woman, and I can't honestly say that I'm sorry I was up in that tree."

Matt noticed a blush cover her face, but with quick recovery she spoke.

"In case you've forgotten, my name is Star, and this is my sister

Fawn. We'll be going now if you think you're all right."

Matt got slowly to his feet. He felt dizzy. He was sore all over, but as far as he could tell, he wasn't hurt seriously.

"I guess I'm all right, but in a way I wish I weren't. I was enjoying that attention. You are sisters?" he asked looking from one to the other.

"That's easy to explain," said Star. "I look like Mother, and Fawn looks like Father. We have to go now. Our parents are fishing with some friends up the lake and they're probably wondering where we are."

Star moved closer to Matt and inspected the gash on his forehead. She looked at him with a concerned caring. Matt felt it was as though she didn't want this moment to end either.

"I hope you will be all right," she said and then turned and ran to the canoe, which Fawn had pulled into the water. Star took her place in the canoe, and they paddled away. With a sudden realization that Star was paddling right out of his life, he hollered to the receding canoe, almost pleading.

"Star! Star! I've got to see you again."

Star turned and smiled, waved her paddle, and went around the point without looking back again.

Matt ached in at least one more place now. He got into his canoe and pointed it toward home.

7

The Tryst

As Star and Fawn paddled farther and farther away from where Matt had met them so unceremoniously, Matt's canoe was headed in the opposite direction. With the sickening feeling that she was leaving something behind unfinished, Star felt a kind of depression settling over her. Though the late afternoon air was still warm, she shivered and paddled faster. Fawn, pulling faster to keep the canoe headed right, shot a glance at her sister.

"You're awfully quiet."

"Umm," Star responded absently, busy with her own thoughts.

The idea of marrying Jim Beaver stirred something close to revulsion in her. Their marriage had been planned since they were children by White Otter, who, while he accepted many of the new ways, still firmly believed in the parents' wisdom to make the right choices of their children's mates. She knew that Jim loved her. She also knew that Fawn loved him. Why did everything get so tangled? She had tried to analyze the love or lack of it in other families she knew, as well as her own. Did those marriages start with real love, or were most of them just a resignation to accepting their fate? Hearing the expression, "the old bag" or "the old goat" and, even worse allusions to marriage partners certainly didn't show any mutual need or respect for each other. It was as if both were trapped, living out an unfulfilled existence. Thinking of her own parents, her father seemed to love her mother, but while her mother treated him respectfully, all her affections seemed to be showered on the two girls.

One couple, she mused, that seemed to be close and still very much in love were Maude Thorson's parents. She had felt that, somehow, during her visits to Thorson's store. Then there was Phil Peterson, who had recently lost his wife. Star had visited them, with Father O'Brien, before and during Mrs. Peterson's illness. The Petersons, of Nordic descent, worked together gardening, fishing, or trapping, happy in their way of life with each other. What was this strange cement called love that sometimes endured, but sometimes seemed to fall apart? It was very much like her paintings that sometimes captured and held freshness and vitality and beauty, while others, using colors from the same palette became dull and lifeless. The thought of Matt and his own particular aliveness kept pushing into her consciousness.

"I should just forget the whole thing, but I don't want to."

"If you ask me," said Fawn, "there was more falling going on back there than out of that tree. What are you going to do about Jim?"

"I may have to become a nun, but the way I feel, my heart wouldn't be in it. There's another problem, too. Matt may be spoken for by Maude."

"What I saw back there didn't look like he was thinking about Maude anymore than you were thinking about Jim."

"I don't know what to do. I can't just paddle down to his place and say, here I am, it's your move."

"You'll think of something."

Adam Berglund was making a walk out of flat rocks when he saw Matt approaching the dock in his canoe. Adam noticed that he limped stiffly to the house. Adam followed him in.

"Looks like you met a bear and lost. Do you want to talk about it?"

Matt told his story.

"It seems unreal. Yesterday I had my life planned with Maude. Today, I've met the lady I really want to share my life with, if at all possible, and now nothing is as important as finding out if it is possible."

"I know how you feel," said Adam. He also knew that Matt didn't know how he knew, as the pervading presence of Eva flooded his being. "Do what you have to do, son. I'm in your corner, although it's going to cause problems."

Adam, along with the rest of the community, had long assumed that Maude would be part of his family. He was fond of Maude, but he had wondered if Matt's casual approach to her evident love was as it should be.

Two days later, Matt was again on the lake nearly recovered from the bruising he'd received. As he paddled to the tree, which drew him like a magnet, he again thought of Maude. There seemed to be no way to inform her of the turn of events. He would always love Maude, but that had been preempted by an all-consuming love for Star. There was no turning back to the "bird-in-the-hand" now.

As he approached the tree, the problem with Maude evaporated. Star's lingering presence filled the surroundings. Walking to the tree, he relived every word and expression of Star's conversation, the laughter, the searching inquiry in her eyes.

He sat on a log close by, trying to reenact each episode of the encounter. Suddenly his eyes caught the pattern of sticks laid symmetrically on the ground before him to form a star, and below it were ten vertical lines scratched in the soil. Something seemed to burst in his brain. It was Star's message. She had returned to set a date for a meeting. Matt attributed her manner of communication to her Indian background, and it only heightened his love for her. Ten days, he thought, would be seven days from tomorrow. It was too good to be true. Matt felt a panic of anticipation and elation, like a child waiting for Christmas.

8

The Vow

It had been less than half an hour since Matt had returned home when he heard the sound of paddles on the lake and saw Jim Beaver in the front end of Maude's canoe with Maude in the rear. At the shoot last summer he had invited Jim to visit him.

As Jim stepped from the canoe, he turned to Maude .

"Thanks, Miss Thorson, for bringing me out."

Matt went to her.

"I'll be in to see you in a few days."

"I'll be there," Maude answered and paddled away.

"I came down on the logging train and asked at the store how to get here, so she brought me. She's nice. You sure are lucky."

To Matt, the word "lucky" now had its complications. Doran also had used that word when talking about Maude. Turning to the man beside him, Matt observed that Jim seemed bigger and tougher than last year.

"You're going to be harder to beat at the shoot this year," Matt said, changing the subject quickly.

"Let's hope I put up a better struggle in Doran's arena," Jim grinned.

"I've been swimming a lot, but it looks like I'd better get toughened up myself."

As they sat on the lawn, neither felt the need of much outward show of their friendship. Matt was more at ease with Jim than with most of the men he called friends. It seemed to him there bad been little lapse of time since they had last seen each other.

"Now that you've graduated," Jim asked, "what are your plans?"

"I hope I'll soon be getting an appointment to a church."

"If you're like Father O'Brien, you'll be okay. He's always helping someone and runs the school at the Mission. I'm not sure how he also fits in time for preaching and praying."

They looked out over the lake. The sun was close to the tree line, a blazing ball of red. The panorama was unmarred by human intervention. Fish leaped out of the water at increasing intervals, as to give a

38

final salute to the receding sun. The two, Native American and Nordic, seemed to be equally in tune with each other in the splendor of creation's canvas spread before them.

Jim looked at Matt.

"I want to show you something tomorrow. We'll ride the logging train to the cutting area. Will you come with me?"

"I've wanted to see that area. Sure, I'll go. How about first light tomorrow?"

Dawn found them on a flatcar watching the unfolding heavily-timbered lake country pass by them as the train puffed along. Most of the time, the lake was in view. The track attempted a straight line but bogs and larger bayous had to be circumvented. A bear with two cubs ambled into the trees as they passed. White-tailed deer were plentiful, and great blue herons spread their wings wide in stately flight at the lake's edge. Matt drank in the ever-changing scene. A bobcat in a tree, an unusual sight, caught Jim's attention, and he motioned for Matt to look. Instead, Matt looked at Jim. He was truly a noble red man, yet in the transition from mighty warrior or hunter, some of the deep pride and dignity had been stripped from him. Now he was a tree topper, and no doubt a good one, but to many, he was a second-class citizen. What was his future? Unless he accepted the ways of the white man, he was an endangered species. In Matt's mind, that was one more area that needed a solution. Where, he thought, should he concentrate his ministry? Preaching and baptizing babies wouldn't suffice. They passed the Mission area, where a large log structure pointed its cross skyward. Matt wanted to meet Father O'Brien. Here was a man who had found a way to make a difference.

Miles later, the logging train suddenly came into a ravaged, tree-less expanse so shocking in its unbelievable desolation that Matt stared in revulsion. That man would rape an area so completely was beyond his comprehension. He heard Jim's voice.

"I used to like my work, but I know this is wrong. I don't want to be a part of it any longer."

The train stopped at the place where loaded flatcars were ready to go on the main track.

A woodburner came out of the still-standing trees pulling a flatcar loaded with logs. Jim and Matt walked back into the timbered area where sound of ax and saw rang around them in every direction. They saw Doran.

"He's our timber boss," Jim informed Matt.

A tree had lodged against another instead of falling free where it was intended. Doran raced up the trunk of the standing tree as though it were horizontal, grabbed his ax from his belt, and from the top side, chopped the wedged tree free. It fell to the ground with a tremendous whomp. Men rushed in to remove the limbs from the main log center, and within minutes, the saw team had moved in and cut the remaining straight pole into prescribed lengths for loading.

Doran shook Matt's hand and then looked at Jim.

"Jim, we sure need you. Don't stay away too long."

It was one good lumberman's appreciation for another. Matt knew that their work was honorable and satisfying and that there were many arguments in their favor. Growing cities and increasing population needed lumber for buildings of all kinds. If the average lumberman ever thought about it, he was doing a service.

They left Doran and walked on. The well-ordered operation was doing a good job as they saw it, but Matt had only to look out over the stumpy wasteland to reinforce his conviction that some terrible wrong was being perpetrated and even God must be saddened by all this defacing by man.

It seemed to Matt that he knew so little about everything. Growing up was a constant process of storing ideas, facts, and philosophy. Here he stood at the threshold of manhood with no solutions nor enough understanding to tackle any problems of society, but he knew this much, his job was to take a small step in the direction that seemed the right way. Here, it was evident that man was not only a builder but also a destroyer, leaving gashes of his greed as he passed through. Was this a final flaw, man's raping of frontiers? The end result was what he now saw, a land unusable and dead.

"Jim, I'm not sure what I'm going to do, but this is one thing I'm going to try to change, even if it takes the rest of my life."

Jim sat on a log, and Matt sat beside him. Drawing a knife from his sheath, Jim cut a small incision in Matt's palm and one in his own. Solemnly, in an old, old ritual as their blood mingled, he spoke.

"You are now my blood brother, and we are in this together. There is an answer somewhere, and I know you'll at least try to find it. No one can ask for more."

Matt jumped on as the loaded log train started its trip back down. He waved to Jim who stood there, tall and regal in stature, as though some of the pride and nobility had returned to him. Jim raised his hand as a sign of the pledge of brotherhood that was theirs.

On the way back from the cutting area, Matt spent time trying to decide how to break the news of his encounter with Star to Maude. He came up with no answers. As he hopped off the train at Thorson's Bay, he decided this was as good a time to broach the subject as any. Maude came to the door when he knocked.

"I'll be out in a few minutes."

They walked down to the wharf and sat on the edge with their feet dangling inches from the water.

"You're finding it hard to tell me something," said Maude.

"You're right. I don't know what to say except to tell you everything."

He related every detail of the "tree" incident. He looked at Maude, perhaps more fully than he had ever done. She was pretty, but behind that beauty was a woman of sensitivity and an embodiment of all that was good. It wasn't a matter of looks, personality, or character. It was that Star had set him afire with a burning desire for her. He couldn't explain why Maude hadn't done that to him.

"I had to tell you, Maude, because I think too much of you to hold back anything. I'm not sure of my future with Star, but I have to find out if it's there."

"What do you know about Star?" she asked.

"Nothing more than I knew last summer, except that her mother is light-skinned and her father is dark. That isn't much!"

"Let me tell you about her. Her grandfather was a French fur trader named LeBlanc, and her grandmother was a daughter of an Indian chief. She's a gifted woman and a Vassar graduate. Her paintings are much in demand. She helps Father O'Brien teach the Mission children, and she is a scholar of French, Latin, English, and the Indian languages. I read about her in the college's *Who's Who*." With just a twinge of envy, Maude added, "No doubt there are other areas where she excels, too."

Maude hesitated, then looked at Matt. "You know I love you, but I wouldn't want to share my life with you if your love wasn't given fully in return. You are decent and kind. I know you have to do what you're doing, and I wouldn't be much of a woman if I didn't want your life fulfilled, whatever direction you have to go."

She rose from the wharf and as Matt stood up she smiled at him, though her eyes were glistening with the tears she was holding back. "If you don't mind, I'll run to the house and have a good cry."

He watched her as she ran. A lump came into his throat, and the surging emotions brought tears to his eyes for the hurt he had caused. He also felt sorrow because of the closing of the long carefree chapter of his life, which involved Maude. It was hard to turn the page.

9

Rendezvous

Adam Berglund had been gone on a tour of his fishing stations for several days, and his home looked good to him as he approached it in the early dusk. The replenished stacks of firewood told him that Matt had been busy. Then he saw Matt partly hidden from view by the dock, soaping his body from head to foot. As he watched, Matt climbed onto the dock and went to the far end. He stood there, naked and muscular. A wave of admiration washed over Adam as he viewed Matt's impressive silhouette against the dying day. He wondered if his mother was in some state of being that allowed her to appreciate their handiwork. Matt seemed taller and stronger than a year ago. Again he wondered if all those muscles would be in the proper place behind the pulpit.

Through the years, they had been within shouting distance of each other much of the time. Through Matt, his own horizons had widened, because the questions asked couldn't be ignored. Encyclopedias, history, and classical literature filled the book shelves, which they explored together. They often reviewed the Sunday sermons, and Adam realized the questions Matt asked needed better answers. He wondered if seminary had resolved those questions, and he felt privileged to have watched a potential unfold. They had hunted, felled timber, fished, and filled their icehouses from the lake in mid-winter. He knew there was an above-average toughness and vitality in his son. He also knew that Zeb Hawkins had done much by example to help Matt look beyond himself.

Matt may have had soap in his eyes, because he didn't notice his dad until the boat scraped the dock.

"Hi, Dad," he called and then dove into the lake, coming up far out, bobbing up and under like a loon. Adam watched. There had been times in the past he had wanted to participate in the shoot, but other pressing duties had kept him away. He was only three years older than Doran and still didn't feel intimidated by any man, but now he was content to let Matt represent the family honor. Matt came charging back to shore like a bull walrus, snorting and blowing with abandon. Matt climbed onto the dock and grabbed a towel, burnishing his body as he came toward the house where Adam stood.

"Tomorrow's the day, Dad."

No explanation was needed. Adam knew the overpowering totality of Matt's condition as the sudden nostalgic sweetness of Eva came to him.

"I'll be up in that tree rooting for you."

Matt turned to Adam and embraced him, and Adam joyfully returned the affection. They hadn't done that for years.

"Dad, I know you've spent a lot of time, effort, and love in bringing me this far. Maybe I'm beginning to realize what a dad I have."

"You're really in love," Adam held him a moment longer.

Morning came as a surprise to Matt because he slept so soundly. The realization that this was the day exploded upon his consciousness. It was hard to wait for the sun to make some upward progress. Out of his own eagerness, the lake soon drew him. Although he tried to paddle slowly, he couldn't stay in slow motion. Nature had again poured out her seasonal extravagance, including an almost cloudless sky, but the serenity of the surroundings belied the turmoil and tugging within him. There again was the tree. It stood like a partner in the fashioning of their tryst. Soon his canoe touched shore. Dragging it up on the beach, he began a survey of the area. No signs of Star were evident. Walking the shoreline, he scanned the lake. Nothing was there except the natural noises of cawing crows and the plop of a large fish in the reeds. Doubts began to gnaw at him. Back at the tree, Matt sat on the log and noticed the ten sticks of the star were disarranged. Star had been there. He counted the days again and knew beyond doubt that this was the tenth day. He made a more intensive search and broke the silence with his voice.

"Star!" he shouted and the loudness of his own voice startled him. Had he misread Star's message? A feeling of discouragement settled upon him as he returned to the log. There the regrouped sticks of the star stared back at him. This time he sat quietly, although his heart pounded against his ribs.

"Star, I know you can hear me. Please hear what I have to say. I want you to know I love you and have thought of little else in the last ten days. You are already so much a part of me that I couldn't imagine my future without you. Nothing is as important as having you for my wife." Matt remained motionless. A light breeze came from behind his left ear and then another. He turned, looking directly into the eyes of Star. They reached for each other. Because it was necessary to breathe, they finally drew back. Star's lips were only inches from Matt's.

"I'd like the honor of getting your proposal from close range."

Matt kissed the tip of her nose.

"Star, I love you as much as it must be possible for a man to love a woman. Will you marry me?"

Star brought her hand to Matt's forehead and touched the almost healed place that had been the ugly cut of a few days ago.

"I can hardly believe this is happening. I don't know the probability that a woman will find the one man that will fulfill all dreams and desires and is above and beyond any other commitment, so that there is a feeling of needing each other which is impossible to express in words and knowing if there were multiple choices, you would pick me. I'm sure you know I would pick you. I love you, Matt. I felt foolish about my method of communication, but I had to find out if you meant it when you said you had to see me again." Star kissed the tender spot on his forehead, and then Matt felt the unrestrained giving of her lips on his. He felt the veneer of mores becoming unimportant in the uninhibited honesty of the expression of her love. Matt drew back, knowing that the way he felt, his control was on thin ice. Star smiled at him.

"How are you going to know I love you if I don't show it?" she teased. The garment Star wore was beaded buckskin with long fringes on the sleeves and skirt. Matt could see that Star was aware of his close scrutiny. "It's warmer in the cool of the mornings," Star explained.

"It's beautiful, and you're beautiful. You are a princess by every description, and I'm in love with you completely, happily, and unequivocally."

They were again in close embrace, but soon Star drew back and sat beside him.

"Now, I have to tell you the whole story. This has been my problem, but now it's ours because it stands between us and marriage. You know I want to be with you from this moment on, to be able to love you whenever and wherever. I want to be in your arms, to see you coming and going, to share your thoughts and your problems, to have your babies. In God's sight, if anyone is married, we surely are." Star paused. "I'm now promised to Jim Beaver by my father. I'm Chippewa, and it's still the tribal custom for the father to choose his daughter's mate. I like Jim as a friend. He has never pressed his advantage, and I was in no hurry. Maybe I'd have married him eventually, and I can guess you thought the same about Maude. Now we have to do something, and I haven't figured out how to go against my father's promise or to keep from hurting Jim."

Matt suddenly realized his own entrapment.

"I've complicated it further. When Jim and I were together, we went through the Indian ritual of becoming blood brothers." He told

Star about the visit to the lumbering operations and his vow to try to save the lake timberland. "I consider Jim my best friend, and I know he must love you. I can't be underhanded and continue seeing you until everything is in the open. I want you on almost any terms, but this needs to be resolved before you or I could like ourselves. I'll admit I was thinking of being married by Father O'Brien or Pastor Wiggens or both, as soon as we could get to them. I'm more than disappointed, some of my amour was getting ahead of itself and it's hard to backtrack."

Star brushed Matt's lips with her own.

"Let's be happy. What brought us together didn't bring us this far to separate us forever, I hope. I brought some lunch, wait here." She floated out of sight among the trees and soon returned carrying a basket and a blanket. Spreading the blanket, Star motioned for Matt to sit and handed him a sandwich. "Pemmican, save a spot for some blueberry pie."

"Do you cook, too?"

"My mother's an excellent cook, but we take turns. A Chippewa squaw has to please her husband in more ways than one."

"I think I follow you."

"I have to thank my lucky wooden star for bringing us together. I felt foolish and brash, but I had to know if you meant it when you said you had to see me again."

"To tell the truth, you shook me up the first time I met you at the shoot."

"It happened to me too, but when I saw you with Maude, I tried to forget it."

"We must be one of the fastest romances on record." A sudden foreboding clouded Matt's thoughts. *Here we are, signed, sealed, and delivered, yet kept apart by a wall we can't climb.*

Quite a while after the blueberry pie, Matt tore himself away from a lengthy embrace. "I've just discovered I'm quite normal. I'm going swimming. I'm going down for the third time right here, and I think you know why."

"I know," said Star. "Don't think this is a one-sided condition. I have an idea. One of us should talk to my mother to see if she can get my father to release me from his promise of me to Jim. I know she would try. I'll go up the lake aways and when you say 'go,' we will both take off our clothes and head for the water. The one who gets in last will talk to my mother."

"Every stitch?" asked Matt.

"Every stitch."

"Okay, only don't come too close; my willpower is weakening." At

45

his own "Go" he tore off his clothing, but he heard the splash up the lake just before he hit the water. The swimming was a relief from the tugging tension of restraint. He swam toward Star. When she was twenty feet away, she rose high out of the water, her tantalizing, beautiful breasts in full view, then she turned and swam away.

"That just about destroyed me," Matt said later, back together.

They paddled up the lake together, as Matt was reluctant to say good-bye to Star and to this day. Star had told him that Fawn was waiting up the lake a way.

"Your mother will get a visit soon. I'm not going to drag my feet." Their canoes were together often, so little progress was made.

"Matt, let me quote the poet John Donne, to tell you what I feel about us:

"Only our love has no decay.

This no tomorrow hath or yesterday

Running it never runs from us away

But truly keeps his first last everlasting day.

"I've never been intimate with a man, but once a man almost forced himself on me. I was with Jim, who wanted to show me the lumbering operations. He had to work, so I just roamed around. I was picking flowers, when a man named Rube Finney grabbed me and put his hand over my mouth while trying to force me to the ground. I bit his hand and rammed my knee into his groin like we were taught in a special class at Vassar. He loosened his hold enough for me to escape. I screamed and ran and he came after me. Doran came out of the trees, picked Finney up over his head and tossed him into a tree stump. Finney bounced off that stump and lay there in a heap. Doran asked if I was okay and when I nodded, he went back into the trees. Finney recovered. Jim said he got his pay and left."

"How well do you know Doran?"

"Not well. He's never let me thank him for keeping me from being raped. I'd say he's a real gentleman."

"My story isn't as exciting. I never had any other girl than Maude, and I even thought we would marry some day. Neither of us ever thought seriously about violating our standards of morality. Dad once said, 'Don't do anything that would make me ashamed of you,' and that was enough for me. As a prospective minister I feel the double standard of behavior is wrong. If I want a virtuous woman, why act like a hound dog? One of the professors gave us a lecture on the sanctity of marriage. He told us to keep ourselves for that one woman whom you could honor and respect with a clean slate of your own. He said when you lower your standard, you lower your own effectiveness as the person God hopes you'll be. He also said, when two who love find fulfillment in the intimate expression of that love, it is the most thrilling experience that can happen to man and woman." Matt held the canoes together as he leaned to kiss Star.

"What about us?" asked Star.

"Star, I loved you before I knew about the person you are, the artist, the teacher, the beautiful mind, and the person who loves me. But I'm not ashamed to say there isn't a part of me that doesn't want you completely right now."

"That makes it unanimous."

They paddled soberly silent for a while.

"When the time comes, I'll be inexperienced," Matt confessed.

"I won't know the difference. We'll practice a lot." There was another interval of silence. "Fawn should be around the next bend. I want you to know her. You'll like her. Her desire is to be the wife of a nice young member of our tribe, and her choice is Jim Beaver. I wish I could make it happen."

Soon Matt saw Fawn waiting at the water's edge. The garment she wore was similar to Star's. Her straight statuesque figure stood in relief against the forested background, lending a fairyland enchantment to the scene. Matt climbed out of his canoe and ran to Fawn. He picked her up off the ground and whirled her around. He grinned at her startled expression.

"I'm going to marry your sister, so you might as well get used to me in a hurry." He held Fawn at arm's length. "Please take good care of Star until we get our problems ironed out." Fawn nodded her head in the affirmative and then ran to Star, where the two sisters hugged, laughed, and cried in pure feminine happiness. Matt was launching his canoe when Star came to him. She unbuttoned Matt's shirt and kissed his bared chest.

"I suppose I should thank you for keeping me a virgin." Matt grinned at her and then kissed her vigorously. "I guess we did the right thing, but I'm looking ahead to those practice sessions."

"Let's look at it this way. It's a beautiful parting thought. Like a good play, you look forward to the next act."

10

The Start

At breakfast the next morning, Matt told his dad about his day with Star.

"Dad, I'm happy and apprehensive at the same time, like being out on a small limb wondering if it will hold until I get to marry Star."

Adam nodded. He had spent what seemed a lifetime doing just that, but what Matt didn't know was that the recipient of his love wasn't Matt's mother. He handed Matt a letter that he had picked up at the post office at Thorson's store. "I'm glad you've found each other. Many never find that special relationship, and settle for less. Here's something that may give you other things to think about."

The envelope showed the official letterhead of the governing board of his church. Matt read the letter and then handed it to Adam.

> We have been considering the establishment of a church in the Mission area of Father O'Brien's parish There are those of the Protestant faith who have expressed their need and the names are enclosed. It has been suggested that the old Trading Post building can be renovated for a place of worship. It will begin as a mission project where your salary and operation expenses come from our mission fund until such time that aid is no longer needed. We have honored your request for a church in that area and pray that you will find a fertile field of endeavor to make God's kingdom come alive in the hearts of those you serve. I will personally follow your progress with expectation and prayer.
>
> Dean Caldwell
> Chairman of the Board of Missions

Now that the gauntlet had been flung, Matt felt a sense of being overwhelmed by the enormity of his task, but at the same time, a direction, a purpose made him eager to get started. At least for a time, he wouldn't be restricted by the conformity of an established church. He would charter his own course, even though he knew the church wasn't strong on backing causes. They talked for three hours and most of the conversation had to do with gleaning ideas about how to attack the

48

problem of the lumbering operation.

"It's quite possible, Matt, that I love this lake country as much as you do. You're not going to stop people from wanting money for their timber. Maybe you can show them that it doesn't need to be as drastic and that most of the beauty and smaller trees can remain. Some of the eastern states even replant where timber is cut. What about a volunteer group that can prove it can be done? By the way, I hope you won't feel I'm butting in."

"No, Dad, and if that's butting in, I want all I can get."

"You get it started. I'm afraid I'm in this to the hilt."

"I've made one start, Dad. I'm homesteading a quarter section near my church. Maybe I can start an epidemic of homesteading or land purchases by those who want to keep things something like they are."

11

Progress

The immediate order of his priorities might not seem in proper sequence to some, but to Matt, Star was first, saving the lake country was second, and his church third. The next morning, he rode the logging train to the Mission to see Star's mother. He had already decided that Jim Beaver would have to know what had transpired because there was no other honest course to pursue. The same question plagued his thoughts. How do you tell a friend that you and his promised wife are in love and plan to get married as soon as possible? He knew Jim was going to be hurt badly which clouded his otherwise bright outlook. Matt wanted Jim's friendship and was proud to have been chosen his blood brother. How he would like to put the day of reckoning off, but acting like nothing had happened would be the worst kind of deceit.

These thoughts ran through Matt's mind as he approached Star's home. The house that LeBlanc built for Star's grandmother stood in a partially cleared area with tall pines lending their protection against the bitter winds of winter and providing cooling shade in summer. It made a striking picture, no doubt built along architectural designs familiar to LeBlanc's French background. The ornate metal work and huge windows made Matt wonder how these had been brought to this place in the early part of the century. Fur must have been a lucrative business. The saw mill in the distance lent its music of whirring teeth chewing into logs as Matt approached the house. He rapped the knocker and Fawn soon opened the door, beaming her easy smile of recognition.

"Star said you might be here today." She invited him in. A large picture of the Frenchman and his Indian wife looked down from the entrance hall wall. An ornate case with racked muskets filled the space below the picture. *LeBlanc and Star's grandmother*, thought Matt.

"Mother knows about you two." She pointed to a room on her right. "Go in the parlor and wait while I tell her you're here. Star is at the Mission."

As Matt started to sit down he looked through a door to another room, where he could see books on the shelves. He went in. Books lined

50

three sides from floor to ceiling. A huge fireplace stretched across the remaining side. Above its mantel were paintings of lake and wooded scenes with children at play, both Indian and representative whites from this area. Star's work, he thought. The portrait of a beautiful woman caught Matt's eye. Her eyes showed the same direct intensity as Star's. He heard a movement behind him and turned to look at the living portrait of the picture. Matt bowed out of instinctive deference to Marie, the mother of the one he loved.

"Come, let's talk." Marie placed two chairs facing each other, and they sat. As they surveyed each other, it ran through Matt's mind that she was the result of the best of two races, the adventurous, resourceful Frenchman and Indian nobility. "Star has told me everything," she smiled. "I don't think she left anything out. She said you were supposed to tell me, but she couldn't wait. I know she loves you, and now," she looked at Matt searchingly, "I think you feel as strongly, and I'm happy for Star and you."

"I guess it shows. You can be sure I love Star with every ounce of me. I know if ever two people were meant for each other, we are those lucky mortals."

"They say a mother feels no man is good enough for her daughter, but I don't feel that way. I think I know you quite well already. Star's a good persuader, and I'm convinced you two should be together."

"I want to share her life, not to dominate or prevent her from fulfilling hers. She is more than any man could expect from this world. If loving her and wanting the best for her is enough, that makes me eligible."

"I am going to use what persuasive power I have to get White Otter to rescind his promise to Jim Beaver. I also know you two are going to get married with or without his blessing in the end, but I hope you'll be patient for a while. He isn't going to change without a struggle. For me, you're already my son."

"We'll wait because neither of us want to cause more problems than are here now. I would be proud to call you Mother." Marie held out her arms and Matt came into her embrace.

"You couldn't know how much I want you and Star to be together."

Fawn looked through the door.

"If anyone wants some strawberry shortcake, it's being served in the kitchen."

As Matt approached the Mission, he saw the door was open. Hesitating before going in, he listened to the chatter and laughter of the children in the playground nearby, but he didn't see Star. The structure next to the chapel had to be the school building, he thought. As he

51

entered the open door, he saw the life-sized crucifix in back of the worship center. A table with a lace cloth covering was on the platform, from which the sacraments of the mass were dispensed.

Father O'Brien soon came through the door, dressed in work clothes.

You must be Matt Berglund." He came closer and studied Matt for a moment. "You and I have a lot in common to talk about. Come into my study." The study was small, the walls lined with important looking volumes, mostly unfamiliar to Matt. "Let's talk about Star first," said Father O'Brien as he motioned Matt to a chair. "I think you know she's no average person, and it has been my privilege to see her develop from a gifted child to a person of achievement and grasp far beyond her tender years. She's told me about you two. I'm responsible for your first meeting because I suggested she enter the swim in last year's shoot. I feel I'm more her father than her father, if that makes sense. She's a thoroughbred, and excellence is the only terminology she knows. I know the love you two have is genuine. Otherwise you'd both be happy not to cause the hurt that will result. I also rejoice in the fulfillment for you both, and am hoping your problems can be resolved without too much trouble."

Matt was discovering that he liked Father O'Brien.

"Jim Beaver told me about you, he is my friend and, according to their customs, my blood brother. I would do almost anything to hold that friendship. When I see him, I plan to tell him what happened. I imagine he loves Star as I do. I know how empty my world would be without her. It sickens me when I dwell on what I have to do."

"If it means anything to you, you have my blessing. I know you are necessary to Star's fulfillment. Not to see this through would be a travesty against God's plan for the union of those who truly love. Now, let's talk about your church."

Matt showed surprise.

"Oh, you know about it?"

"Yes, things like that get around, and I'll be glad to help you get started. There are settlers around here with Protestant backgrounds, and they need a place to be reminded that God is important to them also. In spite of what you've heard, I know that God judges us beyond our separate systems of faith. Star also told me about your feelings on conserving our timberlands. I hope you won't back off until you halt this unrestricted ravaging of this beautiful part of God's green earth. If I can nudge you into action, I'll do all I can."

Matt warmed to his new ally. "The first step is to get all those together who are concerned enough to want to do something about it.

52

From this group, we can plan a course of action to resist and change, without violence, the present lumbering methods. You would add clout as a member of this strategy board. I don't want people to think this is just a whim of some kid out of college."

"Do you have any direction in mind?" asked Father O'Brien.

"My mind keeps coming back to one main course of action, which was suggested by my dad, and that is to organize a volunteer lumber crew from those interested. They will select an area, possibly one of their own places. If we just harvest the mature trees, leaving the rest unmolested and the other greenery just as it is, we may have proven a point that the return will be as large and the harvested area is still habitable instead of an eyesore. If it works out, no one will want or allow the present Monarch operation to come in. It is my hope the legislators could be invited to view the two methods and put pressure on Monarch to enact similar conservation methods. Because much of the land is still unsettled, Monarch can do a lot of damage. Most of this land is best suited to be forest and should remain as such. I plan to homestead near my church and to encourage others to homestead or buy land so they will have a right to decide what will happen to it."

"You've been doing your homework. It's iffy, but it's got to work Count me in. Let's get that church of yours in shape and call a meeting. God must be hoping we do something fast." Father O'Brien leaned back and studied Matt again. "How are you going to preach, visit, and nurture the needs of your people with all this other activity?"

"I'm not afraid of work. I'll give it all I have on every front, but I'll have to admit that next to Star, the preservation of our lake country is my strongest interest. This may be my ministry."

"Do you have a list of names of your prospective members?"

"I have." Matt unfolded a list from his pocket.

"Good. I know every inch of this territory, and I can steer you to where these people are. The Trading Post needs some work, so you need to set a day for volunteer work to get it in shape so we can get on with that meeting to save our beloved lake country. Allow me to make one comment. After you've baptized a couple of babies, your priority may change. This is God's world."

12

The Canvas

True to his word, Father O'Brien alerted those of Protestant leanings in his parish, but he also asked his members to make a special effort to help in the reconstruction of the old Trading Post. He and Matt had divided the list, and Matt knew that his prospective members would heed Father O'Brien's invitation because they admired and respected him as a positive force in the community.

Distances between prospects were long.

"Take my horse. He needs some exercise," Gunnar Anderson told Matt.

It was the same with a canoe.

"Take it. You'll get there faster," someone offered.

There was an Abrahmson and a Zuber. Some were happy to know there would be a church for them. Some heard him out and smiled politely. Enlisting them to help rebuild and repair the Trading Post was an incentive because they sensed a gathering with the presence of food and sociability. The threat of the invasion of Monarch and their innate love for their woodland way of life, with the appeal to change or stop the devastation, made most say, "We'll be there."

Bob Dahl's place was a surprise to Matt. By the use of a windmill he had constructed, he pumped water from a bayou to his land for irrigation. Monarch and Thorson took all the strawberries, tomatoes, and sweet corn he raised. Matt estimated his cleared land at twenty acres, which was mammoth for this part of the north country. One reason for his success was the use of remains from the fishery that cleaned and sold fish. The covered containers would be unloaded by the track close to his farm. Bob Dahl contracted for the amount he could use as fertilizer. He hauled the container to his field and spread the innards, heads, scales and skins before he prepared the soil for planting. If the wind was in the wrong direction, the Dahl family would endure the smell for a few days, but the crops tripled their production.

Matt was invited to dinner, after which Susie crawled onto his lap and kissed him.

"Thanks for saving my life."

Matt hugged her.

"You've been coached."

"Anyone who can build a system like this should surely be on our 'how to' committee," Matt told Bob Dahl.

"I want to help." There was no reluctance in Bob Dahl's answer.

Because Star was never out of his thoughts, Matt was curious how married life bloomed or faded in the way people reacted to their spouses. He wondered why that glow of love and respect for one another was often absent. Was it never there, or did the stress of living and surrendering of dreams for reality drain their togetherness to a passive acquiescence and enduring? He came to Bill Carnahan and was invited to dinner. There was little evidence of substance, but the cottage was neat and cheerful.

"My wife makes blue gill, and corn bread taste better than roast duck," he said by way of introduction. Bessie Carnahan turned from the stove, where the odors of cooking promised that her husband had told the truth.

"Bessie, meet Matt Berglund, our new preacher."

She nodded, as Bill kissed her on the cheek. She threatened him with her spatula and kissed him instead.

"Bill, act your age."

As they ate, Bill spoke.

"We didn't have any children, but we adopted Bessie's sister's boy, Clark, when she died. Her husband wasn't much and was glad to let us have Clark. He's seven and visiting the Bannisters today."

Matt left them with warm good-byes. He knew here was a difference between living and enduring. Why was it so rare, he thought.

It was fifteen minutes before the time of Matt's first sermon. Noises of assembling people could be heard from where Matt sat in his recently constructed study of his Trading Post church.

The events of the last three weeks since he had received his appointment raced through his mind. He and Father O'Brien had canvassed all of the families to invite them to take part in the revamping of the Trading Post and to ask their attendance to the meeting following the first service concerning Monarch practices. Last Wednesday, these neighbors had come from the outlying areas and converged on the Trading Post in number beyond his expectation. Matt had asked Zeb Hawkins to organize the work groups and oversee the renovations. Zeb had been everywhere, lifting, nailing, directing, and lending a hand where necessary. Now, minutes away from his first sermon, he wondered how many would respond to the meeting to discuss the invasion of Monarch.

It was time. He opened the study door to his recently constructed altar platform and his pulpit just two steps away. Zeb had made his pulpit. It was a professional, well-finished piece of furniture, which stood out against the rough hewn interior. The church was filled. The plank benches, furnished by the saw mill, were hidden by human density. Looking out over those present, his eyes met those of Star's. For a moment the intensity of his need for her seemed to eliminate all others. How he wanted to rush to her, hold her and tell her again and again of his love.

Recovering from his trance, he noticed Star sat with Fawn, her mother, and a handsome well-groomed Indian, who White Otter. Matt wondered how much coaxing it had taken to get him to come and see what this young usurper was like. As he looked over his audience he recognized several whom he had called upon, but there were more he'd never seen before. Then he saw Jim Beaver and a cold apprehension enveloped him as he realized how much he wanted Jim to be his friend. His dad and Zeb were there also.

It didn't occur to Matt to be nervous. He had prepared his talk and had decided the congregation couldn't expect a spellbinder from a twenty-one-year-old beginner.

The service began. The invocation he gave was a prepared one from his manual which ended in the prescribed, "Through Jesus Christ our Lord. Amen." The scripture he selected was from the Epistle of James, chapter two, verses fourteen to twenty-five, ending in "Faith without works is dead." There was a short pastoral prayer. "God, we wish to thank you for these days of our lives, especially for the cooperative spirit which has allowed us to work together to be able to worship here this morning. We hope we can continue this spirit of togetherness so that, at least some of the time, you will be happy to be among us, to love us, and encourage us to serve you better. We also thank you for the privilege to have lived in the majesty and beauty of this lake country. Help us to seek out your purposes so that we can be a people worthy to glorify your name. Let our voices rise in praise and honor to You, our Lord and Counselor, amen."

The sermon began. "I want to welcome all of you who are here today. Some of you came because you felt a need to worship, some out of curiosity. Still others came to enjoy the basket dinner immediately following the service, while others came to take part in the meeting which convenes after dinner, to which everyone is invited to attend. We also have a number of Father O'Brien's flock here, and he is among them.

He scheduled his services at different times to pay respect to those whose background of faith is different. We have worked and will continue to work together in open-minded support for each other. There is much here today that is new, a new place to worship and a new preacher. I probably don't need to remind you that I'm new at this job. My name is Matt Berglund, just out of seminary.

"This is my first sermon beyond some practice sessions at school. I don't know many of the right answers on what is the best way for us to reach out for God, but I know all of us need love and sometimes a helping hand. There was One who walked among us less than two thousand years ago, who loved, helped, healed, and invited us to follow His example. Fancy prayers and expressed platitudes are of little value if there is no further participation. Scriptures have been used to prove many points, but it's hard not to agree with James when he says, 'Faith without works is dead.' Let us think together on the simple down-to-earth implications of what is said here.

"God sees us as we are. He knows we are happiest when our hearts and minds are reaching up and outward to express the potential of love and goodness in us that are often suppressed by pressures that make us surrender to lesser living. Often, each of us have looked inward and seen what we are, and that image will not be covered by paint or false fronts. According to this scripture, our faith must be expressed with works. If you are looking for a church that is a comfortable place to spend Sunday mornings, you may have picked the wrong church. Some scriptural encouragement will be a part of our program, and I'm hoping we will want to be motivated to make a difference in our own lives and in the quality of living in this community.

"Someone has said, 'We are God's fingers.' Little will happen here unless we help God mold and shape our destiny. You may say, 'We are too selfish, too discouraged, too set in our ways to believe that life can have more zest, more quality, and more fulfillment.' Well, I'm too young and too stubborn to believe that we here can't make a difference, so I'm asking you to come along for the ride. Some day, it could be said, 'This was just another church with an average profile of faith and expectations. Then something happened. A chemistry of God's love and action burned in its heart, and it wasn't just another church.' It's not my desire to be a great preacher, but I pray that what happens here will renew our determination to live as we already know we should."

After the benediction, Matt hurried to the door as people got up to leave. One of the first to greet him was Mrs. Meek. She was a widow, who still lived on the place she and her husband had home-

57

steaded. She had a goat and a mangy dog that looked more like a wolf. Matt remembered his first confrontation with that dog. The bared fangs and the snarl had given every indication of immediate attack until Mrs. Meek said, "No! Buck!" The dog had then backed away almost apologetically.

"Pretty good for the first sermon, Preacher." She took his hand and smiled mischievously. "We may not have the best preacher, but I'll bet we have the biggest."

The greetings were warm and congratulatory. Star's mother, Marie, took his hand and patted his knuckles with the other.

"I want you to meet my husband, Chief White Otter." The clasp Matt received wasn't unfriendly, but it seemed neutral.

"I'm glad to meet you, Chief White Otter. If you ever want to talk to me, let me know, and I'll be there. Thanks for coming."

Fawn shook his hand and smiled, and then Star stood before him. No words were spoken. The strange situation they were in seemed so unnatural to him. In the squeeze of her clasp, her love swept over him as their eyes fixed on each other. Then she loosened her grip and went with her family.

Jim came by.

"Jim, I've got to talk to you. Will you stay around till after this is over?" Matt said.

The potluck dinner was served on the plank benches brought outdoors, which made respectable tables when placed together. It was a time of banter and feasting and a good time for Matt to get acquainted. Zeb, as usual, was deluged with the small fry so much that he had little time to eat. He liked it that way. Venison, ham, fried chicken, biscuits, blueberry pie, and strawberry shortcake were some of the more obvious dishes. There were some big black pots of coffee steaming over a fire. Matt furnished the lemonade for everyone who felt like a kid.

The well-fed frame of mind was general as almost all came back into the church for the meeting. No doubt, some of the wives were more interested in the problems to be presented, but it was evident that the issue at hand was strong in their minds. Father O'Brien started the meeting.

"Although this was your pastor's idea," he said, "he asked me to open this meeting. I might add that I feel as strongly about the problem, as many of you today know. Maybe I should start by asking two questions. How many of you have seen what's happening to our timberland farther north?"

There was a show of hand by most of those present.

"Now, how many liked what you saw?"

No hands were raised. Father O'Brien looked all around.

"I think this is a good time to hear from Phil Peterson, whom some of you know."

A rangy, weather-beaten man with graying temples came to the platform. His raw-boned rugged appearance was similar to many of those who attended the meeting. He was ill at ease.

"Making speeches isn't my kettle of fish," he said, "but I hope none of you will allow what has happened to me to happen to you. Our place, where my wife and I homesteaded many years ago, is now a part of the godforsaken useless area left by Monarch. Two years before they were at my place, one of their men offered me money for the trees on my property at a time when my wife needed to be in the hospital. I signed the papers and took the money. Later when I realized what I had done, I tried to get them to release me by paying back the money. They laughed at me. Now, I'm out in the open with nothing big enough to hide a skunk. In the name of God, don't let it happen to you. My wife didn't live to see this day." Phil Peterson hesitated, choked with emotion. "She would have been heartbroken. She loved every inch of this beautiful northland. Ours was a simple life. My wife took part in everything; the hunting, trapping, fishing, and the garden. You know Monarch will be breathing down your neck soon. I hope you find a better solution than I did."

Matt could feel the pervading empathy as Phil went back to find a seat.

Father O'Brien spoke again.

"We all know that harvesting timber is necessary because of the great demand for building material. It's obvious that we are not going to stop lumbering, and to try would be wrong. Our reason for meeting today is to consider the alternatives. There has been some head-scratching, and we want to present a possible solution that will involve each and all of us. After we have presented it, we are open to other ideas if they have merit. Now back to Matt Berglund, not as your pastor, but as one who can swing an ax with the best of you and wants to keep the land of ours as nearly like it is as possible."

Matt had taken off his coat and tie, and as he stood up, he looked around at the audience.

"First, I want to get things straight. There is a very special young man among you this afternoon. His name is Jim Beaver. He's the one who invited me to the cutting area and hoped something could be done about it. He is my friend and my blood brother by their tribal custom. Credit him for being the first one to want to see some action." The spirited applause seemed to embarrass Jim.

"I'm not an expert in this field," Matt continued, "but I've done some homework lately, and the experts tell us we are in an area that is best suited for trees. Climate and fertility keep it from being the best place for large crops. It took centuries to grow the mighty pines and other trees that we have here. It is insane to think that it can be mowed like grass and made unfit for human habitation, and that is just what's being done farther north and will continue to be done unless you and I grab hold of this knotty problem and change what's happening.

"We propose this effort for your consideration, which, I hope, will start the change. Father O'Brien made this remark, 'God must be sickened by what is happening and hoping someone will do something.' Here is one idea that could be an answer. We will form a lumbering operation of our own, which could involve every able-bodied man and woman. We will harvest only the mature trees from whichever plot of land is decided upon as a showcase to prove that it can be profitable and still leave much of the trees and undergrowth untouched. Much of the beauty and natural habitat will be left intact. It will be hard work, and that's where you and I come in, offering the time necessary. We would be a volunteer crew that won't quit when the going gets rough, which it will.

"If we can prove our point, we then can let the legislators come and see for themselves and make laws that will force other lumbering interests to do as well. After the verdict is in on the first phase, we'll decide whether to continue or use other tactics. We're not going to lie down and quit. It's possible we may have to become a full-fledged operation. I'm also sure that some of those now working with Monarch would be happier to be a part of a crew where sensible harvesting was the end product. If people have a choice, Monarch will be stymied and forced to change. It's time for immediate action, and whatever final plan we decide on here, let's throw our combined weight behind it and get started. One other thing. I have filed for homesteading on a plot of land near this church and adjoining the railroad track, and I suggest if there are others who can, now would be a good time to even buy more land. If it is ours, we can at least decide what to do with it. I will also offer my land as a starting point for this new venture if no one else wants to start it, or we can vote to see who gets the nod."

Matt hesitated. "I want to see this happen. I believe in it so much that I will donate the money from the lumber removed to help pay some of the expenses we will incur. It's about the average amount of mature pine and should give us an idea of what to expect from your own properties."

He sat down. Father O'Brien again took the center of the platform.

"This is a time for serious thinking. Nothing much can happen unless most of you are willing to put in long strenuous hours of hard labor to see this through. Let me say one thing for Matt. I knew he was homesteading a piece of land near here, but I didn't know he was willing to donate the profit from the sale of his timber. It's plain to see that he's in it all the way. Those who work will be paid according to the pay scale used by Monarch as soon as the money for the lumber delivered comes back to us. You won't be wasting your time. Now, let's hear what you have to say."

Olaf Hedberg stood.

"I doubt if any of us have given this much thought. Let's try this plan until we can honestly say we have a better one. It's going to get some of us off the seat of our pants. Unless someone has a better plan as well thought out, let's do what has been put in our laps. This has got to work, or we'll be sitting here with a few trees while the rest of our lake country is ruined. I'd like to see how many of you agree with me by standing. A plan's no good unless we have the people to back it."

Just then Jim Beaver got up, and, in what seemed like one leap, he was beside Matt. There they stood. One could feel the admiration of those present as the two tall young giants stood side by side. Most of them knew Jim worked for Monarch.

"Count me in," said Jim. "You're going to need all the help you can get. We've got to make this work."

To a man and woman they rose from their seats. There was loud clapping, and the women were hugging their husbands or the closest male. The men were shaking hands and back-slapping each other.

Father O'Brien stood at the center of the platform and waited until the first wave of enthusiasm had allayed.

"Now is the time for each of you to sign your intent in this notebook," he said. "If you have experience with ax or saw and any equipment we can use, let's get it down so we can see what we have to work with. It's quite possible we are starting a new lumbering operation that will need to continue until such time as we have made our point and the present lumbering methods are changed by law and public opinion. Our main purpose is to bring that day into reality as soon as possible. It should be democratic, so you need to be thinking about who'll be the crew bosses, and then put the best man in the best place. It may take some of you a while to get things tended to before you can go all out for this project. I'd like to advise you to have another meeting next Sunday

61

after church, where definite plans will be made and crews selected for the various jobs of cutting, logging, cooking, and whatever. This has been a long day. Sign up before you leave, and consider yourselves adjourned."

13

Betrayal

The church was empty with the exception of Matt and Jim Beaver. Matt's mind was in turmoil. The moment he dreaded was upon him. He and Star had fallen in love. He wanted Jim's friendship badly. Jim certainly loved Star, and she had been promised to him by tribal protocol. Matt knew it wasn't going to be easy for Jim to accept that Star had chosen him, Matt Berglund. He feared it would be the end of a friendship that he cherished.

"You asked me to stick around," said Jim. "What's on your mind?"

"What I have to say has caused me more mental anguish than I've ever had to cope with before. I have to tell you because it's the thing to do. It's Star. We are in love. I didn't know she was promised to you when we met by accident, but I'm glad I didn't know."

He related the tree incident as Jim sat frozen.

"We are not seeing each other until we have her father's and your approval. I know you love her, and, hopefully, that will make you understand why I love her. I wasn't aware of that kind of love until we met, and Star feels the same."

Jim sat. No change of expression had shown on his features. He stood up after what seemed an interminable time and looked at Matt as one who had betrayed him.

"I promised I would help, and I will," he said. Then he walked out of the church.

After Jim Beaver had gone, Matt went to his study. The cloud of Jim's frozen countenance remained like a toothache. He scanned the notebook, which showed what he knew with certainty already. Axes were plentiful, and there were a few saws and an old winch that Monarch had scrapped. The odds seemed insurmountable to him, and his usual optimistic resilience flagged.

He couldn't sleep. It was 1:00 A.M., and there was no use trying to sleep. He got up from the cot in his study, dressed, went to the lake dock, and climbed into his canoe.

14

Help Comes

The sun was rising when he approached his dad's place. He wanted to catch him before he started his day. The smell of bacon and eggs suddenly hit his nostrils, and Matt realized he was hungry. Adam opened the door before he knocked.

"I kinda figured you'd be here," Adam said.

The breakfast was nearly over before either of them mentioned their new project, but as Adam was sipping his coffee, Matt showed the sign-up notebook to his dad.

"About what I expected," Adam said as he checked the names and equipment, "but none of these mentioned horses or mules, which they have. I know; right now, you think we've bitten off too big a hunk to chew, but maybe you've got to stop thinking you're the only one who is doing something. As you know, I was in the war, and my job in the Engineer Corps was to cut down trees, build bridges, make roads, lay track, and do what needed to be done to keep the army moving. I became adept at improvisation. Now, if you think we're going to be licked before we start, you don't know your dad. I'm turning over the managing of my fishing stations to Ed Swedberg so that I can devote full time to helping save our lake country. Here's what I've done so far. I went down to the city and talked to my old army buddy who is in charge of the rolling stock of the railroad. He has offered an old switch engine which is too small for their bigger operations but will be just right for us. A couple of gaskets will put it in good shape.

"There are several old railroad spurs around here. We can recover rails and ties and put them in our cutting areas so the logs will not have to be moved so far, just like they're doing up north. The only cost will be our labor and the usual charge for hauling logs on the main track when we start delivering. I've used and reused rail and ties so much that I can do it in my sleep. And one thing more, I've written to a General Green, who once told me that if I ever needed a favor to ask for it. He happens to be in charge of quartermaster supplies. I've asked him to check over the war surplus and ship some of the cable, pulleys, winches, and block and tackle that we used to move logs in the army. I should know what the outcome of that will be very soon."

Matt put his head between his hands as he felt an upsurging flood of relief. How little he had known about his dad, the qualities of giving of himself, the astuteness and intelligence to make things happen. Adam came behind him and pressed Matt's wet cheeks with his hands.

"We're in this together. Let's go get 'em."

At Adam's suggestion, Matt lay down on the sofa for a short nap. Adam had been told of Jim Beaver's reaction to Matt's love for Star. It was a knotty problem. Time is a fickle mistress, giving, denying, and separating. His heart sorrowed at the uncertainty of Matt's future with Star. Here were two young lovers, whose desire was to literally devour each other, kept apart only by their own acquiescence to an unfair and, for the most part outmoded, custom. Jim was a casualty, and Adam hoped he would come to the realization that he wasn't the first or the last where love is concerned.

Two hours had gone by and the sound of heavy sleep emanated from the sofa, when there was a knock on the door. Adam opened the door to Zeb Hawkins.

"Come in, Zeb. You didn't come out just to say 'hi' this time of day. What's on your mind?"

The sound of conversation woke Matt. Two hours had lifted some of the burdens from his mind and body. He greeted Zeb.

"Hi, Cub, let's all sit down. I think I have something to say that you'll like to hear." Zeb looked at Matt and Adam with his warm uncomplicated and friendly smile.

"When I came from the South, you accepted me as one of you right from the start. It was like moving into paradise with the beautiful people and country that are here. My happiest years have been here. I tremble at the thought of looking out one day on an ugly landscape without trees. I didn't do anything about it, but the cub here did." Zeb hesitated. "I don't know how to say it, but I have money, lots of it. I never needed it. Now I'm turning as much as is needed over to you, Adam, to spend and administer where necessary. I want you to buck and beat 'em, not with just one little space, but to continue until you can force a change.

"Now," Zeb continued, "I don't want anyone to know that I'm doing this other than the two of you. I plan to work alongside the rest just as I am and have been."

"I'd like to tell Father O'Brien," Matt added, "It will go no farther."

Matt paddled back north with a feeling of joy in every stroke. He looked again at the familiar shoreline with a more vivid appreciation of its grandeur and beauty. He thought how different his own attitudes were. It seemed that God opened a window to let light in when the darkness seemed most suffocating. Maybe, there was a sermon here in all of this.

The Trading Post came into view, but Matt went on by to the Mission. He wanted to see Star and wave to her. Temporarily, that would be enough, just to see her to let her know by this much that she was the most important reason for his facing the tomorrows ahead. He was almost to the Mission door, when Star came out. They stood face to face. Matt felt an overpowering urge to sweep her in his arms. Father O'Brien stood in the doorway.

"You two better go inside and do what you're thinking about doing. I'll stand out here and keep off the wolves."

They went inside the foyer.

"Kiss me, hold me, love me," said Star, and Matt did. If God were looking on he may have said, *Here is true love expressed. Love beyond and above what few mortals seem to attain and it breaks my heart that you are held apart by that sense of honor that I also commend. Because of free will which I have given you, I cannot intervene.*

"Matt, you could send me a little note now and then, and I'll do the same. Father O'Brien can be our post office. Maybe we can find out little things about each other that we don't know now, and you could tell me you love me every time."

Matt gave his "will do," just as Father O'Brien came in. "Time's up. Try to make that last for a while."

"Have you talked to Jim?" Star asked, as they walked out.

"Yeah, he's still going to help us, but he hates me."

"Poor Jim, I think I know how you feel about him. I hope he can return your friendship again some day."

Star kissed Father O'Brien on the cheek and started toward the school. They both watched as Star walked with a lithe graceful stride, pleasing to the eye. She stopped, turned, blew a kiss, and then disappeared through the school door.

"We both love her," said Father O'Brien.

It was Matt's turn to let Father O'Brien in on the day's events.

"I also stopped at the post office and picked up my mail, I am now a homesteader."

"Glory be," said Father O'Brien. "We're going to do it, and we're going to do it right. I think God is answering a few prayers. We'll get a group together and build you a cabin so you can start living there to make it legal."

The mile and a half to the Trading Post church hurried by as Matt leaned into his paddle, expressing his joy of living with every stroke. The world never seemed lovelier as the moon rose over the pines and smiled her benediction upon him. There was much to do, and he was glad. He would sleep tonight and face the new day and its beckoning demands with exhilaration.

15

Ready to Go

The surveyors had come and marked the corner boundaries of Matt's one hundred sixty acres. The land between the tracks and the lake was railroad right-of-way. Matt's section bordered the right-of-way east of the tracks, into the virgin timber.

The second meeting for the planning of the volunteer lumbering experiment was held. These were people who were used to coming to grips with emergencies of existence and this, by bringing it into the open, was an emergency they were ready to tackle. By vote, the Trading Post was to be the bunkhouse. The crew couldn't be going home every night because of their scattered and often distant homes. Each would bring his own bedding and mattresses to be placed on the benches which were pushed together. Matt's section was to be the starting place. "We can't beat an offer like that," was the verdict.

Mr. Thorson, Maude's father, who owned the grocery store, promised to furnish the staple groceries necessary on a pay-later basis, after which Mrs. McCormich, president of the Ladies Aid Society, stood up.

"I'd like to announce that the ladies will see to it that meals will be served to the workers, thanks to Mr. Thorson."

Father O'Brien took the floor.

"I know you are chomping at the bit to get started, and I think we should set a possible date. However, there are some loose ends that need to be brought together, so let's give ourselves time to set up, then we can continue without trusting too much to luck. Since our last meeting, I have been informed of some things that will give our operation more possibility of success, but it will take more time to put it together. Some of you have suggested that we start the Monday after the shoot on Saturday, four weeks from now. Your pastor has stated that he hasn't time to defend his championship this year, but his congregation has voted him down. So they took up a collection and have the dollar for his entry fee." He rattled some coins in a cup.

"Matt, will you come and stand beside me?" As Matt presented himself, Father O'Brien continued. "Matt, these people of yours have dug deep in their pockets and come up with a dollar for your entry fee to the shoot. You're pretty busy and they thought you might forget to enter. You have been a champion in more ways than one in getting this project started, so whatever the outcome this year, they want you to know that you'll still be a champion to them. It's a good idea to play together as well as pray together." He handed the cup to Matt. "The money is yours, but be sure to give the cup back to Mrs. McCormich."

The whistling and cheering gave Matt a warm glow as he grinned at his people. They were his kind of people, rough, tough, and dependable. In this area where man struggled with and against each other, guts and brawn were respected as leadership qualities that rated above words and appearance.

"I'll give it a go."

"Now," concluded Father O'Brien, "we need to set a date for raising a cabin on Matt's homestead."

16

The Cabin

The railroad company had built a bridge across an inlet that made a small bayou on Matt's property. Matt had picked a slightly elevated spot close to this bayou for his homesite. He had selected the trees for logs and cut them himself into prescribed lengths. Most of his congregation had shown up to help. It was a good cabin. Adam did the notching and Zeb supervised. Again, Matt could see the smooth unobtrusive manner in which he kept things going. It was a fun time. The ladies brought enough food to overstuff the participants and children. A small stove with a flat top for cooking and heating was installed, and curtains were hung on the two windows, compliments of the ladies. As Matt walked through the door, someone joked, "When you going to get married, preacher?"

The cutting of timber for home and firewood had resharpened Matt's skill with the ax. Sometimes when he saw a tree similar to the one used for the tree climb at the shoot, Matt would race up its trunk and into the branches to get some first-hand practice. When he called on his church members, he often ran at full speed for a spurt, hoping no one was watching. Maybe he'd be in shape for the shoot, after all.

Matt began to know his people more fully and hear the undertow of what was wrong or not fulfilling in their lives. When he decided whom he would call on, he wore clothing to fit the occasion. He felt more at home in most places in dungarees. Little Susie Dahl would run to meet him to be carried with her legs wrapped around his neck. He helped Si Webb snub down a cow so the horns could be sawed off. Mrs. Meek's porch was sagging at one end. Matt sawed a section of a large stump the right length and put it under that end to make it level again. The wolf-like mutt who had bristled and growled when they first met was now a friend. Ted and Mary Bannister were barely thirty, but the stair-stepped children came from every corner of the place. She looked drawn, worried, and unkempt. When Matt finally got a smile and she brushed back her snarled, uncombed hair, he could see that she was pretty. Ted had worn his present garb too long and smelled of old sweat. There were eight children, and it was obvious they didn't need any more. She seemed to be holding Ted at bay, literally, by being unattractive and frigid. Some of the children went to school at the Mission.

"I like my teacher," little Sarah, who was eight, said.

"Oh! Why?" asked Matt.

"She's pretty, and she smells good when she hugs me." Matt reflected that he had noticed that, too, and thought he and Sarah had a lot in common.

Matt had read an article on the syndrome of childbearing. Too many women had babies until they died, as a result of exhaustion, never really recovering from the last one, or of complications made more severe by their rundown condition. Ted was looking at hopelessness. He and Mary hadn't thought it would be like this. They were in the early threshold of their lives, disillusioned and bewildered by the trap of their expression of a love that had turned into a nightmare-struggle to feed the many mouths. One had only to visit the graveyard to see how many families had children who had been decimated by disease, were stillborn, or did not survive the first year. To put it crudely, the Bannisters were the lucky ones. But here were eight bright, healthy children who were destroying the bonds of marital coexistence. Was there an answer to the Bannisters' dilemma? He had read some of the manuals explaining methods of preventing conception. As he ran and walked back to his cabin, he decided to get some authoritative information on the subject and bring it to the Bannisters.

These were problems that needed solving before God could infiltrate into their lives. Matt knew he didn't have many of the solutions, but some could be found if the effort was made. One thing that helped was the inner assurance that his dad and Zeb had what it took to make the lumbering operation viable, and though he continually felt a surge of eagerness to get on with the project, he was no longer bogged down with the crippling fear of inadequacy.

17

Time to Play

The day of the shoot arrived. In light of everything else going on in his life, the event had seemed unimportant to him, but as he saw the whole population converging on this one day of festivity, Matt began to catch some of the excitement in the role-playing to come. He was in good shape, but he had never really been otherwise. Maude was there, and he wondered if their paths would cross before the day was far along. He knew they were still good friends. She was all the things he had seen in her—pretty, kind, thoughtful, and intelligent—but now there was a barrier that separated them and kept them from talking together freely.

Jim Beaver came to the judges' stand to pay his entry fee the same time as Matt, but he ignored Matt completely. The smell of liquor came to Matt's nostrils, and he wondered which of the contestants had imbibed. As he was waiting, his dad approached. They hadn't seen each other for two weeks.

"I'm not going to bother you with other business right now," Adam said. "I'd like to see you win this one for the Berglunds. Enter everything, and you may pick up some extra points that will come in handy."

"I hope I can come through for you, Dad."

The shoot was the first event. It took more time as each contestant fired ten shots, three at a stationary target, three at a moving target drawn jerkily on a cable, three at some cheap pottery saucers thrown in the air from behind an embankment, and one shot fired through a small hole in a tree stump which set off a loud cap used to set off explosives. When it boomed, it made enough noise to make young and old clap their hands over ears.

It was said that Doran had filed the tang on the firing mechanism so that it released the firing pin with the slightest squeeze of the trigger. Matt's rifle was the same as Doran's without the hair trigger. He and his dad had hunted through the years. Deer meat was an acceptable addition to be drawn and frozen after the first heavy freeze. His rifle was from army surplus, like Adam had carried through the war. Adam was a good instructor.

72

Doran, with seeming casualness, put three shots in the bull's-eye of the stationary target. The moving target rang like a bell the three times he shot. He broke the three saucers, and then set off the first boom by centering the last shot through the hole in the stump for a score of ten.

Phil Peterson, the widower, whose homesteaded land was destroyed by Monarch, had his turn. Matt had encouraged him to enter just to get his mind off his troubles. A rifle was second nature to him, and he scored eight out of ten, but he didn't make the noise of that exploding cap reverberate through the trees. It was a popular event, and many displayed their skill or lack of it. Matt shot a respectable score of six, to get one point for third place. He finished with a boom.

The foot race was next and it didn't take long. The distance was approximately one hundred yards from the warehouse right through Main Street, if you could call it that. It was the only street and hardly wide enough for the fifteen hopefuls entered. The race was on. Jim Beaver was a step ahead, but Matt, straining every sinew, stayed close by sheer determination. It was almost over and Jim, who had gained another step, was slowing, and Matt pulled almost even. Eighteen-year-old Hank Osborn flew past with his arms pumping like pistons. He won, Jim was second, Matt was third.

Score: Doran three, Osborn three, Beaver two, Berglund two.

The archery event came next, and Jim Beaver won easily. Matt enjoyed trying to hit the target but did poorly. Doran was second. Now Jim Beaver and Mike Doran had five points, Hank Osborn three, and Matt only two.

The log rolling, where two contestants tried to topple each other from a log, was easy for Doran, but Matt had been working on this skill most of his adolescent years. He stayed with Doran the longest. Now Doran was ahead with eight points, Beaver five, and Matt four.

The wood chopping contest had only five entries. Adam had honed Matt's ax and Matt felt on even terms with Doran. His long, powerful arms went through his log seconds before Doran separated his log.

Score: Doran ten, Matt seven, Beaver five.

Doran didn't enter the ax throw. Maybe he thought it unnecessary. Matt had often spent a few minutes tossing the ax at a stump in their yard, so he wasn't a total novice. Axes were flying from several competitors, most of them missed the tall stump used as a target or chipped a sliver of bark from its side. At thirty feet, Matt called his placements, top, center, or below, and he sunk his blade within a foot of his callings. Jim sent his first two throws within inches of designated areas. He pulled his handkerchief from his pocket and wiped his forehead before the third attempt. As he let go of his handle, he sank to the ground and vomited. The ax hit the stump flat-sided and bounced away. Matt hurried to Jim, but the look he received told him not to try to help. Matt had three points, Jim two. The three points he received for the ax throw were not to his liking. He tried to get the judges to give Jim another chance, but they said "rules were rules." Now it was obvious why Jim had slowed at the end of the foot race. Drink had sapped his performance. In a backhanded way, Matt knew the reason for Jim's condition. He thought of the venomous look in Jim's eyes as he came near and knew that Jim's love for Star was destroying him. He wanted to forget the points on the ax throw, but then he remembered his promise to his dad and knew he must continue.

Score: Matt and Doran ten, and Beaver seven.

Fifteen canoes lined up for the race, but soon, the front runners were Doran and Matt. It was a seesaw race, with each man ahead several times. In the final ten yards, Matt won by half a canoe length. Matt thirteen, and Doran twelve.

The tree-climb, one of the most exciting events, was in progress. Because the lumberjacks were good at it, there were a great number of them competing in this event. Jim, a tree-topper, was no doubt one of the best, because he had told Matt he was going to give Doran a run for it. He didn't show up to try, so that finally narrowed the challengers to Doran and Matt. When the results were in, Doran was the winner, and, to his surprise, Matt almost equaled Doran's time. Doran fifteen, Matt fifteen.

Doran was now on the spot. He had to enter the swim to try to keep pace with Matt. No doubt now he wished he had entered the ax throw to get some extra points. Doran was a good swimmer, but Matt knew he himself was a better swimmer than last year, and he won by ten yards. Matt eighteen, Doran seventeen.

The crowd fever was rising as the final event approached. Many still called this Doran's arena, because, with the exception of last year, when Matt beat him, Doran had always won this event. This time, Matt had his share of backers, and the vociferous rooting for each side was a competition in itself. Maude and Star were together rooting for him. Matt marveled at their unselfish friendship. Fawn didn't seem to be in evidence. Jim was probably in a stupor somewhere, so he was no longer a contestant. Now Doran had to win to tie. Matt knew that to lose and tie was unpalatable.

No one else wanted any part of either Mike or Matt, so they were in the ring together waiting for Zeb to give the "go" signal. No doubt Doran felt Matt had lucked out last year, and Matt knew Doran would be more formidable this time. There was to be a half-hour limit. At the "go!" signal, they met in the middle. Matt didn't try to elude Doran, probably to Doran's surprise. They locked in a tangle of arms and legs, this time muscle against muscle, which eliminated to some extent the cunning and trickery of either opponent. Doran lifted Matt off the ground, but Matt had his arms tightly locked around Doran as Doran moved toward the rail. Matt's grip was not to be broken. Doran knew if Matt went over the rail, he would take them both out, so he set him down. Matt had trained with the wrestlers at seminary and learned some of the holds and breakaways. Matt fell backward, cartwheeling Doran against the rail. This time, Doran hung on. They separated and probed for a different attack as their bodies smashed together in a heaving, wriggling, maneuvering intertwining. Matt now invited the close contact because he knew he was as strong as Doran. With his fifty-pound-weight advantage, he could try to anticipate Doran's next move. They broke apart again and as Doran backed off, he kicked his feet into Matt's neck and jaw. It reeled him back but not off his feet and as Doran came down, Matt moved in, grabbing Doran's leg, and began to swing Doran in a circle around him. Doran curled up like a coiled spring. He held on until Matt had to stop before he got too dizzy. Doran had been in orbit, and the crowd cheered at the action packed spectacle.

Matt was gaining confidence. He had wrestled on even terms with Doran and, on some test of strength, had made Doran counter to keep from being bested. In one exchange, Matt clamped a headlock on Doran and held it. Doran tried several tricks to break the hold, but Matt merely applied a little more pressure. Doran seemed to be tiring and relaxed, as though giving up. It was an old ruse. Matt let up slightly. Doran kicked violently and twisted out of the hold to come back like a bull moose facing the next attack.

"Time," said Zeb. "It's a draw."

With the one-point advantage, Matt was the champion.

18

New Venture

The designated Monday came, and the preliminary preparation had been done. Adam was voted to take charge over all. Zeb was called the coordinator, which meant what everyone knew, his job was to see that things ran smoothly, to be at every place that needed solutions when problems arose. He would be there. Matt's quarter-section was divided into several parts. The first part was ready for cutting. A rail spur had been extended into the segment selected, and Tom Bannister was in his element as operator of the woodburner. In his teens, he had worked in a switchyard but had been nudged out of a career by an engineer who had a son that needed a job. The quartermaster department of the army had shipped and unloaded large quantities of cable, tackle, and winches like those Adam had used in the war. Adam received a short letter, which concluded with these words: *Win this one for Conservation. General Rick Green.*

Adam met with Jim Beaver and discovered a powerful ally in lumbering. He made him straw boss. Jim threw his unstinting energy into making things run smoothly. He and Zeb exchanged ideas often, and Jim began to feel the strength and influence of Zeb's character on his outlook on life. A friendship developed out of mutual respect for each other.

Matt didn't work full time because of his other obligations. He worked where needed the most and was often where Jim was. There was no camaraderie shown, but at least there was respectful communication. Matt could, by osmosis, inject some extra energy into any crew with which he was involved. He loved the action it induced and felt a sense of purpose more fulfilling than his pulpit duties. He and Zeb gravitated to each other. He knew that Zeb had a strong faith, which glowed unobtrusively. Matt wanted what Zeb had—something so real it made him feel he was in the presence of an angelic force. Zeb should be the one in the pulpit, he often thought.

Large cables were extended over long areas or ravines from one tall tree to another. Pulley-supported carriers moved along these cables after lowering block and tackle to the ground to pick up logs, then raised and carried them to be let down on a flatcar on the spur. The efficiency was evident. Admiration for Adam, Jim, and Zeb showed in morale and desire to be good lumberjacks. Father O'Brien remembered that Matt had called this a "new venture," and that became the name of the operation.

The ladies divided the cooking duties, with different crews taking turns. The present headquarters for meals was under a huge canvas tarpaulin close to Matt's house. The men were carried on flatcars to and from the Trading Post. Children were divided among those off duty. As the men and women welded into a unit, one could feel an upsurging, an elation, a pride in working for a cause that gave each a status as a person of destiny.

Timothy Barnes became a pivotal figure in the success of New Venture. Matt made a belated call on him when he happened to be in his path of visitation. Mr. Barnes invited him in, and Matt noted the meticulous housekeeping.

In their conversation, he learned that Mr. Barnes had worked at a bank. He was a bachelor and had come north on a vacation just to look around. When he came to church at Matt's invitation, Matt asked if he would handle the collection and allocation. He seemed pleased. After showing his method of bookkeeping and accounting, Matt knew he had found the man for the more difficult job of disbursing treasurer for New Venture. He also kept a close check on the amount of lumber cut and shipped.

Others were volunteering their land even before Matt's was finished. It was very evident that the method they were using left the lumbered area still easy on the eye. Trees of various stages of maturity dotted the terrain. Brush was dragged to the ravines by mule power to slow erosion at flood times. The land had given much of its treasure, but what remained one could live with, including much of the wild life. Any comparison with Monarch's results should convince the most skeptical of the need to minimize devastation farther north. Those tracts of timber adjoining the railroad right-of-way were tackled first to present a more extensive picture of selective cutting to those who made the laws.

It may have seemed unimaginative, but when there was a special occasion, it always included a potluck. Timothy Barnes had done his job well, and when the check came for Matt's lumber, a Saturday was set aside for all to celebrate the results. Payday had been observed each week, and though some might have wondered where the money came from, there was a feeling that things were going well. They were glad to be allowed to share in the total picture, so a talk and share time was held before the feasting. Timothy Barnes started it.

"It's my job, to deal in facts and figures. I've written them on this blackboard for you to see. The seeming huge profit is due in part to your pastor's donation of all profits to New Venture. Without that, we can still pay more than what Phil Peterson received from Monarch and have money to pay current obligations. If this bears out in the future, we can pay our way, keep up our equipment, and apportion the extra profit back to you."

After the noisy approval, Mrs. Meek stood. She had given more of her time than any of the ladies, because she was free to do so. A new stature had come to her in the eyes of the workers because she could make a tastier pot of beans, fry the fish more golden brown, tenderize the venison, and stir up a stew that was a gourmet treat to those large appetites.

"You may think I'm out of character, but I've been listening and thinking. The more I dwell on it, the more I think we have a miracle happening here. In the first place, if our pastor had not gotten all stirred up by Jim Beaver showing him that Monarch mess, and if Adam Berglund hadn't been in the war, he wouldn't have known the right people to get all this equipment. Without him or Jim Beaver, we wouldn't have had the know-how to hack it. I don't know how to talk about God, but I think He wanted us to do this even more than we did and has been pushing us all the way. One more thing. I've come to know the people of this community more than I could have in a hundred years, and I'm so proud to be one of you." She sat down to a noisy response as Father O'Brien rose.

"I know you all came here to eat, so let us bow in thankful appreciation to our God. God our Father, we want to thank You for the miracle that has happened. In spite of blisters and aching muscles Your people have united in a common endeavor that has made them more responsive to You and to each other. Two of Your church families have gathered in a spirit of communion, unselfishness, and love and also with a feeling of honest pride in reaching the first plateau of our goal, the preservation of our beautiful part of Your world. Be with us as we laugh and feast together. We give You praise and honor for Your watch care and presence among us. Amen."

19

The Bannisters

Ted Bannister and Matt became good friends. When the woodburner didn't need his complete attention, Ted lent a hand elsewhere. He even came to church with some of his brood, but Martha stayed away. Matt knew their lives had polarized and he knew at least one reason why. He had written for and received some pamphlets on birth control, but he hadn't figured how to get through to Ted. It was resolved in this manner.

Ted's son, John, the ten-year-old, was large for his age and a good worker. He was one of the brush crew when he wasn't in school. A cable was fastened around a pile of brush and then taken to the nearest ravine. Joe was Ted's mule, a powerful specimen, who responded to any command with a complete lack of enthusiasm. On this day, John had hooked Joe to a cabled pile of brush. With the usual "giddy-up," John nudged the mule with a blunt stick. After the third nudge, old Joe decided to move out. He stepped on a forked stick, which hit hard under his belly. In a flick of an eyelash, Joe's sagging ears came straight up. He made an unearthly noise, kicked out over his traces, hunched like a jack rabbit, and bolted, taking the brush pile with a series of fast lurches and also dragging John, who had the halter rope looped around his wrist.

Matt was on the end of a saw when he looked around to see old Joe dragging the pile of brush and John toward him. He ran toward the mule, grabbed the halter with his arm around Joe's neck, and dug in his heels, forcing old Joe's head to the ground. Joe stopped in a very few feet and dropped back to his usual docile pose, as though he had forgotten what he had done. John regained his feet, scratched but unhurt. Ted, white and shaken, ran to his son.

"You all right, son?"

Matt could see that although Ted had too many children, he loved John as no doubt he did all the others. In a few minutes everything was back to normal and John finished the journey to the ravine without the rope around his wrist. Ted came over to Matt.

"I owe you one."

"I'll collect tomorrow," warned Matt.

The next day, Matt climbed on the woodburner and handed Ted some pamphlets.

"I want you and your wife to read this literature. Our church isn't ready for it yet, but the time will come. You and your wife are too young to just stare at each other. Honestly, I'm no authority. It just seems to make sense. Read it and use your good judgment."

As Matt went back to his saw, he thought it would be great just to be able to stare at Star, but he knew they wouldn't stare long when the obstacles were erased. There were few times when Star wasn't in his thoughts. Each moment of the first day, when they had made known their love for one another, burned in his memory. The holding, the uninhibited expression of Star's love for him, and the completeness of those few hours stirred him to a fever pitch. At times, he pictured her nakedness, the perfection of each tantalizing contour, combined with the excellence in every other category. How could he feel otherwise? He also knew the love they had for each other transcended the physical. She was his to have and hold, and yet barriers of custom and friendship stood between them. He dreamed of her, and that made the waiting more difficult. Yet, through the heartache and separation, there was the euphoria of anticipation.

In this mood, Matt went to see Father O'Brien, hoping that Star may have left a letter for him. She had, and Father O'Brien grinned as he handed it to Matt.

"I know what you came for, so take it with you and come back when you have both feet back on the ground."

It was dark when Matt walked back to his cabin. In his own lamplight, he read Star's letter.

Matt,

That's the most intimate way I can address you. When I first heard you call me "Star," when I left you bruised and standing there and paddled away, I prayed you loved me as I knew I loved you in return. I have a pillow that I hug at night and sometimes call it "Matt." It doesn't seem to mind at all. New Venture has a rooting section here. Mom, Maude, and I want you to know you have our wishes and our prayers for its fast success.

There hasn't been a dull moment since school started this fall. Some day I'll bore you with the extracurricular activities we have. When we get married, I hope school is out so you'll be my chief distraction. "How do I love thee, let me count the ways." When you look at the stars, I'll be waving back from every one and smiling love to you.

Star

20

The City

Two more quarter-sections along the track had been harvested, and with the further experience, New Venture had done an even better job of conservation, which added to the esthetic appearance of the harvested landscape. It was autumn, and Matt had written a letter to the Committee on Land Use in the state legislature. He asked for time to talk to the legislators, to tell the story of New Venture, and to invite a comparison of the harvesting techniques by having them come to see the difference.

After three weeks, he finally received a letter, saying that he would be told when to appear in the near future. After waiting three more weeks and receiving no answer, he rode the train down to the city. The letter he had received was written by a secretary who worked for Representative Sam Bender. There was a debate on the floor of the House of Representatives, but many were milling around the halls. Matt asked a page where he might find Representative Bender.

"That's him over there, talking to two others." The page pointed to the trio.

Matt introduced himself when he felt he could get a word in without being rude. He told Representative Bender about the letter he had sent and the reply.

"Oh, that letter...you know things move slowly around here. You'll get your turn when the time is right."

"Now let me get this straight. What is it you want to do?" asked another representative who had been listening.

Matt had found an interested ear and told him about the New Venture project.

"I don't want to stop their lumbering. I just want them to use similar methods to ours, so they won't ruin the Northlands. All I'm asking is that you come and compare."

"My name is Wade," the representative said. "I'll get you a few minutes this afternoon. Sounds more important than what we have boiling now."

Representative Bill Wade turned out to be the floor leader of the House, and he opened the afternoon session.

"Before we start on the bill before us, I've promised Matt Berglund a few minutes to present something that should be of importance to all of us."

Representative Bender got to his feet.

"The chair recognizes Representative Bender," said Wade.

"I think we should take these requests in order," he said, "and not break in on the very important bill coming up."

"How long have you known about this project?" asked Wade.

"It came to our committee about six weeks ago. I had my secretary answer it."

"Does anyone else in your committee know of this?"

"No one else showed up." Bender didn't like the corner he had brought himself to.

"Some of us might ask why we haven't heard of this sooner," said Wade. "Those present who would like to satisfy their curiosity, raise your hand." Most of the hands were raised.

Matt stood up. The representatives saw a young man who would make two of the floor leader.

"I have no doubt that all of you love this great state of ours and we in the Northland feel the same. The Monarch Lumbering Company has devastated the land. We who are close to it have been sickened and revolted by the desolation they have left behind them. They are creeping farther south each day. Out of this revulsion and apprehension about our own impending doom, we put together an operation of our own, called New Venture. If you will take the time to get on that passenger car behind the logging train that goes up and back daily, you can see for yourselves the utter waste, the uninhabitable eyesore, where trees, animals, or humans want no part of it. That is Monarch's work. You will agree that something terribly wrong is being perpetrated.

"I know lumbering is a necessity for our growth and it is honorable work. But if you will compare the Monarch methods and results with the areas we have harvested, I won't need to tell you which is the way to go. We have left the land still beautiful, harvesting only the mature trees, allowing space and sunlight for the remaining trees to be productive in the future. We know it is more work, but we can show a profit and still pay those who own the land more than double what has been given by the Monarch Company. We ask you to come and see for yourselves and then, by legislation and public pressure, insist that Monarch and other companies use conservation methods similar to ours. This is your state, your beautiful part of this country. We need action in haste.

Greed and indifference have done far too much damage a}ready. I am also aware that there are those here today who will oppose any reforms because the vested interests are concerned only with profit. All that we're asking is that you come and see for yourselves and, in honesty, make your decisions. Thank you for listening."

Bill Wade came to the podium.

"Someone who knows about this man gave me some interesting information. Matt Berglund has been the 'All Events' champion of the north country for the past two years; ten events, including shooting, wrestling, swimming, canoeing, throwing the ax, wood chopping and log rolling. If any of you care to tangle with him personally, let us know. We'll pay to see it. And here's a clincher. He is pastor of a newly established church of one of our well-known denominations."

They were laughing and applauding as Matt left.

21

The Epidemic

During the fall as New Venture continued, the logging train brought many people north to see what was happening. Mr. Barnes and Matt often met the train to answer questions and show the harvested areas after they had already seen the bleak devastation of Monarch's spoilage. Soon the metropolitan papers were giving space to voice the opinions of those who had seen the difference. There were editorials urging immediate action. Monarch replied, saying they couldn't operate like those "eager beavers" and pay dividends to the stockholders. A cartoon appeared with the New Venture mouse hanging the bell on the Monarch fat cat.

A bill was presented to the legislators, but it was sent back to the committee for revision, which was the delay tactic of the heavily lobbied pressure placed on the representatives. Accusations were made of pockets being lined with greenbacks for votes against change.

Winter came and, with it, an epidemic of smallpox swept through the Mission area and spread even beyond the families of the two churches. For Star and the still healthy, there began an ordeal of caring for the sick. The Mission school became the hospital. Zeb came, caring, holding, cajoling, and telling stories to the little ones as everyone, sick and well, listened. Matt had other obligations, but his job was to minister, to help keep things as sanitary as possible, and to carry out the dead. Maude volunteered. Star warned her of the danger.

"You're here," said Maude. "Am I better than you?"

The dead bodies were frozen and stacked in a shed. The frozen ground wouldn't accept them, and timber wolves had no qualms about flesh of any origin. Bob Dahl's brother, Floyd, didn't survive. The Zubers were found dead and frozen in their house, showing the pock marked ravages of the disease. The Indians were hardest hit, and Matt found it a sickening chore to remove the dead from among those still breathing. He, Maude, Zeb, and Star worked long hours taking their rest in catnaps. Father O'Brien had been in the middle of it from the beginning, giving encouragement to those who fought hard and last rites for those who were waiting for the end. Matt and Star often worked side by side, so busy with the problems at hand that their only reward as lovers was their eye contact, still honoring their hands-off agreement.

Once, as the three of them sat together, Maude asked, "Why aren't you two married?"

Star told her their problem.

"Oh, that's cruel!" Maude said.

With the lessening of winter came the decline of new patients. Twenty bodies were buried as soon as the ground would accept them. White Otter became a patient after it seemed that the epidemic had run its course. When he was brought in, Maude appointed herself as his nurse, and he responded to her solicitude and caring.

"Why are you keeping Star and Matt apart?" she asked one day as she brushed his hair. "Don't you know they love each other, and that's the only good reason people should marry? Do you really know what it is to love someone?"

Just then, Marie came in and took his hand in hers. White Otter looked at Maude.

"I know."

There hadn't been a new case of smallpox for ten days, when Maude came down with the disease. The Thorsons kept her at home and hired a doctor to be on hand around the clock. She continued to worsen in spite of the doctoring. Maude became weaker and more emaciated with each hour. The doctor warned her parents of the possibility of her succumbing. Star came to see Maude and was told that Maude wasn't expected to live much longer.

"Let me see her," said Star. She came to Maude's bedside and took her hand. "Maude, can you hear me?" Maude gave a slight pressure to Star's hand. "You have to live, Maude. Matt will need you. I can't explain it except that I know it's true. You have to live for him. Believe me, he will need you. Don't try to understand, but live for Matt, please." Star stayed with Maude, saying softly as she washed her face, brushed her hair, and patted her hand. "You have to live, Maude. Matt is going to need you."

Hours later Maude looked at Star.

"Get me something to eat, please. I'm hungry."

Her convalescence was speedy, and Maude wondered at her recovery. There were no pockmarks. She really hadn't realized the depths of her despair at losing Matt to Star. It had to be the hope that what Star had told her about Matt needing her at some time had kindled her desire to live. She wondered how that could be. It had to mean that by some trick of fate, Star would be out of the picture. Maude knew that

Star had intelligence and insight and was gifted in so many areas. Did she really possess that gift of divining the future as far as she and Matt were concerned? In their association together during the epidemic, they had become close friends. The hope that Matt would sometime be hers, which had made her want to live, could only happen by Star's elimination in whatever way, and she didn't want that to happen to Matt or Star. But she couldn't dismiss the feeling that Star had told her an awful truth. Maude felt like a pawn in circumstances over which she had no control.

White Otter lived through the smallpox, but the disease had sapped his vitality. He was suddenly old. Spring came and the north country brightened with a profusion of flowers and greenery. The difference of the two methods of lumbering stood out in such contrast that it stirred a mounting crescendo by the public and private sectors to force Monarch to change.

White Otter died. There was only a gentle sadness shown by Star, Fawn, and Marie. Marie said he seemed to will his death.

"He couldn't be an invalid," she said.

Matt wondered about White Otter's promise of Star to Jim Beaver.

22

Sadie Meeks

Maude took her turn helping prepare food for the New Venture crews. She and Sadie Meeks hit it off from the start. Her assessment of Sadie was the same as others who thought they knew her, a widow, clean but untidy, and seedy in her appearance. She had a quick rejoinder for any small talk, and everyone liked her but didn't include her in their lives. Maude and Sadie enjoyed working together, and gradually Maude began to look at her more closely. Sadie was fit and agile and had a good set of teeth, which was good background for a pretty smile. Maude just couldn't stop there.

"Do you like to live alone?" she asked Sadie.

"Not really, but a tough old crow like me don't get any proposals."

"How long have you been a widow?"

Sadie thought for a moment.

"About twelve years."

"Did you love your husband?"

"Oh, Lord, I guess so. He was a good provider. Maybe this is a little rich for your ears, but he was a lover. We spent a lot of time in bed and other places, and, would you believe it, I was as willing as he was ready." She was reminiscing with stars in her eyes. "We had a great relationship."

"Did you ever want to get married again?"

"Don't be silly, Maude. Look at me I'm a mangy whelp that can't even attract flies."

She was right, those baggy clothes and that stringy gray-brown hair wouldn't set anyone on fire, thought Maude.

"I'm coming over Sunday afternoon, and we're going to make a new woman out of you."

Sadie didn't protest too much, and Maude knocked at her door early Sunday afternoon. She brought a bag, which included a comb and brush, some soap and cosmetics and two dresses that Maude and her mother had selected. Maude shampooed Sadie's hair and snipped some straggly ends. The tints of gray in the healthy sheen of brown didn't detract at all She brought the soft contours down slightly over Sadie's forehead and around to the back in a neat bun pinned in place. Then she told Sadie to look in the mirror.

Sadie caught her breath.

"Is that me?"

Maude gave her one of the dresses.

"Mother and I picked out this dress for you. Actually, she's about your age. Put it on please."

Sadie removed her sagging, poorly fitting garment and slipped into the new dress. It wasn't fancy but well styled. It looked good on Sadie's well-formed frame. She surveyed herself in the mirror.

"I can't believe it. I feel twenty years younger." There were tears on the still-firm skin of her cheeks. "You are my fairy godmother." They hugged. "Could I tell you a secret, Maude? I hope someone we both know looks at me."

"Who?" questioned Maude.

"Phil Peterson. He now owns the property next to mine."

"He doesn't know it, but I think he's a goner right now," laughed Maude. "Here's another dress, and we're going to get you some more. You're going to look like this every day from now on."

The following day, the New Venture crews lined up with their dishes to get their food. Among those serving the meal was Sadie. You could hear the undertow of conversation enough to know that Sadie was the topic. There she stood, "neat as a bug's ear," according to one comment. Gabby Barnett blurted, "My god, Sadie, is that you? You look like you've been resurrected!"

Sadie was all smiles, and when Phil Peterson came by, she smiled her prettiest. He just stared, took his food, and went by. A little later, he brought his dish back for a refill.

"I'll take a little more," he said, "but I came back to ask you if I could call on you next Sunday. You are a lot of woman, but you managed to hide it pretty well. I hope I asked you first. You hit me right between the eyes."

"Come for dinner," Sadie smiled.

23

Jennifer

A light could be seen through the window of Matt's cabin. The April dusk showed a faint glow in the western sky as Adam canoed to the dock. The door of Matt's cabin opened as Matt filled the doorway.

"Hi, Dad, good news I hope."

"Well, I'm here to get something off my chest," Adam said as he came into the cabin.

"Relax and unload." Matt pointed to a chair and his dad sat down.

"I'm going to be gone for awhile. Things are in good hands here, and I have to do something I want you to know about." Adam told Matt about Eva. "She's never been out of my thoughts for any length of time all these years, but in the last few weeks, I've had that same feeling that I did when she wanted me to come once before. I can't explain it, but I have to find out what has happened. I'll be leaving tomorrow."

Matt sat in silence. He had read about mental telepathy, and he felt that he would know if Star really needed him. It also gave new insight on the depth of character of his dad, who kept himself for that one great love. With different circumstances, he and Star had a similar situation.

"Go to her, Dad. I'll be rooting for you all the way."

The town seemed to have changed little in the intervening years. Adam's journey had moments of joy and anticipation along with the wondering if this was the better or worse in their vowed love for each other. He wondered what could sustain him if the bubble burst completely. The Variety Store was still there, newly painted, but otherwise the same. As he came through the door, he saw a young lady who looked a lot like Eva. When a customer left, Adam went to the counter.

"My name is Adam Berglund; I knew someone whose name was Eva Mason. Are you her daughter? You resemble her."

"I am," she smiled. "My name is Julie Mumford. My mother is a nurse at the hospital. You can see the building from here." Julie went to the door as Adam followed. She pointed to a large modern structure. "You'll find her there."

Adam walked to the hospital. He wanted to run, but reason slowed his steps. *She's married*, Adam thought. Where do I fit in? He asked for Eva at the information desk with subdued eagerness. *To see her again*, he thought, *was more than he expected out of life.* Who can say with complete authority that life is happenstance? It doesn't explain that intertwining thought that kept Adam and Eva bound by ties beyond comprehension or that single-mindedness of loves' embracing constancy initiated at their tryst. Perhaps from his celestial rampart God looked at them and said, "You have been sorely tried, but now, enjoy!"

Adam saw Eva coming down the hall. A constriction came into his throat. She was as lovely as the first time they met. Reason told him that was impossible, but there she was, strikingly beautiful in her nurse's uniform. She stood in front of him with eyes that spoke that same message—love in its richest potion. They were in each other's arms. This time, the kiss was long and lingering. Her pretty mouth still close, she looked at Adam.

"Tell me your thoughts," he said.

"You haven't changed in twenty years," Eva said as she reached for Adam's lips again.

"I thought the same about you as you came down the hall. I'm afraid to ask. Do I have the right to kiss you?"

Eva gave Adam a quick kiss.

"You have every right. My husband died a year ago, and I waited until it was somewhat respectable, and then I prayed for you to come. Somehow I felt it was going to be today. How did you know that I needed you?"

"I just knew," said Adam, smiling, "but I'd like to be sure this isn't a mental aberration. Another kiss might help." Their lips blended in total consecration of the purity of giving love, and Adam drank the sweetness that seemed to increase with each kiss.

"There, if you're sure now that I'm real, I want you to meet my closest friend." She led him to the information desk where Adam had inquired of Eva. "Adam, I want you to meet Ada McPherson. Ada is the only one who knows about us."

"I don't know about this," she said. "First you win the war, and then you steal my best friend."

"I'll admit I'm guilty," laughed Adam, "on both counts."

"I've been watching you two put on your act," she said, "and if I've ever seen two people in love, you are the prize winners." Ada sobered for a moment, feeling a sense of privileged closeness to be a part of all this. "Something tells me that you're going to be very happy, and that makes me happy."

"You've just made another friend." Adam kissed her cheek.

As someone came to the desk, Ada excused herself.

"Back to business."

Eva reached for Adam's hand.

"Come with me, I want you to look in on someone with me." They walked down the hall until Eva stopped at a door and brought out a piece of paper from her uniform pocket. "Before you go in I want you to read this note."

This is Jennifer. Five years ago, your husband charmed me into bed, and Jennifer was the result. I had been a virgin, but now I am a whore. I didn't know who your husband was until I read his obituary, which told me things he talked about when he was drunk. You may remember seeing me at the funeral. I had to be sure he was the one. Sometimes I can't feed and clothe Jennifer properly. She is a darling child and I love her enough to want something better for her. I've done my own investigating and know you would be good to her.

Please take care of her. She's the one pure part of my life. Don't try to find me. God bless you and good-bye.

An unfit mother

"I slightly remember a young lady at the funeral, but I didn't connect it with anything unusual," Eva said as Adam handed the note back to her. "I found Jennifer on my porch when I came home a week ago. She was tied to a column with a scarf and this note pinned to her. The next day, the paper said a woman had run in front of a moving train. There was no identification. The coroner said the mangled remains were of a woman about twenty-three years old. Assuming she was Jennifer's mother, that makes Jennifer an orphan. "Now let's go in. She had a cold and fever, but she's okay now."

A child sitting on the hospital bed stared at Adam and smiled at Eva, who kissed her forehead. She had a book in her hand.

"Jennifer, I want you to meet someone. His name is Adam."

Adam knelt at her bedside. His eyes were even with hers.

"Hello, Jennifer."

"I guess it's all right to speak to you. Are you a nice man?"

Adam grinned broadly. "Well, I could be very nice to you." Adam thought she talked like a grown-up.

"Do you like her?" Jennifer asked, looking at Eva.

"Yes, I do. I love her. Do you know what that means?"

"Uh-huh, you like her a lot."

"How would you feel about living with us as long as you care to?"

"I'd like that. My mama said I'd have to find a new mother."

"Okay, that's settled, you will be our little girl. Let's shake hands to show we mean what we say."

Jennifer slowly placed her hand in Adam's and looked at him quizzically.

"Does that mean we'll live in the same house?"

"That's right. Now you think about that while I ask Eva a question."

Tears ran down Eva's cheeks as Adam turned to her. She kissed him.

"I love you. I love you," she said.

"You know I love you. Will you marry me today if we can get a license and a preacher or priest? I don't want to spend a moment more away from you."

"I thought you'd never ask, Yes! You know I will, and I don't want to be away from you any longer. Let's get moving before it gets too late. I'll ask Ada to be a witness."

"Can we take Jennifer with us? I could carry her if she doesn't feel like walking."

"She's really quite well again, so let's ask her. Jennifer, did you hear what we talked about?"

"I heard everything. He asked you to marry him, and you said yes. Then he asked if I could go with you, and he said he would carry me if I didn't feel like walking."

"You're exactly right. Do you want to go with us now?"

"Yes, I do." She reached for Eva and received a hug and kiss on the forehead. Jennifer turned to Adam. "Do you love me?"

"I love you very much already. How could I resist?"

"Then I love you." She raised her arms to him as he responded with a hug.

"That makes you our Jennifer. Now we are a family that wants to be together."

Eva reached for a paper sack.

"I bought some clothes for Jennifer, which we'll put on right now and do what needs to be done to get this family legalized."

"I've put my foot in it. I've proposed to two ladies today," Adam mused vocally.

A spectator might have seen a man, woman, and child emerging from the front door of the hospital, squinting at the midafternoon sun.

The man was six feet four or five, muscular and trim, with an erect military bearing. He walked beside a four-year-old miss who skipped about every third step. Next to her was a neatly attired lady who stepped with the lightness of a thoroughbred horse.

Before they arrived at the courthouse, Jennifer turned to Adam.

"Will you please carry me?"

"Are you tired?" Adam lifted her far above his head and brought her down to eye level. Jennifer giggled at the quick elevation.

"Oh, I'm not tired, but I can see better from up here." Eva laughed, and Adam remembered the trilling vibrancy of its sound from twenty years ago. They reached the courthouse. A clerk filled out their license and had them sign. It was a short distance to the Variety Store. Julie was wiping a counter when they entered.

"Hi, Mom. Hi, Jennifer." She looked at Adam. "I see you found her and her new acquisition."

There was a counter with an assortment of jewelry under the glass. Adam spoke to Julie.

"Show me a wedding ring that will fit your mother. I want to marry her before she changes her mind."

"You work much faster than my boyfriend. There's more to this than I've been let in on."

Jennifer grabbed Adam and Eva's hands and looked up at Julie.

"We're going to be a family."

"If that's what you want, then that's what I want." Julie gave Jennifer a hug.

Adam tried a ring on Eva's finger. It fit, so he paid for it.

"Can you close the store and stand up with your mother, so you could give her to me when the question is asked?" he said to Julie. "Believe me, I love her. I want to take you to dinner afterwards. Then you can get the whole story."

"I believe you, and I'm happy for both of you." Julie reached up and kissed his cheek. Adam smiled.

"Some young man's going to be very lucky."

Ada McPherson came in. She sang as though she was walking down the aisle.

"Here comes the witness."

Reverend Clayborne had worked in his garden and was cleaning his fingernails when the wedding party arrived. Eva wasted no words.

"Hello! Reverend Clayborne. I want you to meet Adam Berglund, and here's Jennifer, who soon will be ours by adoption. We want to be married. We have the license."

The reverend shook Adam's hand.

"You're both of age," he said, "and I'm sure it's not as sudden as it seems. Let's get on with it."

Adam produced the ring. The reverend stooped and smiled at Jennifer and handed her the ring.

"You'll be one of the prettiest ring bearers I've ever had," he said. "When I ask for the ring later, will you hand it to me?"

"Yes! I will." Jennifer said, in her precise enunciation.

There was no music except in the hearts of those present, but Reverend Clayborne neatly tied the knot. Julie gave her mother in marriage. Jennifer handed the ring at the proper time, and soon, all heard the familiar words:

"I now pronounce you husband and wife."

Adam and Eva warmly kissed and Reverend Clayborne wished them happiness.

"We'll miss Eva, but I predict this will be one of my best marriages. Ada, if you'll sign this certificate, we'll have everything in order."

The dinner was at a private home that served meals for such occasions. Adam discovered that even lovers get hungry, and they enjoyed the family bounty on the table. While they were eating, Julie tapped the table with her knife.

"Now I'd like to know how this came about."

Eva swallowed a grape.

"I think it's worth retelling." She gave Julie the story of their twenty-year interrupted romance, leaving nothing out. "No one has explained it to me, but somehow we can communicate across the miles. I think it has something to do with the certainty and depth of our love for each other. We knew we were meant to be together, but I had promised, and Adam had his obligations to his wife and son."

Adam looked at Julie.

"I hope you find or have found someone who loves you like I love your mother."

Eva suddenly sobered.

"Mother would have liked to see this day."

"Oh, isn't your mother still around?" Adam queried, "She wouldn't have been old."

A tear rolled down Eva's cheek.

"She died after falling down the basement steps. A broken rib pierced a lung, and she didn't survive it. She knew I loved you, and her last words to me were 'I think you and Adam will get together.' I've wondered if she had insight that this world can't explain."

"I have to believe she knows we're together." Adam leaned to kiss his bride.

It was dark when Eva, Jennifer, and Adam waited on the porch for Julie to unlock the door. Julie went in first and lighted two lamps as they entered. The living room was neatly furnished with a horsehair sofa and rocking chair. A stairway circled to the rooms upstairs, and on the other side, a breakfront glistened with glass and china. The bookcase beside the stairs bulged with classics, novels, and a long line of large books, probably encyclopedias. The shadows partly hid the table and chairs in the dining room.

Julie kissed Jennifer.

"Come with me. It's time for us young ladies to get some rest. Say good night."

Adam went to Jennifer and knelt.

"May I have a good-night hug?"

Jennifer crept into his arms.

"If we're family, am I supposed to call you Dad?"

"Oh, I would like that, but only if you feel like it."

"Good night, Dad," she said and hugged him tightly, then giggled as she went to Eva who had knelt beside Adam. "Good night, Mom."

Eva received her hug and kissed Jennifer on the cheek.

"Good night and sweet dreams, little princess. Remember, this is Julie's family, too."

"Oh, I had that all figured out. We're sisters." She followed Julie up the steps. Adam hurried to the staircase as Jennifer stopped to blow a kiss.

"Jennifer, there's something else you ought to know. You have a big brother, too."

"Wow!" Jennifer giggled, "all that in one day."

The bedroom took form as Eva lighted a lamp. Adam felt uncertain of himself in the role he should play. Eva came and loosened his tie. She smiled at him.

"I'm not sure of myself either. I think you've gathered that my marriage wasn't a fulfilling experience. We know we love each other. Let's just let what happens happen."

Adam awoke. Eva was kissing him. Adam returned the affection with total enthusiasm.

"We have some catching up to do, and it seems we're working on it. How long do you think it will take to catch up on twenty years?"

Eva kissed him again.

"A lifetime, I hope."

Adam had kept Matt informed in the letters he wrote. In one letter he tried to describe Eva.

I used to think that when you found Star you found "your Eva," and now that I'm with Eva again, I'm with "my Star," so you know the completeness of my happiness. We are adopting a little lady between four and five years of age. Now you have a sister, and whether you have your guard up or not, she'll creep into your heart. Actually you have two sisters, because Eva has a daughter, Julie. We're settling some business affairs for Eva and pursuing the adoption. Look for us when you see us. You know I'm proud to be your dad.

Matt saw his new family in church about three months after Adam had gone to find Eva. Letters told him of the time-consuming adoption process, along with Eva's turning the Variety Store over to Julie by sound legal procedures. There was New York City with its theaters and Coney Island, Niagara Falls, a steamboat to Chicago, and finally Thorson's Bay.

On that Sunday morning, Matt saw his new family in the well-filled lines of benches. In his mind, he had pictured a matronly stepmother, but Eva was a stunning picture of beauty and form, and that cute four- year-old made his heart flip just as his dad had warned. Emotion overwhelmed him as he thought of their twenty-year separation. His lips quivered, and tears flowed down his cheeks. He looked around at his congregation.

"Please, excuse me; there's something I must do." He stepped down from the platform and walked up the aisle to where his new family was. Eva, sitting by the aisle, stood and hurried to meet him. They hugged, and Eva kissed his salty cheek. Matt stood by her side and looked around to those assembled, "This is Eva, my new mom," he announced proudly. "Mrs. Adam Berglund, and there's more," he continued. He escorted Eva back to her place.

"May I hold you, Jennifer?" Jennifer raised her arms, and Matt picked her up. He sat her on one arm and walked around the benches. "These are our friends, Jennifer, and they'll soon be yours." He brought her back where Adam and Eva sat. "Before I give you up, will you give me a big hug?"

Jennifer threw her arms around Matt's neck. She giggled as she looked into his face.

"You're my big brother," she exclaimed, "and you are *big.*"

The church rippled with laughter.

Matt returned to the pulpit with tears still evident.

"You see my tears," he said. "They aren't always a sign of grief. There have been few times in my life when I have experienced as much joy. I want to ask my dad to stand."

Adam stood.

"Dad, I wish you and yours much happiness. I love you, Dad."

There was sniffling and a display of handkerchiefs.

24

Problems at the School

The Mission school was an integration of Indian and white children. Whatever parental bias existed, it seldom raised its head at the school. Star kept the upper hand by treating the students alike. They respected her because they knew she would draw out their better efforts with a caring love. Jim Beaver's younger brother Jud was eleven, and had been advised by Jim to learn as much as he could from Star. Sid Duncan was the same age. His dad, an Indian hater, who went by the name, Moose, was a newcomer to the community. He couldn't explain why he hated Indians, but he believed what someone had told him at some time in his life that "the only good Indian was a dead Indian." Sid had this same attitude.

During a recess period, Jud had beaten Sid in a foot race, and Sid had taken it badly. He pretended to be friendly with Jud and offered to shake hands, but then grabbed Jud and threw him to the ground like a bag of grain. Jud sprang to his feet and pulled Sid's head down, coming up with his knee into Sid's face. That knocked two of Sid's teeth loose and bloodied his nose. This took all the fight out of Sid, and he began to bawl at the top of his lungs. Star rushed out. She washed Sid's face, stopped his nosebleed, and examined his teeth. She told him if he was careful, they would tighten up again. Sid seemed subdued, but the next day, Moose came to school with him.

Star had just rung the bell and was greeting her students as they went inside. Moose's anger was out of control.

"I want you to expel that savage!" The children crowded around to get in on the excitement.

"Sid," Star looked at him, "I want you to tell your dad just what happened. Everyone here witnessed it, so you'll have to tell the truth."

Sid squirmed and looked at his dad.

"Well, he beat me in a foot race, and I acted like a friend and held out my hand to shake his. Then I slammed him to the ground, and he did this to me."

Star looked at Moose.

"I think you taught him to dislike Indians."

Moose glared at Sid.

"Son, you lied to me."

"Let's all forget this happened, Mr. Duncan." Star held out her hand. "I hope we can be friends."

"I'd love to be your friend; you're pretty and you're smart." He reached for her hand and Star smiled at Moose as they clasped.

"Maybe I'm your first Indian friend. I'm a Chippewa Indian."

"Good Lord!" Moose guffawed, "It won't be hard to be your friend. I'm honored." He looked at Jud and Sid. "Maybe you two can be friends, too. You can teach each other a few tricks."

John Bannister caused some problems, too. When he came to school in the fall, he had made up his mind that he didn't need any more schooling. He was being paid for a part-time job on the brush crew with New Venture. He felt he could be working full-time and making more money, which had always been scarce in his family. Going to school was a waste of time. There was friction from the first day. When, on the third day, Star called his grade to the front, John didn't leave his seat. When Star went to him, he looked at her coolly.

"I'm quitting school." He picked up his jacket and began to put it on to leave. He had both arms in his sleeves when Star pulled the jacket over his head and immobilized his arms like a straight jacket.

"We'll discuss this further after school is out. Your parents sent you here, and here you'll stay unless you can convince me otherwise. I want to know what your problem is." Star angled John back to his seat and helped him out of his jacket. He sat staring sullenly ahead until the class was finally dismissed for the day.

"Come up to my desk and bring your books," she ordered. She placed a chair by her desk for John to sit in. He obeyed with a let's-get-this-over-with demeanor. As he sat on the chair, his notebook clattered to the floor. Star glanced at the open sheets of paper, then looked again. There were neat drawings of trees, landscape, and animals. "Is this your work?"

John looked sheepishly at the notebook and then at Star.

"Yeah, I gotta do something while I'm here."

Star turned more pages. It was there, a talent far beyond his years.

"Put on your jacket," she ordered. "I want to show you something, but you'll have to walk home with me."

In her study, John stared at Star's pictures with an awed expression on his face. He studied each canvas with complete absorption.

"Would you like to do this?" Star asked.

"How could I? I'll never be anything but a farmer or a lumberman

99

or worse." Star could feel his despair.

"Let me help you with this, and you help yourself by studying hard at school. The more you learn about things and events in this world, the better artist you'll be. The world won't open itself to you. You'll need to prepare yourself to get the proper training in an art school. They won't accept a dummy." Star reached in a drawer and put together some paints, brushes, sketching accessories, and a palette.

"John, you promise to learn as fast as you can at school, and I'll promise to teach you how to improve your drawing and painting."

"Oh, I will, I will." Happy tears rolled down his face.

Star loved her day-to-day interaction with the children. The little girls and boys liked to be hugged, and even the older boys were receptive to the warm pressure of her hands on their shoulder when they shared a victory of learning.

Suddenly, lice was a problem. The Whitakers had two daughters in school, ages six and eight. They came to school unkempt, uncombed, and unclean. Star had noticed them scratching their heads more often than the others. When little Annie came for a hug, Star suspiciously searched her hair. Lice! It was a sticky problem. No one likes to be told they have lice.

Star brought some kerosene to school and warmed some water in the sun. At noon, while the others were playing, Star applied the kerosene to Annie's and Abby's hair, and then washed their hair in soap and water. She dried and combed their tresses and attached a little ribbon to the braid. Then she let them see themselves in a mirror. They were pleased. She hoped that that would be message enough to eliminate the lice problem, but soon, the lice reappeared. Uncertain of the right course of action, she confided her dilemma to her mother.

"Let me see what I can do," Marie offered. "We'll have to get their mother to change her habits, and that might not be easy."

When Star saw Marie the next morning, Marie was dressed in old, but clean clothing. Marie noticed Star's quizzical stares.

"I'm going to the Whitakers, and I may need to burn these when I come back."

Star went to her mother.

"Mother, I hate to see you do this, but I honestly believe you're the only one who can get some good results. I love you." They were used to hugging each other. This hug was one of love and sympathy.

"Pray for me," Marie smiled, half joking.

Marie hitched her horse Dan to her buggy. She took a gallon of kerosene, some soap for hair and more soap heavily impregnated with lye for laundry and scrubbing. She had visualized in her mind what the

Whitakers' place would look like and wasn't surprised when she surveyed the actual scene. As she approached, she saw Velma Whitaker standing in the doorway. The yard was as disheveled as she was. Marie felt some qualms about what she was going to do. She had dealt with Indians who were in a similar state of shabbiness, but she had some leverage as wife of Chief White Otter to tell them to shape up or be ostracized by the tribe. This was going to be harder. This would take some tact. Marie reined Dan to a stop. Out of the corner of her eye, she saw Mr. Whitaker as he emerged from the ramshackle barn. He seemed more neatly attired and cleaner than his wife. She stepped down from the buggy and went to the door where Mrs. Whitaker had remained.

"Mrs. Whitaker. I'm Mrs. White Otter, and I've come to talk to you. May I come in?"

"I guess so. It's kind of cluttered in here, but I'll find you a chair." They both sat by the side of the kitchen table.

"You have a problem," said Marie, "and it's no use mincing words or dodging the truth. Your two daughters came to school with lice in their hair. We have to do something about that."

Velma cringed and brought her arms together until her elbows met, as though to ward off a blow.

"Let me see your hair," Marie said, as kindly as she could. She didn't need to explore long. "You have lice in your hair, too," she said. "We'll have to clean you and this place before the Health Department has to take action."

Velma cringed further into herself. Her despondency made Marie wish she'd stayed away, but she steeled herself to continue.

"My daughter, Star, is your two daughters' teacher. She says Annie and Abby are lovely children. It's not my job to find out how this happened, but I'm here to help you get back on the right track."

Velma remained frozen.

"You're not saying anything, so I'm going to ask you a question. Do you want to mother your children properly, or are you a quitter?"

"That's what I've been, a quitter." She broke into sobs. "Please, please help me."

"I'll help you if you'll help yourself," said Marie. "The first thing is to wash your hair, and then we'll need to wash every piece of bedding in this house. We'll scrub everything that can hide a bug."

As Marie washed Velma's hair, the smell of kerosene filled the house. Marie was firm but not unkind. Velma pitched in when instructed. Ignorance was part of her problem. *It probably was the way her parents had lived*, Marie reflected. The mattresses were opened and the straw was burned. The cloth coverings were washed in lye soap and hung in the sun. Bedbugs were evident, and Marie was almost sickened at the sight.

Most of the sanitizing was completed when the daughters came home from school. Velma had bathed and put on a clean frock, and her hair sparkled. Annie was impressed.

"Mom, you're pretty," she said.

Earlier, Mr. Whitaker had looked in long enough to be introduced and had retreated, but when Marie went to her buggy to leave, he came over to speak to her.

"Thank you so much." He was pleased when Marie asked about his physical problem.

"I worked for Monarch. The accident wasn't my fault. A cable snapped and knocked me off a load of logs and left me in this condition. This thigh bone seems to be torn out of its socket. Monarch gave me a pittance of a pension, and here I am, a cripple with a lot of pain. The company doctor said he did all he could, which was nothing."

"You're going to see another doctor," said Marie, "but right now, wash your hair in kerosene and soap." She smiled. "You've probably got 'em too."

25

The Cure

Marie talked to Father O'Brien about Alan Whitaker being crippled while working for Monarch.

"I don't think they did all they could for him."

"I understand that Eva Berglund, Adam's wife, is a registered nurse," said Father O'Brien. "Maybe you two should pay Alan a visit."

Soon Eva received a letter.

Dear Eva,

Somehow I feel I know you. My daughter Star, and Matt are kept apart by unfair customs and a sense of honor that makes them wait until the barrier is lifted. They should be married, and I pray that time will be soon. We will be more than friends some day, so I want to invite you to my home. Matt will tell you how to get here. The reason I want you to come now is because you are a nurse. I want you to see Alan Whitaker who was crippled in a lumbering accident. Monarch refuses to do anything other than give him a small pension. You have seen everything in your time as a nurse, and I'd like your opinion if something more can be done. Also I want you to see Star. I pray you have a new daughter and I a new son soon. Bring your husband if he can get away from his work. Don't dress fancy. We may get messed up a little.

Marie White Otter

Eva read the letter and handed it to Adam.

"Let's all go," he said. "I'd like to see Star, too. I've seen them in church once, but I really don't know them. Let's go day after tomorrow. I've got to give a few instructions to the crew on laying some new track first."

The train ride to the Mission didn't take long. Jennifer enjoyed everything from the toot of the whistle to the continually changing scenes of lake and forest. When Marie answered the door, she had to be a little surprised at the handsome family that entered. Eva and Marie looked at each other in honest admiration, and they hugged. Marie gave Adam a friendly handshake and stooped to Jennifer.

"This is Jennifer. Jennifer, this is Mrs. White Otter."

"I'm glad to meet you, Mrs. White Otter." Marie noted the precise enunciation.

"I haven't held a pretty girl like you for a long time. May I have a hug like your mother gave me?" Jennifer walked into Marie's arms.

"If I call you Jennifer, you must call me Marie."

"How do you do, Marie." Jennifer giggled as they rubbed noses.

Star came into the room. She had been painting. The frock she wore showed a few blotches of paint. Adam stared, almost stunned by the picture of perfection before him.

Marie spoke.

"This is the woman your son is in love with."

Adam didn't hide his admiration.

"Matt described you, and he's right. I don't know how he could let you out of his sight. I want to welcome you into my heart, too."

Star came to Adam, embraced him and kissed him on the cheek.

"You'll be a dear, dear dad."

Eva went to Star. There was an easy responsive respect for each other as they embraced.

"And this is Jennifer. Jennifer, say hello to Star."

Jennifer looked up to Star as she held out her hand to her.

"Hello, Star." She touched Star's hair. "Oh, you're pretty. Now I know why Matt likes you a lot."

They called it a "snack," but it was really a complete meal with strawberry shortcake as dessert. Fawn wasn't present as she was helping with the bookkeeping at the saw mill. Marie and Star learned of Adam and Eva's separated romance, with which Marie and Star could empathize with understanding.

"I want Jennifer to stay with me while you go to the Whitakers," said Star. "We're going to have fun."

Adam, Eva, and Marie filled the buggy seat fully, but no one complained. They reached the Whitakers around two o'clock. Abby and Maybelle were home, clean and combed. It was their vacation time. Velma was neat and scrubbed. The house smelled fresh.

"We're here to see what can be done for Alan," said Marie. "This is Adam and Eva Berglund. Eva is a nurse."

"I'll get Alan. He's hoeing the garden." There was a new look of competence in Velma's eye.

Velma went to the rear of the house to call Alan, and he came limping painfully.

"We're here for one reason," said Marie. "Alan, this is Adam and Eva Berglund. Eva is a nurse, and she would like to see the extent of your injury and decide if anything can be done."

"We'll have to put you on a cot or a bed to examine you." Eva reached for Alan's hand. "Don't feel embarrassed. I've been a nurse for a long time. Adam, I think we'll need you."

Alan was embarrassed, but not to the point that he didn't want help. He was stripped and given a towel to save face and laid on his side with the injured area up. The problem was easy to diagnose. The end of the thigh bone had been wrenched from the hip socket. It protruded above and out of place.

"It can be repaired," said Eva. "It would have been easier the first few hours or days. Now it has tried to start a new socket but I think we can get it back where it belongs right now. It's worth a try."

Eva took a vial out of her kit and poured some powder in a glass of water. "Drink this," she said. "It will help deaden the pain. Now Adam, you get at the foot of the bed. Marie, you and Velma keep him from sliding toward the foot of the bed when Adam pulls. It'll take a good pull to get it where it belongs." Eva showed Adam how to hold the ankle and foot. "Now, pull!" she ordered.

Alan was pulled away from the women's grasp and slid to the foot of the bed by Adam's tug. He screamed from the pain. Eva looked at Velma.

"Have you got another sheet?" she asked.

Velma produced a tattered sheet from a dresser drawer. Eva folded it to make a triangle. She slid the sheet under Alan's shoulders and tied it to the head of the steel frame of the bed. She brought Alan to his side position again.

"Now pull again!" she ordered.

Adam pulled, and this time, they could hear a slight tearing sound as the leg lengthened. Eva pressed the protruding end inward. It gave a thump as it found its proper place in the hip socket. Though heavily sedated, Alan screamed just before the final thump. Eva untied the sheet and placed it under his buttocks.

"We need something stiff to hold against his hip and thigh while it heals," she said.

Velma was thinking hard. Her face brightened.

"He has some leather army leggings," she said. "I'll get one."

She dug it out of an old trunk and handed it to Eva. Pulling out the laces and opening it wide enough to cover the hip, Eva then wrapped the sheet around it like a wide belt. Alan was still under sedation.

"He won't be hoeing the garden for a while," said Eva, "but he should move enough to perform his own duties. There'll be pain for a while, but he's used to that. He'll walk again and maybe run a little. In time, it will be almost normal and without pain."

"When he gets around pretty well, tell him to look me up. He's a lumberman, and we can use his expertise," said Adam. "I'll open an account for you at Thorson's and you can get what you need until you're able to pay it back a little at a time. We'll keep in touch with you."

26

The Swim

Star and Jennifer watched the buggy disappear. Jennifer was carrying a little bag.

"What do you have in that bag?" asked Star.

"Matt said you might want to go swimming, so I brought my bathing suit."

"Matt tells me you're a little fish in the water. Let's go inside and change to our bathing suits, and then, the first one in the water gets the biggest cookie."

They soon reappeared.

"You can see the lake through the trees. Now, let's get an even start, and when I say go, you run for the water."

"I'm ready," Jennifer giggled.

"Go!" They raced for the shoreline fifty yards away. Star discovered that Jennifer could really scoot but allowed Jennifer to reach the water just before she did. They splashed through the shallow water and dove into the sloping contour. Matt had told Star in a note of Jennifer's quick adapting to water, and Star could see she swam well. Star swam out farther as Jennifer stayed close. Star stopped and trod water. "Show me how fast you can get back to shore."

"Okay, I like to go fast. Did you know Zeb calls me 'Buzz Saw'?" She churned the water neatly as she raced to the shore and scampered onto the sand.

Star extended herself for a distance, and as she walked the last few steps in the shallow water, Jenny came to her with her arms up. Star picked her up and received a hug.

"I love you, Star," said Jennifer. "Matt said I would."

Matt had mentioned in his note to Star that Jennifer might be another Star in the making.

"I love you too, Jennifer, now we both have a new friend."

After swimming some more, they headed for the house. In the kitchen, Star brought out the cookie jar and placed several cookies side by side.

"You get to pick the biggest one."

Jennifer giggled.

"Okay, I know you can run faster if you wanted to."

Star was more than intrigued with Jennifer. Though they were years apart, she felt that Jennifer's comprehension was far beyond her years. The time sped by. Jennifer's ability to read and understand exceeded many adults she knew. The grand piano attracted her. Star saw her intense scrutiny as she played a portion of a Beethoven sonata, and the almost instant comprehension after she taught her some fingering. Soon they were playing short bars together, and Star caught the rapture in her expression as she mastered the chording. Being in the presence of one so gifted seemed almost unreal.

Star now knew more clearly Father O'Brien's interest and attachment to her.

After a successful duet of a simple sonata, they grinned at each other, and Jennifer suddenly reached for Star.

"Oh, Star, I love you so much, it kinda hurts. I hope you and Matt get married so we can be together a lot. I guess you and I love Matt more than anything in the whole world."

To Star, being in the presence of one so gifted, and yet so totally normal and unaware of it, made their time together an unforgettable experience. She hoped that she could help mature this little girl who was seemingly devoid of limitations. It helped her understand herself.

When Marie, Eva, and Adam returned, it was too late to get back to Thorson's Bay. Marie negated all argument to the contrary

"You'll spend the night with us."

Fawn came in. She had been helping with the inventory at the saw mill.

Fawn had worn her buckskin attire, and Jennifer, sitting by her at the supper table, asked about it. Fawn's easy friendliness had captured Jennifer.

"I think I like you almost as much as Star."

Everyone laughed at the frank appraisal. Later, they all went to the parlor. Star and Jennifer demonstrated their accomplishments of the afternoon at the grand piano, and everyone applauded.

"Now we're supposed to curtsy." She demonstrated a curtsy as Jennifer looked on, and then they held hands as they both curtsied to more applause. Jennifer giggled, and Star looked at Eva and Adam. "If you don't mind, I'd like to have Jennifer share my bed tonight." Jennifer received good night hugs all around. "Come on, Buzz Saw," said Star, "let's brush our teeth."

Eva must have anticipated a possible overnight stay and had put a night gown in her bag. Jennifer put it on as Star slipped into a silky, clinging gown.

"Oh, you're so pretty," said Jennifer. I'll bet Matt will like it when he gets to sleep with you."

Star kissed Jennifer on the forehead.

"I know I will," she laughed.

"I have to say my prayers," said Jennifer. She knelt by the bed, clasped her hands, and closed her eyes. "Thank you, God, for this wonderful day with Star. Help me to be the little sister she will love. Bless Star, Matt, Zeb, Mom, Dad, Fawn and Marie. Amen."

Jennifer was asleep with one arm in loose embrace on Star's bosom. She didn't pull away. Jennifer had hit a responsive chord of love in her. Such fulfillment of trust and love made her want to stay awake and treasure every sweet breath that came from Jennifer. It surprised her when she realized she was thinking how to capture a moment like this on canvas.

27

The Plot

Trouble began. Matt had expected internal problems with New Venture, but due to the expertise of Adam and Jim Beaver, they had been minimal. Still, it didn't surprise him that the heat generated by New Venture and public opinion called for some retaliatory action from Monarch. Olaf Hedberg's house was burned to the ground at the same time they were cutting his timber. A note on a nearby tree said, "This is the beginning. New Venture must quit or all will suffer."

New Venture took time out to build Olaf a better house and voted to continue, with a watchful eye for the perpetrators. The following Sunday, when many of the crews were in church, they heard a series of explosions coming from the cutting area. Matt looked out to his apprehensive audience, bowed and prayed.

"God, we knew there would be good and bad moments in our endeavors to build you a better world. Help us to keep our faith and New Venture alive." He looked up at his people. "How many of you want to continue this service?" No doubt, there were a few that wanted to go on with the service, but no hands were raised. "Let's see what happened."

When they reached the cutting area, the first damage that met their eyes was several sections of ruptured track. Ted Bannister wondered why the woodburner looked intact. As he neared it, he noticed a piece of fuse entering the firebox. He opened the door and removed enough bags of gun powder to have blown it to bits if not for the faulty piece of fuse. Total damages were one crippled flatcar and the mangled sections of track. A note on a tree made this demand: "Give up, New Venture."

"This won't take long to put back in shape," said Adam, "but we're going to lose a little sleep and place guards around the clock and, at the same time, keep our eyes open for any strange faces in the area. I don't know if it was an act of Providence or not, but if that woodburner had blown up, we'd be in real trouble right now."

When the church service had been cut short by the need to find out about the explosions, Adam told Eva to go to Matt's place where they would meet her. She explored his icehouse, and when the two men neared Matt's house, the smell of frying venison steaks whetted their appetites. They were soon making the steaks, biscuits, and gravy disappear. Matt watched the radiant happiness of Eva and his dad and knew he and Star were going to be like that.

"I notice you two haven't lost your appetites," said Eva. "I also found some strawberries in the icehouse, so you get shortcake for dessert. Someone's being nice to you, Matt."

"Yeah, Mrs. Meek gave them to me."

There was a knock on the door, which was partly open. Doran stood there. Matt invited him in and introduced him to Eva. Adam and Doran knew each other. Doran looked at Eva with approving appraisal.

"The Berglunds seem to attract beautiful women."

"How far away do you live?" asked Eva.

"Oh, I guess I paddled about three miles."

"Well, that should give you an appetite. Now you sit right down to the table and wade in on that steak, biscuits, and gravy. If you don't give me any trouble, you'll get some strawberry shortcake, too."

Doran performed well at the table. Before he had finished the shortcake, he had extracted the history of Adam and Eva's twenty-year romance. He leaned back.

"I'm truly happy for you." Then pointing to Matt, he grinned at Eva.

"What do you think of this part of your family?"

Eva kissed Matt on the cheek making an "mmmm" sound.

"I couldn't have done better myself."

"I don't know when I've had such a delightful meal. I feel I'm with good friends."

"You are," came almost in unison.

"What I came here for doesn't seem as important now as getting to know this family. I just wanted to tell you that I talked to the manager of operations at Monarch and told him if they didn't start lumbering like you are doing, I would quit and take many of the men with me. He seemed glad that someone stood up to him and said he'd see if he could get the board of directors to vote a change. Whatever happens, I've set my course, but I'll give them a couple months to make up their minds."

"We hope Monarch will change." Adam's eyes met Doran's, but if they won't, we want your know-how and those who want to come with you."

Matt spoke up. "This is good news after what's been happening to us." He told Doran about the two attempts to stop New Venture.

"There are those whose greed will make them try anything, but I don't think that kind of action was voted by the board. Anyway. It needs to be stopped by whatever methods it takes, and the sooner the better," Doran affirmed.

That same afternoon, young John Bannister, who had been in on the excitement of the morning, took his sketching pad that Star had given him and went to look for some scenery suitable for a picture. He walked on and on, looking for the right composition in the varying landscape. Coming over the crest of a hill, he looked out over a lake with several fingers, and in the center of the nearest finger, he saw a small pine-tufted island with a log cabin in a clearing. From his vantage point, he studied the picture of lake, sky, trees, and cabin and started to sketch.

After some time, he saw smoke rising from a place near the cabin, and soon, three men came out of the cabin, going to and from the fire. John decided that they were preparing a meal, and then it struck him that these men could be the ones trying to stop New Venture. He crouched lower and backed out of sight and then ran toward home. He had come a long way. By the time he reached home, he was exhausted as he blurted out his discovery to his dad.

"Do you think they could be the ones?"

"Well, son, we gotta find out. I'll head over to Matt's and discuss this with him. He'll know how to proceed."

The sun was still hours away from setting when Ted Bannister came through the clearing as Doran was taking his leave. Ted told of the three men on the island in the lake.

"That's Hand Lake," Doran said. "We can get there by two short portages. I say we find out about this tonight. This is my problem, too. I want to find out just how low the company I work for can stoop."

Two canoes were soon heading for Hand Lake with Mike and Matt in one and Ted and Adam in the other. It was Matt's idea to be with Mike. The more he knew him, the stronger the desire to know him better became. He viewed Doran as the embodiment of the lake country, strong, resilient, inspiring, mysterious, friendly, but aloof. Doran had his rifle with him, and Adam brought his binoculars. It was nearly sundown when they reached the finger of the lake where the island was located. Pulling the canoe ashore, Adam looked at the island through his binoculars.

"We're here just in time. They're putting stuff in their canoe. Looks like white powder bags to me. I'll bet they come this way pretty soon."

"Who's supposed to get it tonight?" Doran wondered.

The three men soon climbed into the canoe and headed toward the foursome. Mike asked for the binoculars.

112

"Well, one of them is my old friend, Rube Finney. I wondered who they picked up that knew this area."

When the canoe came abreast of them, about fifty yards out, Doran raised his rifle. He spoke just above a whisper from behind the bush that concealed him.

"I'm not going to hurt anyone," he said, "but I'll put a hole in their canoe and see how they respond to that."

Man and rifle followed the canoe for a second, and then a sharp report echoed back and forth from across the lake. In seconds, one man was trying to stop the incoming water. They turned toward the shore, threw out some white bags and what appeared to be a can of kerosene.

Adam nudged Mark.

"You swim out and retrieve all the evidence you can, and we'll grab the rats as they come close."

As Matt swam out, he saw the canoe go under and heard the cursing and splashing of the three men struggling to get ashore. He soon found the powder bags and can and put them in the sunken canoe and started dragging it in. He had to come up for air several times but he wrestled it to shore, dumped out the water and dragged the evidence onto dry land. There were also two rifles and some fuses in the canoe.

Adam looked at the evidence.

"This should convince any judge. We'll stay here tonight, repair the canoe in the morning, and get these troublemakers off our hands on the afternoon train."

The three men were bound hand and foot.

"We don't want to lose them. I'll take the first watch," Matt volunteered.

The moon came up over the trees and lit up the faces of the prisoners. Matt knew which one was Rube Finney because Doran had tried to question him. Here was the man who had attempted to rape Star now hired to do Monarch's dirty work, which made Matt wonder if Rube had exploited his base nature to the point of no return. This caused Matt to wonder if he had been exposed to the same day-to-day life style, would he have been any better? A feeling of sympathy replaced the hatred he thought he would have for this man. He thought of Stuart "Stud" Monroe in seminary who had bragged about his conquest of women. He seemed to be of the baser nature. No doubt "Stud" was preparing a sermon right now to hypnotize his congregation for next Sunday. It rankled in his mind that much of society had succumbed to a new commandment that inferred you could ignore the first ten.

He thought again of that attractive coed who had been the playground for many young men. She would be walking down the aisle to be

113

married, still beautiful, possibly diseased, into someone's arms of equal promiscuity and exposure. And even worse; he thought again of Stud, who looked out from his pulpit with pious lust at the attractive females of his congregation as he mouthed morality. He felt a futility, but he also knew that someone had to try to halt the erosion of moral values of the Judeo-Christian ethic. He had set his course. He would give God an honest effort.

Doran came over and sat close to Matt.

"Are you and that young lady I danced with last year making any plans?"

"I guess the only way I can explain that is to tell you the whole story." He then told Doran. "I didn't know Star had been promised to Jim Beaver when I asked her to marry me. Jim was my best friend, and is my blood brother. Star and I aren't seeing each other as lovers until Jim frees her from White Otter's promise. I explained to Jim what happened, but so far he can't bring himself to step aside, and he wants nothing to do with me except in the line of work. My love for Star is a once-in-a-lifetime happening, and I know she feels the same. I guess Jim loves Star as I do, so I can understand his reluctance to let her go." Matt looked out over the lake. "Star is my life. She's never out of my mind. I keep busy and hope and wait."

Doran laid his hand on Matt's shoulder.

"Count me in on the hoping. We don't need any more long separations," he hesitated, "like your dad's."

In a note to Star, Matt wrote about Doran.

Dear Star,
Here is a man who is larger than life, and I'm drawn to him. There is a spirit of the indomitable, a keenness of mind, and a toughness that helps him rise above pettiness and trouble. I can't explain this tie, but I'm glad I'm his friend. You once called him a gentleman. I wish you really knew each other. I know you've met my little sister Jennifer. Sometimes I try to visualize you in your earlier years and when I see the quickness of mind in Jennifer, I imagine what Father O'Brien discovered in you. Over and over, I think of the miracle of our meeting. You are a necessary part of my world, and I feel I'm a necessary part of yours.

Impatiently yours,
Matt

28

Success

With the promise of a lighter sentence, Rube Finney talked. The instigator of the attempt to stop New Venture was Ira Thatcher, a member of the board, a hard-bitten curmudgeon, whose only credo was profit. As New Venture began to make inroads on the more accessible timber, he took it upon himself to start the sabotage maneuvers. The newspapers splattered their front pages with this caper. Thatcher was fired, and the Monarch board faced up to the internal trouble of losing much of their work force with Doran's threat to quit. Doran was instructed to make the changes necessary to use the New Venture methods of timbering.

With the green light, Doran wasn't to be outdone in the results. The heartless devastation was a thing of the past, and a feeling of elation spread beyond the boundaries of the lake land. The certainty of the passing of the bill to force compliance to strict conservation methods for lumbering was no longer in doubt, although the legislators still dilly-dallied.

Into the atmosphere of victory, Matt invited Dean Caldwell, chairman of the board of missions, to take charge of the service for the following Sunday. Because he held such an important position in the denomination, the congregation thought he should share in a "potluck" immediately after the service.

Dean Caldwell sat in the pastor's study, waiting for the time to begin his sermon. Matt glanced at the calendar and suddenly realized it had been just a year since he had fallen out of that tree, which seemed to have been the start of everything. So much had transpired since then. New Venture wasn't even being incubated at that time, neither did he know the church's plan for him. He still was at odds with some of the prescribed approach to preaching. Quoting scripture troubled him because it was often used to prove man's manipulative ideas. He had developed a credo of his own, at which his church would probably shudder and which, in essence, was that God was too big, too all-embracing to be fenced in with petty rules and beliefs that shut those out whose hearts were just as pure, loving, and desirous to help build a better world. To him, the love of God couldn't be exclusive.

It would make God too small if He didn't look at the heart. No one could possibly have all the right answers in this imperfect world.

They came out of the study, and as Dean Caldwell sat down, Matt came to the pulpit to begin the order of worship. He looked out over the congregation. There was Star, Maude, Marie, and Fawn. Star and Maude had been close friends since the epidemic. They were two beautiful women who had given him so much. He smiled at Eva, his dad, Jennifer, and Zeb. Eva and Adam beamed with the happiness they had found. Matt resisted the desire to go down and hug Jennifer. Ted and Martha Bannister were sitting side by side with their stair-stepped brood all neatly attired. This was the first time Martha had come to church. The steady paycheck had given a new outlook to many in the congregation. Matt wondered if the birth control pamphlet hadn't also helped to turn things around for Martha and Ted.

Matt carried out the order of worship and gave the dedication prayer for the offering, then introduced Dean Caldwell to the congregation.

"He comes with a long line of credentials," said Matt. "I'll give you a few. As Doctor of Theology, he teaches at our seminary. He formerly won many collegiate honors in wrestling and now, as Chairman of the Board of Missions, he wrestles with problems like us. It is an honor to have one of the great minds and Christian examples of our church with us. Dr. Caldwell."

Dr. Caldwell was a large man. Though beyond the half-century mark, the muscular evidence of his athletic frame was still apparent. As he looked around at the congregation, his easy smile emanated friendliness.

"We call ourselves Christians," he said, "because someone whom God loved very much spent a few years among us. The scriptures say, 'He grew in wisdom and stature and in favor with God and man.' He left a new enthusiasm and an assurance that your life and mine counted, telling us God wanted for us what every father and mother wants for their children, a challenge to find our potential that will bring happiness and fulfillment. There is no mention of a soft, easy life without struggle and adversity. Abraham Lincoln, our martyred president, once said, 'Let me do the right as God gives me to see the right.' The Church has done many things of which, in retrospect, we can't be proud. Causes, wars, and twisted beliefs have tarnished the image of Christ, and our prejudices still cloud our vision. In spite of this, God uses us, and history also reveals that much good has been accomplished, overshadowing our mistakes. In an imperfect world, our church must keep seeking better answers, and God must smile when we do something right. You here today have done something that is right, bright, and shining.

"A little over a year ago, a young man who was ready to graduate from seminary sat in my office. His name is Matt Berglund. He told me several things, among which was that he wouldn't be satisfied to marry, bury, and preach. He said that the people he wanted to work with needed help, understanding, and answers to problems that kept them from letting God enter their lives. He said, 'I believe God is more concerned with results and that He is willing to overlook a lot if one is trying to help Him make a better world.' My answer to him was 'I'm all for you. If you want to reshape lives more than listen to your own pipe organs, let's see what happens.'

"What did happen? Well, the first thing I noticed was that you got off the Mission roll almost immediately, and, not only that, you gave back to missions far above the average of other congregations. Neither has happened so soon in the history of our church." Then Dr. Caldwell paused and looked around. "I began to hear rumors of a church and community project to save the lake country from the lumbering ravages of what was happening farther north. I trembled a little, because we don't usually get in the middle of controversial situations.

"But you did it in a common spirit of working together to keep God's world beautiful. You did it without violence or meanness, as though you felt that you were doing what God wanted you to do more than anything else. I've come to believe that you did what God wanted you to do. Some time ago, I received a letter from Father O'Brien, your totally involved neighbor at the Mission. He kept a few notes of your pastor's first sermon. I want to read to you the part that is inscribed on this large plaque, which will be placed by the door for all to see coming in or out: 'Some day it could be said, this was just another church with an average profile of faith and expectations. Then something happened. A chemistry of God's love and action burned in its heart and it wasn't just another church.'"

Dr. Caldwell looked down as though he was trying to control an emotion and then his eyes seemed to seek out each person in attendance.

"You did it. You who are here today made those words come true. You are a very special people, and God must be proud of you. Some of the credit is due your pastor, your instigator and coworker." He turned to Matt and said, "God bless you, Matt. Your people and the church are proud of you."

After the shouting, feet-stomping, hand-clapping, back slapping,

117

and whistling finally subsided, Mrs. Meek voiced the general feeling.

"That's all the preaching we can stand. Let's eat."

Matt and Dr. Caldwell stood at the door and greeted everyone as they filed out. Maude and Star came out, side by side. They grabbed Matt's right and left hands and shook them simultaneously, laughing as they did. He liked it. Ted and Martha Bannister stopped to shake hands. Martha looked impishly at Matt.

"Ted told me to tell you that we read our lesson in the pamphlets."

"Good for you," Matt stooped and kissed Martha on the cheek.

Eva, Adam, Jennifer, and Zeb came out. Matt picked up Jennifer and hugged her warmly. Eva kissed him as he held Jennifer.

"You make us proud."

29

Hope

After the fun, banter, and festive mood had run its course, the families sifted in various directions to their homes. Dr. Caldwell had to hurry to catch the train back to the city. Matt made his way mechanically inside to go to his study. As he approached the altar, he felt a sudden need to kneel and pray, to be thankful. So much had worked out, well beyond his expectations. The turnaround in the attitudes and outlook of this community, the well being and hope that a purpose and paycheck had caused, the Bannisters happy again, the latent talent that had emerged to make it all happen. He felt a soothing serenity of mind as though he were with a presence that approved.

Matt had to admit that some of his early thinking had solidified into a certainty of faith. The early outer garment became an inward conviction of God's presence. When he baptized a baby, he felt a warmth and oneness with God at this new life. He knew those who came to the communion table came for different reasons. It seemed to be the thing to do. It did create a desire to want that total surrender to a faith so obvious in others. Loving your neighbor as yourself made you admit you could do a better job in that area. Here on your knees, perhaps God was helping you think. In their separate ways, many had made a step toward God, and some were finding His open arms. He differed from some of very devout believers. He couldn't believe his God was so small, mean, and unloving that His arms did not reach out to others who were "not of this fold."

The door to the church creaked on its hinges. Matt turned to see Jim Beaver enter. Jim came down the aisle and sat on the front bench near him.

"I have something to tell you. Before White Otter died, we had a talk. He said he was taking back his promise because it was wrong to stand between you and Star. It took me some time to face up to it. You have been more than decent about it and patient with me, and I guess it was because you knew I loved her, too. I'm sorry I wasn't man enough to do the right thing."

"You were my blood brother and my best friend," said Matt. "I want it to be that way again."

Matt held out his hand. Jim took it hesitatingly, and then, Matt drew him in as sobs shook Jim Beaver's frame.

"Maude told me if you really love someone, you want their happiness more than your own."

This broke any restraint Matt had, and his tears rolled down his cheeks onto Jim's shoulders. Jim grinned at Matt.

"Before we become blubbering idiots, I've got something more to tell you. Star is paddling down to your tree. She wants to meet you there. Get going! I'm going down the lake myself to talk to your dad. He asked me to come, but I'm not going to try to keep up with you."

Matt wasted no time getting to his canoe. The record for the time it takes to get from the Trading Post to the tree was in the process of being broken by Matt in his eagerness to get to Star. History perhaps will never put such a combination together again, a young blond giant who handled a canoe with power and perfection of stroke, plus one of the strongest incentives known, true love.

When Matt was still a half mile from the tree, he shouted.

"Star! I love you, I love you!"

A short time later, Matt heard a shot. A wave of apprehension struck a cold fear in him, and he knew something had happened to Star. In panic, he strained into his paddle, the canoe leaped with each stroke of desperation to get to her. As he came around the point he saw Star's canoe rocking sideways against the beach. Before he reached the shore, he jumped out of his canoe and splashed to Star's. A stifled wail exuded from him as he saw Star slumped inside the canoe, with blood covering her dress from a hole in her neck. He picked her up and carried her to the log by the tree, crying, "No! God! No!"

For a brief second, he sensed something was happening to his mind.

30

Rube

Rube Finney had a new trade, which was stealing from defenseless old women or robbing homes when no one was there. It didn't hurt his conscience. His wants were simple, a little food and a constant bottle. When he had tried to rape Star and Doran had thrown him against that tree, he had never fully recovered. He couldn't swing an ax because a broken or twisted vertebra caused excruciating pain. Thievery was easier than lumbering, so that part of the transition was painless. But in those times of unbearable torment when he made the wrong move, he let his venom pour out on Doran and Star.

The short prison term only increased his need for revenge. It was Doran again who had curtailed his lucrative employment of destroying New Venture. The mounting hatred and the need for retaliation goaded him to take the train to the Mission. The train stopped at the Mission and Rube got off. The Mission community seemed to be devoid of occupants, which was all right with Rube because no one would be able to identify him at a later time. *This was Sunday*, he thought, *maybe everyone was at church*. He could still walk, and today he carried a bag with several bottles that would keep him going until he could get some more.

Rube knew that Doran lived in an isolated area about a mile from the tracks. In his liquored condition, he felt a gleeful anticipation of his mission of revenge. He didn't know what he was going to do, and one thing that he didn't want was a direct confrontation with Doran. If Doran was home, he would wait until Doran left before he attempted anything. He had the time and the liquor. Setting fire to Doran's cabin might be the way to go. It was a pleasurable thought. He kept out of sight as he approached Doran's cabin. There was no smoke coming from the chimney or any signs of activity. He came to the side of the cabin and looked in the window. No one was there. Rube took a short log from the wood pile and smashed the glass until he could enter. A sharp twitch of pain engulfed him as he climbed inside. He drank from his bottle to ease the agony, then opened the dresser drawers searching for money or valuables. There were none. He kicked the floor for loose boards with no results. Then his eyes zeroed in on Doran's rifle against the wall close to the bed. *That would irritate Doran more than any other loss*, he thought. He grabbed the rifle and went out through the window, feeling a sense of well-being at his mission accomplished. He headed southward, staying close to the lake. Rube had traveled several hours, and the sun was still high. He estimated the time at about four o'clock. As he held a bottle to his lips, he heard a voice coming from behind him on the lake.

"Star! I love you, I love you."

Out of curiosity he came closer to the lake and looked through the trees. He recognized Star paddling toward a small beach. In his alcoholic mind, his hatred for Star flared. *If she wouldn't have made such a fuss*, he thought, *he wouldn't be in the physical condition and constant pain he was now.* He brought Doran's rifle around and looked down the sights at Star. *He could kill her if he wanted to,* he thought, *but he wasn't planning to be a murderer, although it gave him satisfaction to let the sights linger on her.* The rifle jerked back against his shoulder as the shot rang out and Star slumped in her canoe. Rube couldn't believe it. He had barely touched the trigger. He was now a murderer. Even in his condition, the realization of what happened sent terror and revulsion through him. He threw the rifle away and ran, knowing there was nothing else for him to do for the rest of his life.

31

Revenge

Doran came home shortly after Rube Finney had been there. He sized up the situation rapidly and saw that his rifle was missing. He wasted no time in getting on the trail of the thief. Being the woodsman he was, he read the signs of a man in a hurry going south. Moving at a rapid pace, Doran felt he was slowly closing in on his prey, although he had no idea who the pursued could be. He heard a shot in the distance ahead of him and realized it was his rifle or one like it. Also, it coincided with the proximity of the thief according to his calculations. He soon came upon his rifle lying on the ground. He picked it up and moved into the clearing by the lake. He saw Jim Beaver standing by Matt Berglund, who was sitting on a log, holding Star. From his short distance, he could see the blood on her dress and the sagging position of Star's head. Jim Beaver turned, and Doran saw the vivid rage on Jim's face as he unsheathed his knife.

"You killed her, and I'm going to kill you," Jim screamed as he ran toward Doran.

Doran knew there was no reasoning with Jim at this point. He picked up a rock and threw it. It bounced off the side of Jim's head and he went down. Doran ran into the forest, away from the lake. He was certain that the blow on Jim's head wouldn't slow him for long. As he ran, he began to assess the situation. Running would solve nothing. His job was to stay clear of Jim and go after the murderer at the same time. He swung southward toward the lake. Star's lifeless form remained in his mind as he ran. It dulled his sense of self-preservation. His daughter was dead. Dead! He had read much of the Bible, but he remembered nothing that could explain or ease Star's dying. He had often pictured in his mind a time when he could embrace Star and talk to her as a father and daughter would talk. Life hadn't given him much joy, and now, the agony of his exploded dreams left him with only the ashes of grief. He wouldn't even be able to console Marie in her time of devastation. Marie must have loved Star deeply. Nothing as lovely as Star could have evolved without knowing she was loved in a special way. A hopelessness enveloped him. Could he continue to want to see another day with the tunnel now darker than ever?

He knew his Bible promised life beyond the grave, but whatever faith he had wasn't strong enough to relieve the agony he felt. Yet his mind resisted his unbelief and gave birth to a nagging hope that he and Star would meet again. Resembling a drowning person, he clung to that hope like a piece of driftwood. Hoping was better than not hoping.

The pace was tiring. Doran had been alternately running and walking for a great distance, and he decided to rest for a few minutes. He sat against a large pine to catch his breath, but he knew Jim was not far behind him. It was time to try a diversionary tactic. Walking at right angles from the direction he wanted to go, he made his tracks easy to find for fifty yards, then walked backwards trying to retrace his footsteps back to the tree, which he climbed. Jim soon came, stopped at the tree, and, as Doran had hoped, started out following his tracks.

Doran slithered down the tree and continued south. As he ran, the awfulness of Star's death again overwhelmed him. He thought of the waste, the loss to the mission school children, the unfinished potential, the seeming inexhaustible vitality that had brought her safely through the epidemic. In shocked grief, he ran, with a knife at his back and a murderer in front. An empty bottle caught his eye. The thief had rested here and imbibed. The summer sun was getting low, and as he continued ahead, he suddenly realized the man he pursued was on his hands and knees, judging by the dragging trail he left. A whimper hit his ear. Pushing a bush aside, he almost stumbled over Rube Finney hunched on the ground with his face grimaced with pain. Rube seemed to be relieved that he was found.

"I didn't mean to shoot her," he whined. "I just wanted to prove I could if I wanted to. I hardly touched the trigger."

Doran heard the sound of approaching steps as Jim came around the bush with his knife in his hand. Doran looked up at Jim.

"Here's the one who shot Star," he said.

Jim cried out in anger. The need for retribution was still strong. He dropped to one knee and raised his knife to bring it down on Rube's back, but Doran grabbed Jim's poised arm.

"It really wasn't Finney. It was the hair trigger on my rifle. Killing Rube won't solve anything." Jim made no further struggle. "Let's bed down here tonight."

In the morning, Doran took Jim's knife and cut two poles. Using his and Jim's jackets, he ran the poles through the sleeves and fastened the jackets together to make a stretcher for Rube. The alcohol which numbed Rube's pain was gone. The agony of withdrawal and his pain-wracked body crazed his mind. The pinched nerves had been aggravated by his headlong attempt to flee, which forced him to double up to get some relief. He couldn't stand. Rube screamed in agony as Doran put him on the stretcher, his knees drawn close to his chest.

They started north with Doran as the lead stretcher bearer. Rube wasn't heavy, he was of average height and weight when he worked for Monarch, but the steady dependence on the bottle had emaciated his body. There was no real path, so there was constant maneuvering around the obstacles of brush and fallen trees.

After plodding north for an hour, Jim stumbled and let his end of the stretcher drag on the ground. Rube screamed at the jolt to his twisted spine. Jim stayed on his knees, wiping his brow with his sleeve. He was exhausted. The blow to his head from the rock had sapped his strength.

"We'll rest here," Doran decided. "After all, we can be of little help elsewhere."

Jim struggled upright.

"We have to go on. I have to see Star before they bury her."

"We can try." Doran brought Rube forward on the stretcher so he would carry most of the weight. "We'll move out when you're ready."

They were soon on their way again. The extra weight and no food was beginning to wear Doran down, too. Jim sagged to his knees often, but was up again in a few minutes. They both knew burials were swift in warm weather, and hoped that the funeral would be at the Trading Post because it was closer to them.

In mid-morning the following day, they staggered to the lake's edge and saw Adam's home a short distance ahead. One of Adam's row boats was tied to the dock. Doran dragged Rube to the dock himself, as Jim was barely able to make it on his own. After carrying Rube to the boat and placing him in front, he motioned for Jim to sit in the rear as he took the oars. It was now only a question of time, and both knew the funeral wouldn't wait for them. The boat left a small wake behind them as Doran rowed with a steady pace. Jim was barely conscious and unable to relieve Doran at the oars.

32

The Funeral

By some manipulation of fate, Eva and Adam were also drawn into this tragedy. That afternoon, Adam had asked Eva if she would go with him to meet Jim Beaver, whom Adam had invited to visit them to discuss some possible refinements in their lumbering methods. Eva wanted to be with Adam, but she was also hoping to share in the intensity of Adam's love for the beauty and immensity of the lake land.

On the way up the lake, Adam pointed out specific spots of interest to Eva and enjoyed answering her questions.

"Here's where I caught my biggest northern. It was five feet long, and I had a struggle to land it. I won the prize for the largest northern that year."

They heard a shot, but Adam was too happy being with Eva and his surroundings to let it bother him for long.

"Canoes keep people too far apart," Eva complained. "Let's go ashore."

"I'm all for that," Adam agreed. "Just up ahead is the tree that Matt fell out of and in love with Star."

They came around the irregular shoreline in sight of the tree and saw they were not alone. Adam recognized Doran and watched him as he threw the rock at Jim Beaver, who slumped to the sand. He saw Doran turn and run into the timber. His eyes then focused on Matt holding Star. The explanation of the shot almost unnerved him. Forgetting Jim, he beached the canoe near Matt, and, as he came closer, the awfulness of what had happened seemed to strangle him. Eva came and stood by him, and although a cry came from her, the nurse in her took over. She felt for Star's pulse, knowing there was none.

Jim struggled to his feet and shouted to Adam.

"You take care of Matt," he said. "I'm going after Doran. He killed Star." Jim disappeared, knowing that Star was beyond care. Matt stared vacantly as Adam took Star from his arms and laid her in her canoe. He went back to Matt and shook him.

"Matt, snap out of it." Then he realized Matt was beyond grief. Adam tied the three canoes in tandem and went back to Matt. "Come,

Matt, we're going home." Matt responded mechanically and was led to his canoe. Adam handed him his paddle. "Help us get home," he said.

When they reached their home, Adam knew it was also going to be his job to make the funeral arrangements. It was late afternoon, so Adam packed Star's body in ice to slow deterioration. He had to wait until morning to start things in motion.

The next morning Adam got off the logging train at the Mission to break the news to Father O'Brien and also to ask him to say what was needed to be said. He knew Father O'Brien would be shocked, and he was. He looked at Adam in disbelief for a while and then sat down as the brutal truth hit him.

"This was a day I was sure I wouldn't live to see," he said. "Suddenly I feel that much of me has also died. I can understand why Matt couldn't accept it." He looked at Adam. "I also know that this is no easy time for you, and I will do what I can to help."

The Trading Post seemed to be the proper place for the funeral. Father O'Brien and Adam set the time for 1:00 A.M. Tuesday.

"Now," Adam thought aloud, "I have to tell Marie and Fawn."

"Fawn is helping with the children in school," said Father O'Brien. "She knew that Star and Matt were meeting at the tree and was bubbling over with happiness for them finally getting together. I'll tell her and the children so that the word will get around. Everyone will know about it in a few hours. That's the way the grapevine works. We'll send the children home right away. You've got all you can handle."

Maude picked out the best casket from her dad's stock and helped make Star presentable for her final exposure. Copious tears flowed as she pondered the truth of Star's prediction. She had lost her best friend. It was a rending tear that was unbearable. Although Matt remained in his world of unreality, he obeyed instructions when prompted. Adam brought him to the funeral. Matt, Adam, Eva, Jennifer, and Zeb sat in the front row along with Marie and Fawn. Matt seemed unaware of what was happening around him. Everyone came. They had all been exposed to Star's charm. They crowded the benches and stood against the walls at the sides and rear. Star's school children sat in the front also, each with a bouquet of flowers they had picked. After the obituary, Father O'Brien began his talk.

"This day would probably have been the wedding day for Star and Matt, but now we come to pay our respects to Star's memory. She, without doubt, was one of the most loved, the most gifted and most completely alive young women I've had the opportunity to know. She was struck down by an unknown hand in the morning of her beautiful life. Some may try to answer this calamity by saying, 'It is God's will,' but you and I know that it isn't God's will that shortened her stay among us. It is the result of the gift of free will that allows some to use it to destroy. To react to her death with hatred or disillusionment would be defeating the trust and love she poured upon us. It is a time of deep sorrow, and God weeps with us. His great heart is broken at the loss that is ours.

"Star spent her short years brightening the corner that was hers, in service to our children, in her long hours during the epidemic, and in her outpouring of love to all. As an artist, she has left a legacy of beauty and meaning on canvas. We have been enriched by her mind that absorbed so fast and shared so much. We have been enriched by the example of her love in all its purity, which touched us all and made our lives richer. She instilled joy and hope by her uplifting spirit. There is a new star in God's heaven which will shine among us to bring out the best in those she taught and in the rest of us who learned from her how God wants us to love. Let us pray.

"Now, God, we give you Star reluctantly, saddened, shocked, and unwilling to accept her passing. Heal us as we go from here. Give us a desire to show that her short years among us will inspire us to pattern our own lives in a spirit of love for each other, to make a better world for us and for You."

The children filed by the coffin, placing their bouquets on Star's casket. There were no dry eyes. The graveyard by the side of the church was a new one. The first interments were the result of the epidemic. Star's coffin was placed on her grave and Father O'Brien invited all to gather close. Adam led Matt to a place near the coffin.

Just as Father O'Brien was about to make his final remarks, the scraping of a boat was heard on the dock not far from the church. Many heads turned to see two men start up the path.

"It's Doran and Jim Beaver," someone said.

As they watched, Jim fell to the ground. Doran pulled him to a sitting position and lifted him to his shoulder. With Jim's head hanging down in back and holding his legs with his arms, he struggled up to the grave. As he neared the grave, people stepped aside, and Doran lowered Jim to his feet as he himself stumbled with exhaustion. Jim, who had seemed almost unconscious, suddenly revived and staggered to Star's coffin looking at Father O'Brien.

"Please open the coffin," he pleaded. "I have to see Star once more."

Matt's reaction to seeing and hearing Jim by the coffin suddenly brought him back to reality. Everything fell into place as he heard Jim pleading to see Star again. A choked wail came from Matt as he hurried to the coffin and stood beside Jim.

"Please open the coffin," he said. "We have to see Star."

Father O'Brien opened the lid. Matt and Jim, with their arms on each other's shoulder, looked at Star and poured out their uncontrollable grief together. Father O'Brien had held his emotions in check until this time. Tears fell copiously down his cheeks as the agony he saw tore him apart.

"And now abideth faith, hope, and love, and the greatest of these is love," he said.

Doran walked back to the dock, while Matt and Jim were looking at the woman they both loved so dearly. He couldn't let the world know of the grief he felt. Lying in the boat in almost the same position they had left him was Rube, dead in his own pool of blood. He had cut his wrist with the knife Jim had left in the boat. Doran pulled the boat into the bushes so those who soon would be leaving would not see Rube Finney, who had decided not to face the future.

When Doran returned to the grave, all were leaving except Marie, Fawn, Eva, Adam, Jennifer, Zeb, Jim, and Matt. Maude had come and squeezed Matt's hand and left with her parents. Eva was washing the deep cut and bruise on Jim's head. She ripped some bandages from her petticoat and talked to Jim.

"I know you're Matt's blood brother, and that makes you part of my family, too. Not everybody gets my petticoat bandages." Eva sobered a little. "Jim," she said, "you and Matt are going to need every friend you have and especially each other." Eva stood back and looked at her handiwork. "I'll need to look at that again, so I want you to be our guest for a few days."

Marie invited them all to come to her home. They sat in the parlor. Marie and Fawn poured coffee and served cake, cookies, and pie to the various appetites.

"Fawn and I have done a lot of crying, so we decided to try to bake the ache away. We still cried but it helped."

Jennifer came and sat on Matt's lap.

"I love you, Matt." That was the food Matt needed.

Jim had acquiesced to Marie's suggestion that he get some much-needed rest in a bedroom of hers. Adam was wondering what changed Jim's mind about killing Doran. He looked at Doran.

"Maybe you can tell me what really happened. Jim told me that he was going to kill you."

"I'll try to explain," said Doran. "We have Star's murderer in your boat, which we borrowed to get back here quickly. I hid the boat in the bushes. It didn't seem right to give him any exposure on a day like this. Jim doesn't know this yet, but Rube Finney cut his wrist when we left

129

him in the boat to come to Star's casket." Doran paused. "Rube stole my rifle and used it to shoot Star. He said he didn't mean to kill her. He didn't know about the hair trigger on my rifle. I'm inclined to believe him. He took his own life, and that closes the book either way.

"When I came to my cabin last Sunday, my place had been ransacked, and my rifle was gone. You get attached to some things. I had carried that rifle through the last two years of the war. It kept me alive more than once. I didn't know the thief was Rube, but I tracked him to where he had thrown my rifle away and fled. When I came out in the open, there was Jim looking at me as if I were the murderer. I couldn't shoot him, so I hit him with a rock and ran to keep from being knifed. I was also on the trail of the murderer. I found Rube Finney, and Jim found us. Finney confessed, so Jim and I carried him to your place, Adam. Rube was in bad shape and unable to walk. We took your boat and brought Rube along. Jim wanted to see Star before she was buried."

"I have something that needs to be said," Marie spoke up, "and this seems to be a good time to get things cleared up. There's little reason to keep this a secret any longer, and 1 especially want Matt to know about this." Marie hesitated. "Star was Mike Doran's daughter." Silence seemed to smother the room. "We met and loved. It was a love like Star's and Matt's, total, consuming, complete, and I think like Adam and Eva's. We told my parents but were told I had been promised to White Otter. Mike was warned to go, that it wasn't safe to remain. White Otter was good to me, and I tried to be a good wife. When Star was born, I let them think she was White Otter's child. I wrote Mike a letter telling him about his daughter, but I told him not to intrude. He never did, but I did suspect who the donor for Star's education was. People do adjust, but I never stopped loving Mike."

Doran spoke.

"I have to tell you what may seem strange coming from me. When I ran from Jim after hitting him with that rock, I felt so devastated that I thought if Jim ended my life it might be for the best. Star was dead. Star, whom I loved with all the pride and affection a father could possibly have. My love for Marie had never diminished, and I could see no light at all. Then I remembered some scripture telling me that there is more. I have to believe it. I want it more for Star than for myself. I know when I step across, she'll be the first to greet me."

There was a series of soft "amens."

Matt watched as Doran rose slowly to go to Marie. He saw Doran kneel and put his head in Marie's lap and heard him break into sobs that shook his frame as Marie put her hands on his head and stroked his hair. Now Matt knew why he had been drawn to Doran. Star had been like him in many ways. The magnetism, the vitality, her expressions and mannerisms, the reddish tint in her hair. He remembered Star's remark when they had first vowed their love. "In God's sight we must be married." In a way that made him an in-law. He thought of Adam and Eva and now Marie and Doran who had to wait twenty years. Now, he'd have to wait a lifetime. A deep hollow emptiness engulfed him, and the agony of losing Star hung like a shroud upon his deadened soul.

33

Christmas

The marriage of Marie and Doran was conducted by Father O'Brien with a few of the inner circle of friends present. Jennifer was the ring bearer. With well-wishers like Adam and Matt, Mike knew the feeling came from the heart. It helped Matt through this period to have two mothers who expressed their love and empathy for him. Jim Beaver couldn't feel like a stranger under the spell of Eva's friendly concern for his welfare. He and Matt were back on friendly terms. They walked, talked, worked, and sometimes laughed together, which made them more able to cope with their feelings of depression and despair. At times, Matt still felt it impossible to continue any ordered existence. He wanted to flee and agonize through the days in contemplative solitude. Instead, he worked harder and longer, often cutting and sawing more than two men. He preached on Sundays, visited his congregation, listened to parents, and played with their children to keep from surrendering to the grief, which was always present.

Once, when he visited Marie, Mike, and Fawn, Maude was there. Fawn in her open-hearted empathy came to Matt and kissed him. Matt kissed her.

"What a sister you turned out to be," he said.

Marie kissed him too.

"You are part of our family," she said. Matt still held Mike in a special kind of respect and admiration. They often talked about work, politics, and Star.

"I hope it helps to know we care," Mike said.

"It helps," said Matt. "I at least got to know your daughter."

Maude left with Matt to catch the train back to Thorson's Bay. They walked in silence until Maude spoke.

"Matt," she said, "I don't want to intrude on your love for Star, but I love you and want to be your friend, not an ex-girlfriend. I want the man I marry to love me and need me, so don't think I'm pushing myself on you. As a friend I want to help you. You had it all in Star, but I'm still second best. Some day, you may not think that's so bad." Maude kissed Matt on his cheek. "I'll be there when you need me, but that's not the main reason I wanted to talk to you today. We have something else to worry about.

"I visited Clint Webber's wife, Irma, two days ago. She came to the door holding a washcloth against her right eye. Her six-year-old son, Tom, was in back of her. The eye was discolored, and the cheek was still bleeding. 'I stooped to pick up a potato I dropped and banged my head on the edge of the table,' she explained. Tom, her six-year-old spoke up. 'You told me to tell the truth, Mom. That's not the truth. Dad did it, and he does it all the time, and he hits me when I try to stop him.'

"Irma placed her hands on Tom's shoulders. 'Tom, will you go out and stake the cow in a new place so she will get all the grass she wants? I need to talk to Miss Thorson alone.'

"Irma pointed me to a chair by the kitchen table and offered coffee. We sat. She unbuttoned her dress and bared her body to her waist. Her entire exposure was a mass of bruises, front and back. Purple evidence of brutality covered her torso. I remember her every word. 'He hit me before our first month of marriage was gone. He drinks, chews tobacco, and doesn't take a bath. My mother told me not to marry him, but there wasn't much choice. I certainly made the wrong choice. I know he's going to kill me. Tom needs a mother. I don't know what to do. I can't submit to him without showing my hate and disgust. He has raped me when I'm unconscious.'

"Irma and Tom are at our home." Maude's voice could not hide the undercurrent of fear. "When Clint finds out, there is going to be a ruckus, and I'll need help."

"We have to get rid of that rabid dog." Matt found himself holding Maude, "I would strangle him before I remembered my religious principles. Let's put Zeb on his tail."

Zeb found Clint in one of the New Venture crews. He approached him in the act of felling a large tree by cutting into the side that would make it fall in the right direction. Zeb wasted no words as he looked Clint in the eye.

"You have battered your wife and son for the last time."

"That is none of your business. I work here and earn my pay, and I'll batter you if you don't shut your trap," was Clint's reply.

"I've got news for you," said Zeb. "As of right now, you no longer work for New Venture, and your pay goes to your wife along with anything else, such as your property." A series of foul oaths indicated Clint's murderous intentions as he raised his ax. Zeb grabbed that ax before it had started forward. He twisted it from Clint's hands, and hit Clint's jaw with the handle. He lay there, not unconscious, spitting out pieces of teeth from his broken jawbone.

"Sorry to have been a little rough, but do what you do elsewhere. If we held a kangaroo court among your peers, they would hang you upside down. You could thank me. I kept you from being a murderer just now. I'll put you on that train going south. Now start walking, the next thing I break may be your neck."

When Irma was informed of Clint's departure, she took a deep breath on life. Reading had been the source of pleasure that preserved her sanity. Before her marriage her mother had read to her out of newspapers, and they both took turns reading to each other. She never thought to ask her mother where she had learned to read, but Irma knew her mother had hopes of a better life for her daughter. She died of a heart condition shortly after Irma had married. Irma's nearest neighbor had given her a book on Shakespeare's plays. "Take it," she had said. "I can't read the small print anymore." Irma's cottage was close to the Mission. She soon became a part of the teaching crew, along with Fawn and Maude, after reciting "To be or not to be." Her arithmetic was adequate. There was the other reason. She would have access to books on history, literature, and the encyclopedias, which would expand her own world. Maude was glad to have her. She wanted to be free to help her father in the store and to be with her parents. The Mission school kept her from doing her own thing, which was helping those in need in her domain.

Tom was a good student and a happy schoolboy. To allay some fear, a sawed-off shotgun was Irma's constant companion

About six months after his exclusion, Clint Webber's name appeared in a newspaper. "Clint Webber was shot in a red light district. The woman who shot him showed stark evidence of vicious rape. No charges were filed." Irma stashed the shotgun.

Timothy Barnes, the bachelor who handled the New Venture funds, looked at Irma Webber and Tom. In spite of the marriage rape her now dead husband had inflicted on her, there was a new bounce to her still shapely form. Irma was only twenty-six. She wasn't looking for a man. Past images of the male experience continued to haunt her.

Trauma comes in different packages. The young lady who had accepted Tim's proposal of marriage was persuaded by her parents to accept the suitor who had inherited a fabulous fortune. It had hurt, but he had finally concluded he didn't want a life partner whose love was that shallow.

Irma was polite, but Tim sensed that a man wasn't included in her future plans. Tim had been quite happy in his new life here in the lake country. His investments were growing, and he knew that by local standards he was "well heeled." Now there was an invading presence of unrequited love for Irma. His days brought a stabbing emptiness. Hopelessly, he knew he had to try to break through Irma's defenses.

The next day, Tim came to school during the noon hour and sat beside Irma on a bench with Maude and Fawn. He pointed to a bench that was off to one side. Irma honored his presence that much. Tim began.

"I want you to listen to my problem. I have fallen hopelessly, yet completely, in love with you. My thoughts carry you in my mind constantly. I would honor you with every part of the marriage vow. I would never invade your privacy unless and until your desire was as strong as mine. I am already fond of Tom. I want to be his dad without any reservations. All men are not like the one who battered you. My love will be for you until the day we separate in death and, God willing, beyond."

Irma sat there as if stunned. Her face brightened as she moved closer to Tim.

"Why do I want to kiss you?"

They were married. Matt and Father O'Brien helped tie the knot. Ian Bannister, who was about Tom's age, invited Tom to spend a few days with them. Tom liked the idea. Mrs. Bannister kissed Irma.

"If it's eight or nine, what's the difference?"

On their marriage night, Irma led Tim to the bedroom, saying, "Take me to the stars. I want to find out if I'm okay."—Everyone enjoys a happy ending. Here was the happiest of beginnings.

When all else seemed to smother him, Matt found excuses to be under the influence of Eva's mothering concern and be in on the raising of Jennifer. She was becoming a fish in the water under Matt's tutelage. Zeb had also become a solid part of Jennifer's world. He confided to Matt, "That little Buzz Saw has a head on her shoulders." She had an instant retention for words and their meanings. One exposure, and it was hers. Zeb introduced her to music, and they sang together, her voice vibrant and in tune. Zeb's violin intrigued Jennifer, and she expressed a desire to play one. With Eva and Adam's permission, Zeb and Jennifer went to the city by train. Zeb was acquainted with a music store that sold violins, and he found a violin small enough for her, but of good tonal quality. Zeb bought it for her and became her teacher as well.

Jennifer practiced more than Zeb had told her to and soon gave a good account of herself. Often, when Matt came down to be with his family, Zeb would show up with his violin and the two concert artists would put on a show. Jennifer was a performer who loved the challenge and the limelight. Her quick grasp of the music she was exposed to was almost unbelievable. Matt wondered if she and Star had been two of a rare kind. He also wondered how the teacher at school was going to cope with her. It was conceivable that when she started school, she would easily jump several grades in one year.

Jennifer's little giggle came easily. Matt had been told about her mother and evaded that topic until one time when she was snuggling in his lap.

"My mother used to hold me like this and I miss her sometimes," she said.

"I'm sure you do."

"That night she tied me to the post on the porch, she told me she couldn't take care of me, so she was leaving me with a mother who would give me a better home. She hugged and kissed me a lot, and we both cried."

"Your mother wanted you to have the best, so she picked Eva. Aren't you glad?"

"Oh, yes, I have the most wonderful mother and dad and big brother in the whole world." She threw her arms around Matt's neck and kissed him.

"Let's pop some corn," Matt suggested.

The weather for Christmas Eve was mild, but everyone wore warm clothing to the long-awaited annual gathering at the Trading Post Church. Many of the children were involved in the portraying of the Christmas story. Margy Bannister was the mother of Jesus. Jennifer's doll was the baby Jesus. John Bannister had been coerced into being Joseph. Rick Bannister, Jud, who was Jim Beaver's younger brother; and Sid Duncan, who was now best of friends with Jud, all had their arms twisted to be the reluctant Magi. There was an assortment of shepherds. Annie and Abby Whitaker were the angels. The huge reconstructed fireplace and densely packed bodies took off the chill of the night. In that audience were Alan and Velma Whitaker, who came to watch their daughters perform. Alan walked with a slight limp, but his stride was sure and strong. He was on the payroll as a trimmer for New Venture. He asked for no favors. The tree was decorated with popcorn, ribbons, and some baubles brought by many who would retrieve them later.

Zeb started the evening off by asking everyone to join in singing "Silent Night." Eva's voice stood out, almost in solo, and Zeb motioned for her to join him. She walked down the aisle, beckoning with her hands for everyone to take part. They responded, and the church reverberated with vocal enthusiasm. Eva's beautiful contralto brought tears to Adam's eyes as he thanked God for the never-ending wonder of her.

Matt read the Christmas story from his Bible and paused at proper intervals to allow the actors to perform. At the appropriate time Jennifer sang "Away in a Manger."

When the actors finished their performance, Zeb took center stage.

"I want all the children to come up front and form a half circle in front of me." They came. Some of the parents brought their youngest who sat in their laps as Zeb asked everyone to sit. "How many of you have heard 'The Night Before Christmas'?" he asked. Many hands went up. "I hope you'll like the story I'm going to tell you then. 'Before the Night Before' is what it's called."

Santa looked out the window while winding his watch,
Saw Cupid and Comet playing hop scotch.
In the rear, he could hear the rapping and tapping,
The elves were all working, no one was napping.
The room full of dolls was Mrs. Santa's domain
And she hugged each one again and again.
More elves were busy stocking the shelves,
An industrious crew and proud of themselves.

Hurrying around in a pace that was dizzy
Was old Agabub in a toy-testing tizzy.
He looked at a train to try out the toot,
If a harmonica wouldn't, he'd give it a boot.
A bugle he'd blare, a pop-gun he'd shoot,
Over here to spin tops, there to finger a flute.
Then he'd stamp his OK and go on his way
Getting things all set up for the "great day."

Santa turned from the window and buttoned his sweater,
Sat down to read what was said in each letter,
He looked at one and then shook his head.
Wondered if Dick was as good as he said.
The next one he opened and read and reread.
"Dear Santa," it said, "I haven't written before.
I looked for you last year but you missed our door.
I asked around and you missed a lot more.

So I'm writing this letter, hoping you'll read it,
To ask, 'Is Christmas for those who don't need it?'"
Well, that lovable, whiskered, round little guy
Sat there as a big tear fell from his eye.

He pressed a button, and the elves gathered close,
And Santa looked at the, sad and morose.
"Dear friends," he said, "let me read you this note.
We've got to do something, and I'll need your vote."

As he read, there arose a great lump in each throat.
Agabub coughed and said, "If we're worth a dime,
We'll double our shifts and work overtime.
If you can deliver, we'll get you the stock,
Enough for everyone to have a full sock."
"We'll do it," said Santa, "and bless each and all;
I'll enlarge the sleigh and not miss a call."
Then the elves filed out and went back to work
You'd hear some whistling, but not one would shirk.

Santa opened his window and called to his deer,
"I've something to say that you need to hear.
The sleigh will be very heavy this year.
You'll have to stop resting and browsing around
And double your practice to leap and to bound,
If we're going to get this sleigh off the ground.
I'm fond of you all, and I know you can do it,
So what do you say, let's start hopping to it."
Then, Santa sat down and leaned back to the wall,
Gave a happy "Ho! Ho!" which echoed the hall, and said,
"This will be the best Christmas of all."

After the reading, Zeb, Maude, Mat, and Jennifer handed out the
candy and oranges along with a top, ball, or crayons to each child present. Zeb had previously asked Maude to get the candy and oranges for
each sack. "You know the people better than I do," he had said. "Here's
a signed check. I want everyone to get a top, a ball, a little doll or whatever you think is appropriate. You know who won't get much, and I
want them to have a wagon, a sled, or a big doll. And maybe some warm
clothing and mittens would be appreciated. Maybe Marie would know
what her people would like. Don't be stingy, and don't let anyone know
who Santa is."

On Christmas Day, Fawn, Doran, and Marie took a wagon, sled,
doll, or clothing to the Indian and white families in the Mission area
where Christmas wasn't going to happen. Matt, Jennifer, and Maude
volunteered to do the bay area. Zeb couldn't find any snowshoes just
right for Jennifer, so he made a pair that were light, strong, and the

proper size. One of their longest hauls was two large dolls and some mittens for Annie and Abby Whitaker.

Jennifer was a tired little girl as they headed for home. She and Maude had developed a mutual attraction. Jennifer expressed her feelings openly.

"I'd like to have you for a sister."

34

Life Goes On

During this time, Matt had spent many days helping New Venture with saw and ax. One noon, Ted Bannister sat beside him as they eased their hunger pangs with Mrs. Meek's stew.

"I want to talk to you about John. He won't go back to school. He says it's a waste of time now that Star's gone. Maybe he'd listen to you."

Into Matt's mind came a conversation of Star's with Maude and himself during the epidemic. "John's an artist," Star had said. "For a ten-year-old, he's exceptional. I gave him some watercolors after I had found out about his talent when his tablet of drawings fell on the floor."

"I'll try to talk to John," Matt promised.

Matt went to the Bannisters to have dinner with them the following Sunday. "One more or less doesn't make that much difference," Martha laughed.

"John," Matt said after the meal, "you and I are going to have a talk, but first I want to see some of your painting and sketching." John soon brought him some folders, pleased that someone was interested. Matt wasn't an artist, but he could see what Star had discovered. One picture, a watercolor of a deer and fawns at the lakeside, with a background setting of trees, foliage, sun, and clouds had this written on it in Star's handwriting: "Keep it up. Some day you'll be a great artist."

It jolted Matt to see it.

"John, you and I loved Star, and the best we can do is to try to make some of her dreams come true. She didn't know what it meant to quit trying. Our faith tells us that Star is even more alive in a spiritual body. I know she's rooting for us to make our lives count." Tears ran down John's face as Matt continued. "You need to learn all you can and as fast as you can to be able to read the books that tell you how to paint right. You do your part, and I promise you that when you think you're ready, I'll see that you go to the best art school there is, and I'll be checking on you so you know I'm not fooling." Matt held out his hand. "Is it a deal?" John took his hand and cried happily as Matt stooped and put his arms around him.

Winter laid its siege upon the lake land again. The long evenings of summer gave way to longer nights, which curtailed some of Matt's chances to visit people. Even in summer, he'd often slept on his cot in his study at the Trading Post. Now, he had more time to think, and he thought of Star. Because of this, he often stayed at the Trading Post. The loneliness wasn't quite as suffocating when he was with the men of New Venture.

Phil Peterson had become a close friend. He had purchased a quarter-section, then an additional quarter-section adjoining it, with money he had earned at his present occupation as a lumberman. That gave him a mile of lakeshore with the marshes and timber for hunting, fishing, and trapping that was his life. He would have no timber removed.

Matt was making notes for his Sunday sermon when Phil first sought him out.

"I knew Star," he said. "My wife and I came to church at the Mission when we could, and Star knew my Laura well. She even brought her some wild rice pudding shortly before Laura died. I had my wife for twenty-five years, and I know how you feel." Phil was silent for awhile before he spoke again. "What a pair you and Star would have made."

Matt folded his papers and said, "I've done all I need to do here. Let's join the others."

Conversation around the fireplace ranged from talk about work to happenings with their families. There was some needling. Gabe Hartnett liked to keep things stirred up. His nickname was "Gabby." On one occasion, when he was sitting beside Matt, he injected these comments:

"I watched Tom here. He went back three times for more walleye tonight; I guess he needs a little extra to keep up his strength these days." Tom Schultz had been married only three months. "They say you're supposed to put a pea in a fruit jar for every time the first year," Gabby went on, "and start taking them out the second year. Nobody ever gets them all back out."

Everyone laughed and probably cried inwardly at the truth of Gabby's glib remark. Tom looked glum. "There are no peas in the jar. Rose don't want any kids."

Tom Schultz belonged to the Mission Church. Matt broached the subject to Father O'Brien.

"I think people have a right to plan their families. Big, unwanted families deprived of a chance for proper care seem to me to be the greater sin. I feel sorry for Tom and Rose."

Father O'Brien stared straight ahead for a while.

"You and Star wouldn't have had that problem. She told me her mother had instructed her in methods of prevention."

Matt remembered Star's statement the day he proposed to her—"We'll practice a lot."

"Rose and Star were good friends" was Father O'Brien's reply.

"In that case," said Matt, "Marie has some more work to do. I'm going to talk to her right now."

35

What's Next?

The news about the Bill for Conservation of Timberlands came to Matt when Adam brought him a paper headlining the overdue passing. It was merely a final icing because New Monarch and Doran had been in compliance for quite some time. Now it was a statewide edict, and Matt began to assess his future. With spring well on its way, the time for placing the pastors wasn't far away. Indecision plagued Matt. He remembered the statement to Father O'Brien—"Saving the lake country may be my ministry." There were some enticing reasons for remaining. He loved this lake country, these people. It would be hard to walk away from his deep ties with Eva, Adam, Jennifer, Zeb, Marie, Fawn, Doran, and Jim. The sting of Star's death still weighed on him, darkening each hour of his day. But what he wanted to accomplish was behind him, and he knew he couldn't coast or bask in the limelight or have time to feel sorry for himself.

In Dr. Caldwell's study, Matt had just unloaded his predicament.

"I know I can't always get a tailor-made situation. The time, the challenge, the catalyst was there by luck, and perhaps divine approval. People became aware of their potential, and a problem was solved. Much as I love the lake country, I can't relax in the glow of something accomplished to such degree. I know my limitations as a pastor. The creeds and the dogma still make me feel uncomfortable, and if the Trading Post must be nurtured in that direction, I must leave that to someone other than myself."

Dr. Caldwell placed his hand on Matt's shoulder.

"We have many churches where the same hopelessness and incentive to cope is caused by poverty and wrong from both the daily pattern of living and outside influences that keep people down. Our church needs you. You aren't looking for a fast climb in your pastoral career from a mission church to a prominent pulpit, where you soothe your constituents with a careful faith. That often happens, and our church progress is diminished by such leadership. You want to give people a faith in themselves and a right to evaluate their own beliefs. I personally know God comes out ahead when people are given challenges to make them want to improve their lives and their surroundings. We need you. Our church is still a vehicle for good. What a pity it would be if you suddenly became complacent and unaware of the needs around. It's my job to place our pastors, and I can toss you in the middle of some tremendous challenges. There is one thing I can do, which might make me unpopular, and that is to back you with a noninterfering policy and extend you my prayers as I always have. I shall also advise the board to recognize your contribution by proper remuneration."

This was the last Sunday at the Trading Post for Matt. He made it known to few on purpose because he couldn't have stood a pot luck. He began the usual routine of worship services and brought it to the time of scripture reading.

Before he continued, he looked around at the packed benches. Doran and Marie were there. They took turns between the two churches. Fawn and Jim were sitting together. Matt wondered about that. Zeb sat with Adam, Jennifer, and Eva. The Bannisters and their children filled a bench. One time when he had visited them, Martha put her arms around Ted and said, "We're more in love than ever." Sadie Meek was sitting with Phil Peterson, and Sadie looked stunning. Matt had noticed the new Sadie before, and he wondered what had brought it about. *Good for you, Sadie,* he thought.

"Reading from the scriptures: 'What does it profit, my brethren, if a man says he has faith but has not works. Can that faith save him? For as the body apart from the spirit is dead, so faith without works is dead also.' This is the same scripture I read the day of my first sermon to you."

He dealt on some of the verses between, then paused and looked around at the congregation for a time, saying nothing.

"This is my last Sunday as your pastor. You are a beautiful people. You are a strong people. Though I would love to stay here and be warmed with the love you have shown me, you and I know there are other churches who need me, whose problems are so big and their faith and hope at a low ebb. I cannot look away from their needs, and I know you wouldn't want me to. Together we tried to make our little world better, and we succeeded beyond our own expectations because we combined work with faith. We have worried together, cried together, and loved together. Believe me, you will be in my prayers. I shall need yours. Tennyson, one of our contemporary poets, says this about prayer: 'More things are wrought by prayer than this world dreams of. Wherefore let Thy voice rise like a fountain for thee night and day. For what are men better than sheep or goats, that nourish a blind life within the brain, if knowing God, they lift not hands in prayer, both for themselves and those that call them friend. For so the whole round is everywhere bound by gold chains, about the feet of God.'

"I shall face a new challenge because I must if I am any kind of man, but I shall never forget how you faced the challenges that came to you in our two years together. I'm proud to be one of you. May you continue to let God work through you and with you."

Matt's eyes were red from many tears as he took the pain of saying good-bye to his congregation. He hugged the children. Susie Dahl clung to him and bawled as her mother took her away. Eva and Jennifer invited him down to spend the night. Eva knew the punishment Matt was taking. She had been crying. The good-byes had drained him. Matt climbed into his canoe to paddle down the lake and spend the night at his dad's place. Eva always made him feel at home there, and he wanted to see as much of Jennifer as possible in his remaining time in this community.

He heard paddling from behind, and soon, Jim Beaver was beside him. They paddled along, and Matt waited for the breaking of the silence.

"I'm going to marry Fawn," Jim said. "I wanted you and Father O'Brien to give us the works, but I guess you'll be gone."

"I'll figure some way to get in on that. How did this come about?"

"Fawn has always loved me," said Jim, "and now I'm able to love her. I can't explain it. It's not a rebound affair, and it's not the same feeling I had for Star. It's calmer, easier, but real. She will be good for me, and I love her in such a way that I want to be good for her and our children."

"Jim," said Matt as he drew their canoes together, "you know I'm glad for you and for Fawn. That's the best news I've heard for a long time."

He paddled on, drinking in the beauty of the lake and shoreline. There was the tree, and he knew he couldn't just pass by. Beaching his canoe, he sat on the log. His mind raced through the events that had brought Star to him and taken her from him. Then he suddenly realized that though the remembering was vivid, the heavy ache was gone. It was as though a smothering blanket had been lifted from him. Could it be Star taking off the shackles of her hold on him? Had she also done it for Jim and Fawn? He felt a freedom to live and to love again.

Suddenly, thoughts of Maude, sweet, fresh, blonde, pretty, and in love with him, flooded his mind. There was no doubt he had always loved her in a calmer, easier fashion, as Jim had said about Fawn, but now he felt an overpowering need and love for her. He sped on by

145

Adam's place, and in a short time was knocking on the Thorsons' door. Maude opened it, a look of surprise showing in her expression.

"Please come with me, Maude. I need to talk with you."

"I'll take a chance," she said. "You're excited about something. Let's talk."

"Let's walk back to the hill like we did when we were kids," Matt suggested.

They reached the top of the hill and looked down the other side. There hadn't been any talk, and Maude was wondering what was happening. Matt seemed to be more attentive, and she didn't mind that. Matt held her hands as he stood facing her.

"Do you remember how we used to roll sideways down this hill to see the world spinning so fast that you grabbed the grass to keep from spinning into space? Follow me. I want to see if it still works."

Matt lay sideways and kept his arms close and began to roll. At the bottom, the world was spinning again. As it slowed down, he saw Maude coming down, her dress creeping up with every spin. She bumped into Matt. He held her.

"Marry me, Maude. I need you, I love you, and, somehow, I'm free to love you. It's as though Star has released me." Matt kissed Maude. "Marry me," he said again.

Maude gradually pulled away and untangled herself from Matt. She tried to get her skirt back down as Matt ogled her exposed underpinning.

"A lady has to undress to get your attention," she teased.

"Legs like yours shouldn't be hid. Although, in my present condition, I couldn't stand looking much longer without becoming rabid." He pulled Maude to him and kissed her again. This time she returned his kiss with equal ardor. "Say you'll marry me."

"Silly boy, you love me, and that's all I ever asked, and I'm sick and tired of being a virgin," she added, tweaking his nose.

"Would you believe it," said Matt, "I'm willing to dispense with my tenure as a celibate, but I know you want our wedding night to be our night."

"There's one other problem," said Maude. "If we don't wait, you'll be rocking a cute little baby before we get the hang of it."

"Where did you learn about birth control?" Matt asked.

"When I babysat with the Bannister bunch a while back."

36

Next Assignment

Matt asked Father O'Brien to help Pastor Wiggins with the wedding ceremony. He told him of the sudden lifting of grief and the ensuing need and love for Maude beyond any he had ever felt for her.

"Star told Maude when she had given up recovering from smallpox that I would need her because somehow she wasn't going to be in the picture. Star never told me anything about it, and I can't explain it. Star isn't out of my life. My love for her hasn't diminished. It's something I now can live with and am allowed to love another."

"That's Star," said Father O'Brien. "Unselfish in her assessment of what's best for you while here. I'll be happy to be a part of this marriage. If it's possible for two people to be equal in excellence, it is Star and Maude. In different ways, those two have it all. Have you ever wondered if you and Star had been together all those years and you felt the same about Star as you did about Maude, as though she were an old shoe, and Maude had come to that tree, who would you have chosen?"

Matt grinned. "I'm ashamed to say it, but I think Maude would have gotten the nod."

The wedding wasn't a large affair. Just the immediate circle. Zeb and Eva sang. Fawn and Jim were bridesmaid and best man, and Jennifer, the ring bearer.

Perhaps God smiled a little at the resolving of this traumatic realignment. Two of Nordic's best in all areas of perfection combined to accomplish a desire to fulfill their love and make this world better by their efforts to improve it.

After the ceremony, Zeb handed Matt an envelope.

"Put this in your pocket, Cub, and open it when you have a little time."

They went to a hotel in the city after a shower of rice and best wishes. Imagination is a powerful vehicle, so, for the record, let's assume their togetherness was beyond words in its fulfillment.

The next morning, Matt was taking a shower as Maude joined him. Each in turn admired and assessed the perfection of the other and happily assisted in the washing of each other's backs and fronts.

"What are your plans for the day?" Matt asked.

"Let's have them bring up breakfast and maybe dinner later," said Maude. "We have some unfinished business to do." Their lips met.

"That's the answer I hoped I'd get," said Matt.

"I heard about the jar of peas story. From what has happened so far it's going to be a challenge, but I bet we get them all back out and more," Maude said later, as they ate their breakfast.

Matt reached in his pocket and pulled out Zeb's envelope and opened it. The short letter read: "You are now my partner in my financial enterprises. Enclosed is an authorization that will honor your withdrawals from any of the banks named here. Use it unsparingly when the need arises. You are more than a friend, Zeb."

Matt handed the letter to Maude. She read it.

"There's one thing missing. We need Zeb, Do you have pen and paper?" Matt asked.

"Yes, I do," Maude opened a desk in the room. There were pen, ink, and paper.

"Write this—'Dear Zeb, Maude and I have discussed this partnership. We accept it on the condition that you come and live with us and help us make your dreams and ours come into being. Believe us, we sorely need you, your guidance, insight, and faith.'—We'll both sign it."

Maude went with Matt when they visited Dr. Caldwell about the new assignment. Matt introduced her to Dr. Caldwell. He was impressed.

"You are beautiful, and somehow I know it's all the way through." They sat by Dr. Caldwell's desk and listened as he talked.

"Here is an all-white, poorly attended church where seventy-five percent of the parish is Mexican and black. It's been limping along and no one has tried hard enough to muddy the waters. You'll get to open the can of worms, because the church needs to be open to all. Try not to lose much sleep if you lose ground for a time. Right now, it isn't a Christian church by any measure. We are and we need to be ashamed of its present stature."

They were met at the station by the chairman of the official board, Hugh Summers. "Ask me the questions, and I'll give you the answers." He built homes and let it be known that he was one of the larger givers of the church.

The parsonage was well kept, better than the other homes near by. In spite of their meager furniture, Maude soon had it looking cheerful and homey. Hugh Summers had come and offered his help to put the furniture in place. As they sat for a cup of coffee, Matt brought up what had been on his mind. He looked at Hugh.

148

"You told me to ask the questions, and you'd give me the answers. I've been informed that the parish is now seventy-five percent Mexican and black. How does the church respond to that?"

"I'm happy to say that we are all white."

"How do you justify that?"

"I don't justify it. That's the way it has to be. When the others come in, I go out and take a lot of the members with me."

When Hugh left, Maude looked at Matt and smiled.

"Well, Pastor Berglund, what are you going to do about that?" Matt embraced her.

"Before I start on my sermon, I'm going to kiss you right on that pretty mouth, maybe more than once."

After the song and prayer at the Sunday service, Matt looked out at his skimpy audience in a sanctuary that would seat six hundred.

"You and I have problems," Matt said. "If you'll look around you, you will see an all-white, exclusive gathering in this church, and you'll also notice that there aren't very many. I've been searching the Scriptures to see if there is any supportive reason for this kind of congregation in a place where the majority of those whose needs are as great or greater have no part in its ongoing. I am sure that one reason is no one has invited or welcomed those of different ethnic background to worship here. They're also smart enough not to want any part of the frigid reception they would get here. This isn't only your pastor's opinion. Dr. Caldwell, head of the Board of Missions, puts it this way, 'Right now, it isn't a Christian church by any measure. We are and we need to be ashamed of its present stature.'

"Some of you are concerned and would like to let your love reach out. To those, there will be heartbreak and rebuff, but also victory and joy in serving, helping, lifting, and building God's kingdom right here in our midst. Some of you have probably made up your minds you won't be back. You know better how to handle this than the God you profess to believe. I can sympathize with your problem. There are many churches where you can fit right in because their areas are all white, but you'll know you failed in the glorious opportunity to serve where the need for positive Christian action was the greatest.

"It's hard to change. If this is a church where God's needs are uppermost, it will have to change. You are at the crossroads where the need, challenge, and fulfillment is great, and this is your chance to make yourselves a great church again. I know you are basically a good people, who through pressures, discouragement, and acquiescence of a feeble faith have lost your vision. I hope none of you leave, but if you stay, I'm asking you, and God is asking you, to place your lives in His

149

hands to do what must be done. There are no quick solutions. We'll need your patience, your love, and your will to face adversity as we work together to make this a community church. Will you help?"

Most of the congregation, including Hugh Summers, stayed for the coffee and cake at the getting-acquainted session in the church basement. Maude remembered their greetings, running the scale from warm to obligatory. She sat in on the first official board meeting.

"I want somebody there that seems to like me," said Matt.

Hugh Summers stood up as the meeting was called to order. He looked around the table uncomfortably.

"I know what's on the minds of most of you here," he said. "There's a story about the old mule that wouldn't budge after being hitched to a plow. The farmer whacked him with his reins, yelled and cursed, then whacked harder, but the mule just stood there. In desperation, the farmer picked up a board by the fence, went around to the front of the mule and hit him between the eyes hard enough to break the board. The mule blinked his eyes, and when the farmer picked up the reins and said 'giddap,' the mule started off. After that, the farmer only needed to show the mule the board now and then."

Hugh hesitated, and Maude could see that he was struggling.

"You all know me," he said. "I've already spouted off to the preacher about my all-white position. I guess I've been hit with that board. I'm loaded with prejudice, and it's going to be hard to cross over. If I can do it, I know many of you can." Tears rolled down the chairman's cheeks as he turned to Matt. "Pastor Berglund, I want to try, but you may have to show me that board from time to time."

Matt rose from his chair and went to Hugh Summers. He took his hand and then embraced him. Maude could see tears on Matt's face as he turned to the other members. "Your chairman is a big man," he said.

Maude and Matt had already spent their few days on location, visiting and assessing the parish neighborhood. There was squalor and hopelessness, especially in the Mexican and black areas. It was easy to see what no jobs and often hunger had done to the morale and morals of an ignored portion of humanity. Thievery and cheap wine was a way of life for many.

Maude and Matt had purchased a large bed for Zeb, along with a dresser and desk in anticipation of Zeb's arrival. When he came, Maude met him at the door and threw her arms around him. She had been doing that for years.

"You have been one of my favorite huggers," teased Zeb, "even when I used to change your diapers."

She showed him to his room.

"You are family here you know," she said. "If you want to take off your shoes in the living room, join the crowd."

Zeb combed the area for a few days, and then, a meeting of the minds was held. Maude spoke first.

"I can do things for the women, like teaching them to sew or work in homes as housekeeper or nannies. We could use some of the rooms in the church basement. Some need to improve their language skills or learn to be a typist, and a lot of them need to know how to have some control over the size of their families. There is talent out there that has never been allowed to express itself, and we need to find it so they can help each other. We know there are some good voices for our choir. I want in as a full-time partner to help get things to happen. I'd like to see a large community garden, which will get them to work together and also improve the kind of food they consume. Most of all, they need jobs to get back their self-respect and desire to want to thank God for being alive."

Matt spoke.

"Many of the men have been in the rut of unemployment so long, they don't try to find work. We have to get them off their backsides and make lumbermen out of some of them. The railroad needs men to repair and put in new track. It's up to us to put some spunk back in their spines and help them get those jobs and bolster their self-worth until they have acquired a sense of being a whole person again. Almost every home needs paint and repair. We need to form work crews. That empty area, now full of junk, needs to be cleaned up and might be the place for Maude's community garden. I don't know anybody who can teach skills of handling tools as well as you, Zeb. The men will learn as they earn and then be able to offer their abilities even outside our immediate boundaries. You advanced the necessary funds to let New Venture have the pay checks while we were in the beginning stages. If this becomes a healthy community, it will support the church that made it happen. I'm sure Dr. Caldwell will put us on as a mission project and let all our churches help by giving to a mission that does its job. Dr. Caldwell is going to get a note from me in the near future to that effect."

Zeb had been listening.

"I'm for all that; I hear your chairman of the official board builds houses. He could get a good price on the paint and lumber we'll need to repair some of these houses the people are living in. I'd like to see us build a community house on that open area close to the church. We could have room for all kinds of classes that Maude is talking about and have a hall for meetings and entertainment, where local talent could express itself in plays or music and social gatherings for the whole

151

neighborhood, whether they belonged to the church or not. If it is church property, the church could monitor the programming in such a way that it will make people want to know the Christ whose expressed love helped them hold up their heads again."

"How about doing the paint and repair crews first," queried Matt, "to find out if there's enough fire burning in them to want to improve their lives? I know my dad would spend time with those who want to learn how to repair and lay track for the railway. Jim would help to integrate our prospective lumbermen. Zeb, the work crews could use your expertise on doing a job well, and we'll need your assessment of their capabilities and reliability. Also, those of your race may feel better about responding to your high standards of work habits. Perhaps my first job is to visit those in the congregation who want to get into the thick of it and make something happen. They're the ones who will have to lower the bars and invite everyone in."

37

Follow Me

There was a pipe organ, a large one, that filled the wall back of the lectern. Matt was told it needed repair. The piano, Maude found, was out of tune. Sometime in the past, the church had flourished. There was no choir, which figured.

Adam, Eva, and Jennifer had come for a visit. It was chiefly Jennifer's idea because she wanted to see her big brother and her new sister.

Sunday morning, Matt looked out again over his congregation. It hadn't depleted. He estimated there were ten or fifteen more sitting in the pews before him. Zeb and Jennifer were sitting near him.

"I want you to meet my friend and co-partner in this job we have been asked to do with you. His name is Zeb Hawkins. I also want you to know my little sister, Jennifer. My dad and mother are sitting among you. You've all read about the two who were in the Garden of Eden. The ones I call Dad and Mother are named Adam and Eva. Will you two please stand?" There were a few smiles. "Now, I know the pipe organ won't work and the piano is out of tune, but I think you'll agree with me that we're going to have some music this morning." Matt turned to Zeb. "Zeb and Jennifer, it's all yours."

Zeb and Jennifer removed their violins from their cases, and Zeb looked out at those present.

"Most of you will recognize Beethoven, as we play. This, in a way, is our theme song, and we like to think that our Lord is making this appeal to each of us here today in the words we will sing." They played several bars of the "Minuet in G" as a violin duet, and then, Zeb played as Jennifer's voice sang loud and clear.

I am glad that I heard Jesus say,
"Follow Me, Follow Me,
I need you to help Me every day:
There are those who do not know My way.
Please open your door,
Do not wait any longer."

Yes, I'm glad that I heard Jesus say,
Follow me, Follow me."

Then Jennifer played, and the audience knew there were two performing artists on stage. She played for Zeb as he sang the same few lines. His powerful and rich bass voice rolled over the pews, carrying with it the honesty of his faith and the perfection of his vocal control. Zeb motioned for Eva to come up, and as she was approaching the altar platform, he spoke to the audience.

"We're all going to sing our next song together, but before we do, I want to tell you that the pipe organ will be repaired and the piano tuned as soon as we find a repairman. You will have a choir in a short time that may be the best in this city or beyond. It will be made up of many of you and many who are a few shades darker coming from those within this parish. Now, Eva, Jennifer, and I are going to lead you in singing hymn number twenty-eight, 'In Christ There Is No East or West,' and we don't want to be doing it alone."

Eva started it. Her beautiful contralto reached out to the hearts of the congregation as she motioned with her hands for all to sing. She smiled encouragement at those who began to sing with her, and soon the church was filled with the uniting voices. There were tears, but they were an outward sign of inner joy that something really was going to happen.

Zeb and Hugh Summers hit it off from the start.

"Do we have the resources to get this started?"

Matt asked Zeb point-blank as he, Maude, and Zeb discussed the needs and priorities to start their own New Venture.

Zeb smiled.

"I think I used the word 'unsparingly,' and that's the way we're going to do it. Summers will be here tomorrow morning with the paint and lumber and tools to get it going. He's also going to bring some of his crew along to show the workers we get how to use them. We're going to pay our workers but we're also going to insist on a day's work."

The renewal began. Matt had to admit that he was surprised how many of the members volunteered to help, to offer their know-how to the work crews, and develop friendships they had a hard time admitting to themselves. Matt was in the midst of it, and he enjoyed the most menial tasks, getting rid of the junk, scraping old paint, lifting and carrying sacks of cement. The workers warmed to him almost as completely as they did to Zeb. He found some men who wanted to become lumbermen and sent them to the Bay area to learn the skills necessary

154

to become master lumbermen. They were under Jim Beaver's wing. Some were taught how to lay and repair track by Adam.

It wasn't long before Zeb and Hugh Summers decided they had the work force and the skills that could begin the Community House. There was an empty area along the left side of the church. The two families that lived in the dilapidated cottages were offered two in good repair and far superior to those they called homes. This gave them plenty of space for the new building and room for playground equipment and a picnic area in the rear. The city asked only a small amount of money for the additional space because they were glad to see signs of renewal.

Maude and many of the women came to help with the cleaning and inside painting. Here again in the daily contact with Mexican and blacks, each began to find out that friendship knew no color.

From this mishmash of color, a choir began to evolve and talent was unearthed. The organ had been repaired, and when someone wondered who was going to play it, Viola Butts, a black member of the choir who possessed a beautiful voice, spoke up.

"I know someone who can do it if she will. Some of us know Ruby Shelton."

Ruby worked as a housekeeper and maid for a wealthy white family who lived in the more affluent corner of the parish. Maude visited her and found that she had been taught to play the organ when she had been a slave. When Maude asked her if she would like to play the church organ, she held her hands together almost prayerfully. "If I only could."

The piano was one of Maude's skills, and when she thought someone else should be playing it, Zeb put it this way. "This is going to be the best choir in this city, and we need the best at the piano. That's you."

Classes began in sewing and learning how to be a housekeeper or maid. Some of the church women volunteered to help improve language skills, and those who taught found fulfillment in giving of themselves. Maude had a large response from those who wanted to regulate the size of their families.

The happening began in earnest. The workers who had rubbed elbows with the goodness and godliness of the trio came to church knowing that each smile Zeb, Matt, and Maude gave them was an invitation to find the source of love they had. The choir bloomed and expanded. New seats were added to the choir loft and then more seats. Zeb was in his element as he fine-tuned their collective voices, half light and half dark. Before the first year ended, the choir sang in the best churches all over the city. There was new hope in the parish. Those who worked for the logging company sent most of their money back to their families. The railroad took the men that Adam trained into their ranks as fast as they were ready, and the ones who had repaired the once-squalid cottages were in demand for their skills in building.

The Community House was the amalgam that brought the people together. Plays of their own talent were put on, along with outside performances of music and acting from Shakespeare to *Uncle Tom's Cabin.*

Ruby Shelton could certainly play that organ! Mr. and Mrs. Devore were the ones who used Ruby's services as a housekeeper. They had been members some years back, but when they knew they had a talented organist as part of their family, they allowed Ruby to take the time necessary to practice and play. Not only did the Devores become proud and active members, but a deep friendship grew between Ruby and Maude. For these two accomplished keyboard players, music was the language of the soul, the unique binding of hearts together.

Maude was soon forced to display other skills besides her piano virtuosity. The banging on her door signaled trouble. There stood young Peter Finch shouting.

"There's a dead man by the tracks!" Maude saw that Peter expected her to follow him. She hurried along behind as he breathlessly explained, "I was going fishing, and I almost stumbled over him in the weeds."

Peter was right—there was a man lying by the tracks, but as she knelt beside him and put her hand on his ebony brow, she knew he wasn't dead, at least, not yet. His forehead was warm and she detected he was breathing slowly. A swelling bump near his temple was a clue for his unconsciousness.

Hearing the commotion, Zeb had looked out his bedroom window to see Maude running down the hill with the boy. He sensed that he, too, would be needed so hastened to the tracks. He arrived on the scene just as the man opened his eyes and groggily looked up at Maude.

"Am I in heaven?" he asked. She smiled a warm, caring, relieved smile.

"You aren't the only one that thinks she's an angel," Zeb laughed.

Zeb picked up the dirty, ragged black as he would a small child, hurried to the house and put him in his own bed. A doctor had been called. After removing his dirty, smelly clothing, Zeb covered him with a blanket. By now, the young man was fully awake and conscious.

"What's your name, and where's your home?" Zeb asked.

"My name's Sam, and I can't remember ever having a home or parents."

Soon the doctor arrived, checked his pulse, and thumped him here and there. Examining his almost skeletal torso, the doctor questioned,

156

"When was the last time you ate something?"

Sam seemed to be trying to remember.

"Three days ago, I ate some overripe bananas at a city dump."

The doctor turned to Zeb and Maude.

"Outside of a little bump on his head, this young man is starving to death. He needs lots of good nourishing food."

"I'm heading for the kitchen, and I'm going to cook up a storm." Maude grinned at Zeb, "You get to clean him up."

Zeb changed the bath water twice and then supplied some of his own clothing for Sam to put on.

"You go on out to the kitchen and start getting some meat on those bones; I'm going to get some clothes that fit you."

Sam still was a bit wobbly, but he made it to the kitchen. Maude pointed to a chair and started him off with eggs and bacon. A batch of fresh bread was just coming from the oven. Sam couldn't decide if the tantalizing, celestial aroma or the creamy butter, strawberry jam, peanut butter, and slices of cheese he piled on top made slice after slice disappear. It seemed to Maude that a bit of color had returned to his pale lips. Sam found it difficult to take his eyes from Maude; it wasn't only her beauty, but her warmth, concern, and friendliness. She brought him a piece of chocolate pie.

"If you don't like chocolate pie, you may have to stand in the corner for a while."

"Why are you doing all this for me? I didn't think there were people like you any more."

"You are one or God's children. He loves you and we love you. It's what we do; we help His children find their way back into His out-stretched arms. We hope they will help someone else find the certainty of His love."

When Zeb came back from the clothier, he was surprised to see Sam with a newspaper in his hands. Zeb carried a bag with a coat hanger exposed and other bundles. He had had to ad lib the sizes, but, thankfully, there had been a customer in the store who was, in Zeb's eyes, similar in proportions and height to Sam. He had told the clerk, "Let's start from the skin out."

Sam put on the new underwear, pants, socks, and shirt. Maude tied the necktie Zeb had procured and helped Sam into his suit coat. It was quality clothing. The shoes fit, too. Though thin, Sam was quite handsome. Zeb grinned.

"With a haircut, I think we've got something here! He still needs a lot of food."

"He can help me cook and get that big garden started until he

157

puts some meat on those bones. Right now, I'd better check that ham roast."

Zeb and Sam were alone, and Zeb pointed to the newspaper, which was on the desk.

"Sam, I saw you reading this paper." He pointed to an article. "Can you read this?" It was a quotation from Shakespeare. Sam read:

"To be or not to be, that is the question. Whether 'tis nobler in the mind to suffer the slings and arrows of outrageous fortune, or by opposing them, to die, to sleep, to dream. Aye, there's the rub; for in that dream of death who knows what dreams may come when we have shuffled off this mortal coil."

Sam read real well and with understanding. That brought Zeb's next question.

"How much schooling have you had, and do you know your age?"

"I never went to formal school, but I wasn't the only one that was overlooked or ignored. There are men who seem to enjoy the life they've chosen as hobos who are brainy. Some have taught me portions of the Bible and helped me read newspapers. One of them taught me some of the basics of boxing, and I won a few preliminary bouts. I quit when I fought someone who was punch drunk at twenty-five. I didn't want to do that to anyone or me. I'm somewhere in my middle teens. I don't remember being tossed off that freight car. They must have thought I was dead."

Zeb sat in deep thought for a short period of time and turned to Sam.

"Maybe God has reasons for bringing you to our doorstep. As your faith grows, and it will, other young people who won't listen to us may listen more fully to you. Maude likes you already, and you will love her. She does need assistance in the kitchen and garden. We'll let others do the heavy stuff, at least until you get your muscles back."

"Do you really want me to stay with you? Oh! I'll try so hard—I will, I will." Tears poured down Sam's cheeks as he found himself in Zeb's arms.

"Okay, okay! Get yourself to the kitchen, and tell Maude that she's your boss." Zeb looked at Sam. "On second thought, let's get that haircut first."

As they walked to the barber shop, Zeb assured Sam:

"You and I are going to get you a high school diploma. I'll help you in your weaker areas."

"Wow!" was all Sam said.

Sam was just beginning to learn how lives could be changed and renewed. That's what God's love was all about. Not only was his life taking a turn for the better, the entire community was becoming revitalized. As the paint and repair brought a new look to the neighborhood, new hope and well-being filled the pews with those who wanted to express their thankfulness. Sam soon was in their midst. He felt his being alive was a miracle. The teenagers listened to his message of God's love. The honesty of his appeal made them want a part of it. Zeb, Maude, and Matt now considered their team a foursome as they poured unlimited love and money into that neighborhood.

The Community House had become a reality. A pre-Christmas potluck was held, and Jennifer was visiting again. Zeb had asked her to help with the plans for the children that day. After some "Barbershop," sung by parish talent, Zeb invited the young ones to come onto the stage and sit in back of him. They ranged from toddlers to early teens. As Sam helped decide who would sit where, he had to stoop to hug the tots who raised their arms. All could see that Sam was in his own heaven.

Zeb had discovered another facet of Sam's abilities. He could sing. With a little coaching, his rich tenor voice made a delightful addition to the choir. He and Jennifer prepared a skit after she taught him a few dance steps.

The stage was filled, leaving a little room at the front. Zeb talked to the children and then pointed to Jennifer in the front row. She hopped up the steps, did two cartwheels, and stood beside Zeb. Zeb grinned at the audience.

"This is Matt's sister, Jennifer, whom, for obvious reasons, we sometimes call Buzz Saw." He pointed to Sam. "Your turn, Sam."

From where he stood, Sam, with two cartwheels, stood by Zeb. Maude was at the piano at the side of the stage. She struck a chord, then played softly as they began to sing:

Grandma used to dance the minuet,
long ago, long ago,
Grandma used to dance the minuet.
Every step and turn she remembers yet.
She was belle of the ball
in her gingham gown so lovely.
Grandma used to dance the minuet,
long ago, long ago.

In practice, Jennifer discovered she had a nimble partner. She had hoped he could learn some simple moves, but his natural athleticism and timing made rehearsal a joy she hadn't anticipated. Now their feet moved in three-quarter time as they danced the beginning minuet steps, side by side. Two young people just having fun. They returned to center with Sam's feet touching the floor in beat while he kept his finger over Jennifer's head as she whirled in one, two, three perfection. Then he placed his hands under her arms and swept her from the floor, raised her high above his head, and returned her to the floor in perfect three-quarter time. They faced the audience and sang:

Grandma used to dance the minuet,
long ago, long ago . . .

They bowed to each other and to the thunderous applause of their audience. Their beautifully blended voices had filled the hall with nostalgic euphoria. Maybe it wasn't Broadway, but there was loud appreciation.

Jennifer opened her valise, took out large happy smiles made of construction paper with strings attached, and with Sam's help, gave one to each child on the stage.

After all had been given a smile, Jennifer took some more smiles from the valise.

"We have more smiles. If you think your dad has been a little grumpy lately, we want you to take another one and go put a smile on him."

There was a scramble for smiles. Most of the dads laughed when their offspring handed them a smile. There was a general response of laughs and applause. One boy apprehensively gave his father a smile. The father pulled the boy to him and hugged him, tears running down his cheeks.

Under Zeb's direction, the choir soon had a reputation beyond its immediate surroundings. Other churches thrilled to the melodious content of its mixed humanity, and Zeb's prophecy of excellence came true. Before the end of the second year, the church was bulging with its increasing membership and the letter that came from Dr. Caldwell wasn't a surprise.

You've done it again. I know it's a combination of daring and doing, along with a seemingly unlimited quantity of unflagging energy and enthusiasm that makes it happen. Our church salutes you. You know we can't let you stay there because there are so many blighted areas that need what you have. We have set the Hawkins-Berglund Fund in motion, and with the reports we have passed on to the churches, many are making your fund a part of their mission giving. We are sending two pastors whom we've selected with care to carry on your programs. We want you to meet with them to instill a bit of your magic in them. We have selected your next assignment.

Matt met with the two pastors, their wives, and families. They were glad to be part of a flourishing parish, and they would give the church a creditable portion of their time. But he knew they were not like Maude, Zeb, himself, and, yes, Sam, who had given their all. By their God-given natures, they couldn't do otherwise.

It had been hard to say good-bye. Hugh Summers took them to the train in his fringed carriage pulled by his two matched trotters. He helped them unload their suitcases. Tears rolled down his cheeks as he hugged Maude and Matt. Zeb and Sam received the same treatment. Sobs tore from him as he hurried to his carriage and slapped his chargers with the reins to get them to hurry away.

Maude and Matt were in their private compartment. They would spend the night on the train. It was a subdued atmosphere, a mixed feeling of having done a good job and an uncertainty of the morrows to come. Matt was just staring into the small space as Maude came and sat beside him on a bunk. She kissed him.

"I have an idea," said Maude. "Let's work on that jar of peas."

38

A New Challenge

Bishop Caldwell had conferred the title of Doctor of Divinity on Matt as an appreciation gesture for transforming and revitalizing churches. The reassignment letter Matt received read:

> This church seemingly has no problems. It continues to increase in membership. Its members give copiously to missions and emergency relief requests. If they needed a new church, it would be funded overnight, but they fail to see the poverty and needs within their own neighborhood. They are all white, all affluent, and totally ignore those of another color, of which there are many in their immediate area. It is a proud church of good people who haven't been told distinctly enough about what being a Christian disciple implies. Naturally, we don't want to destroy the church, and redirecting and changing their thinking may be asking too much of them. Nonetheless, we're tossing you into this lion's den. I'll admit we're shaking a little, but God has worked many wonders with you. This may be your greatest challenge.

Maude and Matt visited the pastor they would replace shortly before he left. The Reverend Dr. Cranston and his wife had invited them to dinner so they could show them what they were getting into.

We're sorry to leave," Dr. Cranston stated. "This is, no doubt, one of the ecclesiastical plums of this denomination."

The parsonage, of colonial design, was plush and spacious and furnished with artistic decor. Its beautifully landscaped lawn was framed with formal beds of flowers. "It's all part of the package," Dr. Cranston said. "You don't have to lift a finger."

The church was large. The three thousand plus members spared nothing in their effort to make their place of worship beautiful, which was evident in the priceless and artistic stained glass windows. They were shown through countless rooms for Sunday school and committee meetings. The office that would be Matt's was enormous, and the other rooms for the associate pastors were more than adequate for any pastor.

"You'll love it here," said Dr. Cranston.

Matt wasn't so sure he could stomach all this affluence. It reeked with its own importance. The church stored their furniture for them. All the furniture in the parsonage was provided by their interior decorator. Zeb had his pretentious private bathroom, bedroom, and study. The parsonage committee was adamant that the house should be a showcase. Matt, with Maude's approval, had invited the four associate pastors to come to dinner on Thursday evening for the purpose of getting acquainted and planning strategy. In the meantime, over the next two days, he and Zeb toured the neighborhood to see what the surrounding area was like.

Thursday night, Zeb and Sam helped serve the dinner. The four associates enjoyed Maude's cooking. None of the pastors recognized Zeb as anything but a servant in the household. Later, when they sat in the study, they had to readjust their perception of Zeb when Matt introduced him.

"Much of our success wouldn't have happened without him," Matt said. "He is my closest friend and advisor and a part of our family. That goes for our newest addition. For now, his name is Sam. He is our miracle. We found him hurt and dying from starvation. We helped him to be among the living. Young people especially respond to his earnest faith, and, like us, he seems to want to work twenty-four hours a day." Sam bashfully smiled at the four pastors. One walked over to him, shook his hand, then hugged him.

Matt continued, "First, I want you all to read this letter that l received from our bishop. Then I'd like each of you to tell me what your job has been here and how you think you can respond to what is now our problem."

Rev. Allan Putnam read the letter and passed it on. He was impeccably dressed and had a natural charisma. It was he who had hugged Sam.

"My job has been to call on our membership periodically, and they, in turn, recommend some of their friends for prospective membership. That, along with being an *ex officio* member of various committees, seems to keep me busy. It seemed to be the thing to do, and I didn't have too many qualms about not raising any dust. I'm supposed to be an example of Christ's love and His very plain message. I realize any excuses I made for myself don't hold water."

Rev. Stan Berwanger was an older man.

"I do most of the funerals, except for the few most prestigious names, and I also call on the membership as we all do. I'm looking forward to retirement. It hasn't bothered me much before, but after reading this letter, I'm suddenly ashamed of myself. God must be ashamed, too, of the quality of some of His supposed leadership."

Rev. Ray Brown fumbled with his necktie.

"That's about the size of it," he said. "I'd tell myself that they gave a lot of money, and that was all one could expect from this unchangeable congregation."

Matt looked at the Reverend Dan Altman. He was a young man who was also new to this church and had just arrived in town earlier that day. Dan looked up from reading the bishop's letter.

"I don't have to apologize for what's been done here," he said, "but I'm glad to know that, as of now, we're expected to try to make some changes."

"Zeb and I have looked around the neighborhood," Matt said. "We talked about a course of action. What we say here tonight will be refined or altered as you add your input. My wife took some groceries to a family less than half a block from this church. The husband was out of a job, and his wife and their two small children haven't been eating well. No one from this church has ever called on them. For a start, I want each of you to select an area of this community and to spend two days of your week calling on the families that live there. For the present, unless there is an emergency need, just keep a record of their church affiliation. Record it if they have none, and don't pass up families that may have a different color of skin. These listings you make will be for our private inspection for a time, but if you see a need, make it a part of our church outreach."

Matt hesitated and then proceeded, "God expects us to use and deal with what we have. We have a church with the capacity and desire to give. There is an abandoned railroad right-of-way less than a block away. It could become a community center and playground park. With help from the city and some financial backing from our church's affluent members, it could raise the quality of life in our neighborhood. People like to feel important. We'll even have a special ceremony to give credit to the financial sponsors. A complex like this would give our youngest pastor, Dan Altman, an opportunity to serve the youth of this parish. There are some good baseball teams out there who are just getting into trouble now. Many of them could eventually be drawn into our membership."

Dan responded to the idea by raising his right fist above his head and grinning.

"I'll throw out another idea. We could build a recreation building on or close to this church. It would be used for basketball, volleyball, and supervised games in general. I'd like a swimming pool in the basement myself. That's one way I've tried to keep somewhat trim. It would definitely attract the youth and, we would hope, add to their spiritual growth." Matt looked at each of his pastors trying to assess their enthusiasm. He felt that he had at least captured their attention.

"It's going to be hard to preach with a soft approach for a while, but we need the congregation's generous support. By the time our doors are open to all, we pray that many of our people will adjust to the idea by seeing what God has done through their participation. Perhaps they will also feel that Christ has become more real to them in the changes that have evolved. Now, they're telling God how to run His business. That cannot continue. We all need to refresh our lives with Christ's call to discipleship. Our members need to know that their call is the same as ours.

"I won't be preaching every Sunday, so I want this constant nudging to true Christian discipleship to come from each of us as we take our turn. I plan to mention this idea of a community center, but perhaps our youngest associate could promote the gymnasium and swimming pool as the project gets going. He would probably generate more enthusiasm than if I tossed the ball. We have been asked by our bishop to make this a church for all people. What is evident here distorts the vision Christ has for His church. Let's pray we can put a smile on God's face as we work together. We will forget what has or hasn't happened in the past. All I want is your sincere enthusiasm to work toward making this church more Christ centered. I'm sure there will be some repercussions, and a little honest prayer won't hurt any of us."

No doubt many in the pews wondered who that black man was who sat with the bass singers in the choir the following Sunday. The choir director, Joe Abercrombe, was brave enough to sacrifice his job if necessary after he heard Zeb sing. He even gave Zeb the solo part for one verse of the hymn "Are Ye Able." His deep bass voice made the listeners forget the color of his skin for the moment.

Rev. Allan Putnam continued the order of worship and then introduced Matt to the congregation.

"It is my honor and privilege to present to you at this time, our new pastor, Dr. Matt Berglund."

Matt came to the pulpit. The short introduction was the way Matt wanted it to be. He looked around. The church was full, including the spacious balcony.

"Many of you are wondering why I have been selected to be your pastor. To clear the air a little, I have to tell you that it wasn't my idea. It was your bishop's. Looking around now, I see your church is full. Your membership has increased steadily each year. You are a giving church and are to be commended for your financial support for missions. Your church is beautiful as a result of good caretaking. The size and quality of your choir quite possibly can't be equaled by any other church. In the face of all these pluses, God is saying, 'You can be better than you are.'"

Matt paused and came to the center. The thought entered his mind that no one had walked out yet. "I come as your pastor," he said, "but I want to introduce my whole team to you." He turned to the choir. "Zeb, will you come down and stand with me?"

Zeb moved to the end of the choir seats and came to stand beside Matt. "I have observed that you already have the Hawkins-Berglund Rehabilitation and Renewal Fund on your list of mission giving. This is Zeb Hawkins, founder of this fund, and my lifelong friend and partner in the work we have done. You have heard him sing. He is also recognized as a leading virtuoso on the violin. You who spend your days in the world of finance will discover that his success in the market has few equals. He gives generously of his time, energy, money, and faith to upgrade the quality of life around him. Your children will love him because they will know that he loves them."

He smiled at Zeb and then turned again to the members in the pews. "I know I've embarrassed Zeb," he said, "but I also recognize that this isn't an ordinary church. Many of our city's best minds are here today, who respect expertise and intelligence wherever it arises. Now," continued Matt, "will Mrs. Berglund and Sam come up here with Zeb and me?"

Maude came to the chancel She kissed Zeb and then stood with her husband. Sam stood beside Zeb.

"As you suspect," said Matt, "this is my wife, and she hopes you will call her Maude. She is the third and a very important part of our work force. She doesn't wait for orders. This week she visited a family less than one-half block from this church. The wife and two little daughters hadn't been eating regularly. Zeb and Maude have taken care of that problem and have found a job for the husband. His wife told Maude that no one from this church has ever called on them in the three years they have lived here.

"Sam is our miracle, and he lives with us." Matt told of Sam's entry into their midst, and by the reaction, it didn't fall on deaf ears. Zeb went back to the choir, and Maude and Sam sat in one of the front pews.

Matt began. "It would be easy to ignore Christ's command to love your neighbor as yourself, but this speaks of your parish. There is a weedy, junk-laden old railroad right-of-way within a block of this church. I can picture a park with a baseball diamond, among other things, where you and your children and the children of this community can gather. A community center could be built where crafts and skills are taught to raise the quality of life in this neighborhood. There is talent here to put on plays, which, in the doing would enrich the rapport among our members. We are supposed to be a happy people, and we are happiest when we help make God's dreams come true."

There was an interval of complete silence as Matt looked at his audience almost individually. "I know your problems," said Matt. "Bias and prejudice are part of all of us. It has been so ingrained in our thinking that we aren't aware of its presence until we face a situation like this. I'm certain that some of you will not be able to adjust, except by the movement of the Holy Spirit in your hearts. The inner struggle that you will experience will tear the foundations of the faith you have. Prayers don't have to be fancy words. Just ask Christ to help you find your answers. Let Him be the Lord of your life."

Zeb sat by Matt at the official board meeting the following Monday night. Most of the board members were either in finance professions or leaders in the business community. Before the meeting began they had already surrounded Zeb, and one had even asked about a certain stock.

"Buy it," said Zeb, "but only if you'll take my advice on when to sell."

Curtis Peabody, chairman of the board of the largest bank in the city, was also chairman of the official board. Reports were made by the chairmen of the various committees, with some input from the associate pastors. Chairman Peabody introduced the new associate, Rev. Dan Altman, to the board and suggested that he take the place of the former pastor as the *ex officio* member of the Evangelism committee. When asked if he wanted to say anything, he stood up.

"I couldn't accept this assignment," he said, "unless I'd be allowed to reach out to every person in this parish and invite them to this church. I'm not taking a slap at the other associates, because they would have reached out to the area if they had been given a free hand. That restriction won't come from Dr. Matt Berglund. I want to be a part of a new beginning. I pray that I can stay here."

Someone started a weak clapping, and it caught fire. The room reverberated with a unanimous response.

"My wife will kill me," said one of the men. "She's from the South."

Others laughed nervously, knowing this was the beginning of something that wouldn't subside easily. Curtis Peabody spoke up.

"It looks as though we've been handed a hot potato," he grinned. "Let's do something about it. We're not pikers. Here's one idea. The city will probably bulldoze, level, and clean up that right-of-way if we say we'll buy it. We can build a community center there and also hold church services there to create a more casual atmosphere, where people won't be intimidated. Most of the people in this area wouldn't want to sit in our sanctuary with us stuffed shirts and will be more comfortable there until we begin to loosen ourselves up a little. I hope I'm not the only one who's beginning to feel good about this. Besides, there could be another plus. If we don't like the sermon here, we can go over there to hear one of the other pastors."

The laughter that followed loosened the somewhat taut atmosphere that had been pervading the meeting. Jim Donovan, one of the chairmen spoke out.

"All of you here know me pretty well. I'm one among others who have made this statement, 'When the blacks come in, that's when I go out.' Probably for the first time, I've really asked myself why I feel that way. My dad was a 'nigger hater.' What was good enough for Dad seemed to be the way to go. On the other hand, I entrust my children to one of the finest examples of decency, love, and faith, and she's black. For the first time in my life, I can say I would be proud to have her sitting with my family, wherever we are. I'm a little frightened, but I'd like to think we can become a church for all people. Right now, many of us have been a bunch of hypocrites. I've had a hard time turning anything over to God. Now I'd like to help Him see what we can do with this neighborhood if we work together."

Matt reached for Jim's hand.

"That may not be the longest speech you've made, but it's the best. I've noticed that some of you seemed to get along with my partner rather well this evening. Being a wizard at finance was one of the obvious reasons, which I'm sure you'll admit. But I'd like for you to know him a little better. Zeb, will you say a few words?"

Zeb rose. For a moment, before Matt sat down, the board saw two giants, whose reputation for rebuilding lives had preceded them. To see them together seemed to augment the feeling that here was an unstoppable force among them. Zeb began.

"My mother died when I was six...." Held spellbound by Zeb's story of trials and triumphs, the members of the board listened with new respect. Some fought back tears. He concluded with: "Yes, Mr. Jackson gave me my freedom, but I'm not free as you here know freedom. I sit in the back on trains. Few hotels will accept me. I hesitate to even become a member of your church. I understand the bias imbedded in you by your parents and peers, but this Community Center will include all ethnic groups. I hope you are aware of that." Zeb took a piece of paper from his pocket. "Here is a personal check for fifty thousand dollars. We don't want to waste time in getting this started. I hope you'll let me be in the thick of it."

Zeb sat down and Chairman Peabody spoke.

"It's in your laps," he said. "What is your wish?"

Jim Donovan spoke.

"If there's an ounce of honest commitment and Christian love in us, we have to do this. I so move."

The church bought the right-of-way and its adjoining morass of weeds and junk with the stipulation that it would be leveled for the baseball diamond, leaving strategic trees for picnic areas and esthetic charm. The majority of the work force came from the perimeters of the neighborhood: black, white, Indian, and Mexican. They were fitted into many crews, who could handle saw and hammer, carry brick, mortar, and lumber, or use a pick and shovel. Zeb's instructions were kind, though he set the norm when he said, "You will be well paid, but we can't have any loafers. We will start each day with a prayer that we will make this into a place for all people. There will be no prejudice shown for color or race. We are all God's children, and we'll treat each other accordingly."

The Reverend Dan Altman had been a baseball star in college and had been sought by major league scouts, but he had opted for the ministry. He picked out the workers in their teens and twenties, and as the diamond began to take shape, the noon hours were spent in work-up games and shagging flies. The diamond, complete with a screened backstop and bleachers, was first to be ready for use. One of the members who owned a sporting goods store supplied ample equipment.

It took a while before the players wanted Sam on their side, but he was quick to learn. He had sharp eyesight and was nimble on his feet. He liked to shag flies, and the bat seemed to know how to hit that ball. Quite soon he was one of the first to be chosen.

One day Zeb watched as Dan had someone pitch to him. He pointed to the various positions and batted out flies or grounders with precision. Zeb grabbed a bat and started to swing it as he had seen Dan do. Now, Zeb could still read the fine print on the stock market page, and his powerful frame showed no fat or deterioration. He could drive a nail into a board faster and more cleanly than any of his workers. It never occurred to him that he could be starting to go down hill physically. Dan watched his swing.

"Where did you learn to bat like that?"

"I was just watching a fellow named Dan, who seemed to know what he was doing," said Zeb.

"Stand by the plate and let's see you hit one," said Dan.

Zeb walked to the plate and leaned in slightly. He watched the first pitch and wished he had swung at it. The next pitch was high and inside, and Zeb drew back to keep from getting hit. The third came down the middle, and Zeb met it squarely. It sailed over the outfielder and landed in the adjoining creek, about six hundred fifty feet away. Dan hurried up to Zeb.

"God made only one of you and then locked up the pattern. Nobody will believe what I just saw."

Dan and Sam became close buddies, but Dan had to admit that Sam could persuade the young people to come and take part in church activities.

Under Maude's loving care and nourishing food, Sam's muscles had reappeared on his athletic frame, and he sought the heavier jobs. His honest faith and enthusiasm made other young people have a hope of a better tomorrow. A hard core of those to whom stealing and instant gratification were the norm came to harass the younger workers and try to steal a convert to their way of life. Sam was their constant target. Their derogatory and snide remarks were politely ignored until Mrs. Goode, who lived alone, was robbed of several thousand dollars she kept hidden in her home. The notice of her inheritance had been published in a newspaper that some subscribed to in this area. She had come home from getting groceries to find her house in shambles and her hidden stash of one hundred-dollar bills gone. She had done one thing right by initialing each bill.

A few days later, Ross Tyler, who seemed to be their spokesman. showed up with his gang of young thugs and came where Sam was digging a trench. Ross sneered a "Hi! Holy boy." He seemed to have a cold. As he pulled out his handkerchief, a hundred-dollar bill came with it and fell close to Sam's hand. Sam grabbed faster than Ross. On the edge was the initial G . Ross flashed a knife. Sam looked at Ross.

"I'll make a deal. You think you're tough. Nobody but a low-life coward needs a knife. You and I are going to fight. If I win, the money goes back to the owner. And you know who that is. If you win, it's your problem."

Ross grinned.

"You haven't got a ghost of a chance. It's what I've wanted to do for a long time."

They squared off. Ross came in like a fast freight train and swung a haymaker that Sam avoided. The opening was there. Sam's left hook hit Ross's jaw solidly. His lightning right found the same jaw, and Ross settled slowly to the ground.

Sam pulled Ross to his feet. He was too groggy to make further resistance but was beginning to be partially conscious. Tears poured down Sam's face as he hugged Ross.

"You wanted to kill me. I want to be your best friend." Ross looked into Sam's eyes and hugged him in return. Ross's so-called friends drifted away. They stood side by side as Ross wiped the blood oozing from his split lip. "What do we do now?" Ross asked.

"Let's take one step at a time," said Sam. "You're coming home with me. We'll get some advice on how to give that money back and keep you out of jail." Sam suddenly brightened. "You are going to finish high school, and Zeb and I are going to teach you like Zeb's teaching me. Then, you're going on to college. You have a quick brain. God needs it on His side."

No one at the parsonage seemed surprised that Sam brought a friend for supper that night. Ross had a thick lip that had stopped bleeding. He felt the presence of love and fell head over heels in love with Maude as she gave Sam and him a hug.

When the meal was finished, Sam looked at Matt, Maude, and Zeb.

"Ross and I have a problem. Ross, will you state your case?"

"I stole Mrs. Goode's money. I still have it all except the hundred-dollar bill that Sam picked up when I dropped it. Some one told me there was a man who bought stolen money. I hadn't got in touch with him. Now, I want to give it back to Mrs. Goode. Sam convinced me, as you can see. He touched his thick lip. I know I want to be like Sam. He thinks he can help me get a high school diploma."

Sam looked at Matt, Maude, and Zeb. The expression was one of pleading.

Zeb went over to Ross and playfully ruffled his hair.

"We can redo Mrs. Goode's home and make it look better. Mrs. Goode will say her money was returned. There is no need for police action."

Maude spoke up.

"Sam, your bed is big enough for two." She kissed Ross close to his thick lip. "You'll be our boy for awhile."

Zeb brought in some of his crew who knew how to redo a home. They papered the dingy, flyspecked walls with patterns chosen by Mrs. Goode, renewed the upholstering on her faded sofa and chairs, and put new locks on the doors. The house breathed a new elegance. The money went to the bank. Mrs. Goode agreed there was no need for police action.

The next time Ross's old gang showed up, Ross went to Pete Gordon.

"Pete, your mother and dad want you back home. You know you're going nowhere but downhill. Your parents admit that they were a little strict. I'm asking you to go back home where you'll get a little advice and a lot of love. Swallow that stinking pride and eat a little crow. Come on, I'll walk with you." When they reached Pete's home his mother had seen him approaching. She ran out the front door, kissed and hugged him. Ross wondered what his own mother was like. He had never seen her. Having been shuffled around to various care establishments, he had experienced little love.

As Ross started to leave, Mrs. Gordon came to him, kissed and hugged him lovingly.

"Thank you, thank you. We'll need your help to keep Pete. Come often and help us be good parents. I know Pete likes you. Please put him on your must list."

Ross suddenly walked into her arms and kissed her.

"I hope my mother was nice, like you."

When Sam began sending in answers to tests given by the Board of Education for high school graduation, he needed a last name. Zeb immediately suggested the name Jackson. Sam knew that Zeb revered that most important person in his life.

A year and a half had passed since Zeb first tossed him an assortment of books. A letter came with a diploma. The note read, "You have achieved this diploma with the highest grades on record."

"Now it's off to seminary, and there's no time like the present," said Zeb. It was a warm send-off. Maude held him lovingly as her tears mingled with his. Ross had about eight months before he could expect his diploma. Tears on both sides told their affection for each other.

As the Community Center building began its rise from the large foundation, Matt was thankful the planning committee hadn't skimped in size. The meeting hall could seat seven hundred people, and its raised stage area was proportionately large for plays, choir, or entertainers. A portable pulpit, lectern, and altar were put in place for church services, which were being held there even before construction was finished. Joseph Abercrombe, the choir director, met with the crews before they went to work in the morning and taught them lines of some of the well-known hymns. They often sang, "In Christ There Is No East or West," as they mingled and greeted each other with a hug or handshake and then bowed for prayer.

Soon a choir emerged, which included brothers, sisters, parents, and friends. Joe Abercrombe drew them with his enthusiasm, expertise, and love as they belted out folk songs, hymns and spirituals. Maude was in the forefront. She had met with the Ladies Aid and other women's groups. "God has given us this important opportunity to make a difference. We need your help to teach children and adults to read and write, to sew, to learn to be a housekeeper, a waitress, a stenographer, or a secretary. Here is your chance to help someone become a competent person who can make their own way in this world. I'm not thinking only of what it will do for them, but what it will do for you as you make this special offering of yourselves."

Maude didn't wait for the Center to be available. She went to the official board and asked if rooms in the church could be used. "Why wait?" she asked. "Each day is important to God. Your wives are ready and anxious to start. We also need the necessary equipment to do this right, so we need your blessing."

It would have been hard to refuse Maude. She was a beautiful woman. Along with that, they saw the charm, the honesty, the depth of character, and the faith that glowed in her appeal. Matt often spent two hours with the workers in the early mornings. After Joe led the singing, Matt read a short piece of scripture and then gave the prayer. Because he wanted exercise, he chose the hard jobs like carrying sand and cement in a wheelbarrow or digging trenches for the pipe lines that brought in the water to the Center and to the fountains in the picnic area and the ball diamond. He gained rapport with the workers and learned about their needs and feelings. He heard one of them say to another, "He's not just all talk! He can out-dig two of us!"

After his morning workout with the men, Matt showered and began his church day calling on members, the sick, and the shut-ins. He called on Mrs. Bart Macklin, the wife of the board member who said his wife was from the South. She invited him in guardedly.

"I know you're from the South," said Matt. "What are your feelings about the direction the church is taking?"

"I'll admit I have some problems. My dad would disown me if he thought I made a gesture of acceptance of a black person. My husband took some investment advice from Mr. Hawkins and that proved to be the best advice he ever received, so we are indebted to him. And my little daughter adores him. I'm supposed to hate him, but I can't. I want to help teach because I'm qualified, and I know I love children, black, white, or whatever."

"I doubt that anyone could change your father's prejudices," said Matt, "but your final loyalty is to Christ and His way. He also knows the turmoil in your heart and understands. Give yourself to Him. I know you'll be one of our best teachers. Please be a part of the tremendous awakening that is beginning to happen. You will be happy, and so will God."

39

Lorna

Young Dr. James Peabody, the banker's son, had just finished his internship and was home taking his time deciding which of the doctors with large lucrative practices needed him the most. He and young Rev. Dan Altman had become friends when he came to help at the Community Center. Jim also had played baseball in college, so he was a valuable help to Dan in sorting out the budding talent of the workers who wanted to play ball. Cliff Carter bruised a hip painfully when he slid into third. That and other cuts, sprains, and blisters confirmed the need for a "body" repair shop. Jim offered his services and set up a small clinic in one of the partially finished rooms of the Center. When Jim examined Cliff's hip, he also discovered Cliff had gonorrhea. After forceful questioning, Cliff admitted he had been a customer of a certain Lorna Bean and that some of his buddies had been to the same source. Jim immediately recommended that all workers should be examined to establish their state of health. Jim also asked Cliff if he had sex with any other female. Cliff told him he was intimate with Marie Wells, the girl he planned to marry.

"She's my best friend's sister."

"Cliff," said Jim, "you have to get her in here. If she has a baby, it could be born blind or have other defects. You're an intelligent man, but your brains seem to be in your pants!"

Marie Wells was contacted privately, but she became so angry at Cliff that she exposed the disgusting situation to her family. Her brother and dad confronted Cliff with fists flying. Cliff came to the clinic where Jim put one eye back in its socket, inspected his loose front teeth, and stitched his lip.

"I felt like squashing you myself," Jim said. "You'll be all right, but if you don't clean up your act, you're a goner. Didn't anyone ever tell you to be careful?"

"My dad knows I'm playing around," Cliff said. "All he ever said was, 'Don't knock up someone you don't want to marry.'"

Jim talked to Dan about the situation, and they decided that all the workers should come to a lecture on venereal diseases. A syphilitic in the advanced stages was brought in to strengthen the mental picture.

"This could be some of you," Rev. Dan Altman said. "The Bible tells us that you should keep yourselves for each other until you marry. God made it quite clear that there's no double standard of conduct for men and women in the commandments."

Dr. Jim Peabody decided to call on Lorna and threaten her to get treatment if necessary. When he called at the address, a strikingly beautiful young woman answered the door. He assumed he had the wrong person or address.

"I'm looking for Lorna Bean."

"You're looking at her, come in." She pointed to a chair, and Jim sat.

His composure was gone, and he felt almost ill. He knew he had to speak before she mistook him for a customer and invited him into the bedroom.

"I'm Dr. Peabody. I'm convinced you have gonorrhea, because I've treated several of your customers. If you come to my clinic I'll give you the necessary treatments. If you don't, I will contact the Board of Health and they will make a bigger deal out of it," he blurted out.

Lorna Bean seemed stunned.

"I guess the less said the better. I'll come right now."

A few days Later, Maude called on Lorna, who was complying with Jim's request to desist in her trade until he pronounced her clean. She saw an attractive young lady giving her a questioning look.

"I'm Maude Berglund, wife of Pastor Berglund of Lane Park Memorial Church. Dr. Peabody asked me to make this call."

Lorna Bean melted under Maude's smile and asked her to come in. She pointed to a chair. Maude looked at Lorna, the surprise showing on her face at the beautiful person before her. She noted the neat, tidy, and well-furnished room.

"You're pretty. Tell me why you're doing this to yourself. I really want to be your friend."

"I've been asking myself that question because of the trouble I've brought to so many people. What can I do? When I was living at home, my dad beat my mother and made me go to bed with him. In high school, I had sex with some of the boys, and everyone knew that I was a whore. I lost my self-esteem and sense of direction. I've worked as a waitress, but I seem to spend most of my time pleasing the bosses and working for less than I can make in this business. Here I am, suddenly hating what I am and not coming up with any answers."

"There must have been something you wanted to do," said Maude.

"In high school, one teacher told me I was good at typing. I would like to have been a secretary."

"Is this your home?"

"The furniture is mine. I rent."

Maude took Lorna's hand in hers.

"I want to help you, and I can if you'll let me. We'll pay your next month's rent and store your furniture. You can live with us at the parsonage and take a refresher course in typing. We'll see that you get a good job. Somewhere out there is a good man who won't worry about your past if you don't let it defeat you."

"What will people think?"

"They'll think I have a beautiful young friend, and I'm going to agree with them."

If someone in the church knew about Lorna's past, they were charitable enough not to spread the gossip. Lorna was Maude's pretty young friend who came to church with her on Sundays. One of the first young men who was more than attracted by her natural sweetness and charm was Dr. Jim Peabody, in spite of his full knowledge of her past.

Zeb had discovered that Lorna could sing when he played his violin in the evenings. At the first sound of his bow, she came into his parlor to sit in raptured silence at his playing. One night as he played the tune, "When Irish Eyes Are Smiling," she joined in with the words to the song. Zeb had heard many beautiful voices, but Lorna's voice was no carbon copy of any he knew. It was the way she pronounced the words, as though she wrapped each one with a cushion of love that made them tug at the heart.

"Why have you been hiding that voice?" Zeb asked.

"It's about the only song I know. My uncle used to visit us when I was quite young, and he could sing. I can't follow the notes in a song book."

"We're going to start on that right now," Zeb announced.

In a short time Lorna was singing the songs in the hymnal with ease and perfect pitch, and Zeb knew he had a young lady who was brighter than bright. He thoroughly enjoyed the sessions with Lorna because of her ability to absorb and remember after only one telling. Soon she was in the choir, and Joe Abercrombe heard her among the multitude of voices. They were practicing songs for the Christmas season and he asked Lorna to solo four lines of the hymn: "Oh little town of Bethlehem, how still we see thee lie. Above thy deep and dreamless sleep, the silent stars go by."

As her voice caressed each syllable, Joe knew he had discovered a voice uniquely different and rare, so warm, with a touch of pathos that stirred the emotions. Zeb prayerfully thanked God for plucking Lorna from the fire, to let her bloom with a radiance that brightened the world around her.

Dr. Jim Peabody's community practice was booming. With his dad's financial aid, he built a clinic near the Center, fully equipped and supplied. He needed a secretary and nudged Lorna into taking her first step at applying her newly found competence. If one could assess how Jim and Lorna felt about each other, one might start by saying, "Here is another Matt and Star, Doran and Marie, or Adam and Eva." Lorna had that boundless energy that defied fatigue. As a secretary and book-keeper, she was superb, and as a nurse's aid, she seemed to anticipate Jim's needs before the asking. In spite of her diseased condition, he had been drawn to her from the very beginning, and when he had to have her expose herself to treatment, he felt as though it were an act of rape, an invasion of her privacy. Jim thought he could make himself loathe her by telling himself she was the lowest type of creature to allow any-one to lie with her. Outside of the fact that she was diseased, he noted her cleanliness and the freshness of her clothing. When Maude brought her to church, he gave up his attempt to demean her and acknowledged to himself that he loved her. This love wasn't slow burning, but was a raging fire in both of them. Jim couldn't explain it, but it was as though her past had been obliterated. Lorna kept him at a distance.

"It was a mistake to start to work for you, I won't let you do this to yourself and your family. You and I are on opposites of the tracks. You know what I've been, a diseased whore." She choked on her next words, "There's someone out there who doesn't have all these negatives."

"Look," said Jim. "What about those girls I slept with in college? I'm ashamed of it now. No doubt I caused someone to become a whore. None of us thought they had to do it for a living, which in my mind makes me the perpetrator of the greater sin. I am more guilty of wrong doing than you." Jim closed in on Lorna and kissed her and kissed her until she responded. He finally drew back.

"Now, even you must feel you are a miracle, because you have a purity and a strength of character few people ever attain. Invite me over to dinner tomorrow night, and we're going to thrash this thing out with Matt, Maude, and Zeb as referees."

Lorna made the dinner and served it as she often did. Maude enjoyed the reprieve from her household duties. Lorna had crept into their lives and added to the rapport already there. She finished the meal with a chocolate pie that met with approval from Matt and espe-cially from Jim. As the last dishes disappeared, Jim spoke.

"Maybe you know about our problem. I want to marry Lorna for every reason a man loves a woman. She says it isn't fair to me or my family because of her past life."

Matt felt the sudden overwhelming despair at the loss of Star. Maude relived the emptiness and futility of those years she had surrendered to Star's stronger hold on Matt. Though he had never talked about it to those present, Zeb was agonizing over the rape and murder of his one love, Jessica, the night before they were to be married when he was still a slave.

Maude was the first to speak.

"Jim, your parents should get the whole story from both of you. It's going to hurt, but they already love Lorna, and they'll approve of your choice. There is no other option for the two of you."

Matt was recovering.

"Dan and I will tie you so tightly that Jim will have to retire from his practice."

"Do it as quickly as possible," added Zeb.

Jim invited Lorna to dinner at his home. His parents were already captivated by Lorna's charms, and although they knew little about her, they were pleased with Jim's choice. Jim and Lorna held nothing back, and one could see the shock and revulsion for the unfolding past life of their son's chosen mate.

"This could become a front page story of some sadistic news hawk at a future date. I don't want to, but we can move away from here," said Jim.

There was a deadly silence. One could hear the slow tick of the huge grandfather clock in the hall. Curtis Peabody and his wife looked at each other to discern the other's thoughts. They both rose from their chairs and came hand-in-hand to Jim and Lorna.

"We love you too, Lorna. There is no one better than you for our son," Curtis avowed.

"Now," Mrs. Peabody was planning, "there has to be a fancy wedding because of our so-called social status. A quiet little ceremony might raise some eyebrows, so keep your passions in control until the 'I do.'"

As Jim came through the clinic door the next morning, he heard Lorna singing the popular song, "I'd Love to Live in Loveland with a Girl Like You." She sang "boy" instead of "girl."

Jim ran to Lorna and kissed her with all the controlled passion he could muster. While still in the embrace, he wondered how so much love, talent, and beauty could be wrapped up in one package. A silent "Thank you, God" went heavenward.

Shortly before the wedding, Jim was at the parsonage table again.

They held hands as Matt gave a simple conversational prayer of thanks.

"Matt," said Lorna, "I don't know if this is a good time to talk about something like this. I know you feel the invisible Spirit of God is with us here. I want Jim and me to believe that He will be in our home, too. Somehow I know He's here. How can we make it happen to us?"

Matt spoke up.

"Maybe I can help you. When we were asked to come here, I'm sure that God knew you needed Maude and Zeb and Jim and me to help you understand how much He wants you to be His child."

Tears trickled down Lorna's cheeks.

"I have to believe that, and I do."

"And so do I," said Jim.

40

One for All

The Community Center was receiving its finishing touches, when the dedication was held. Most of the church membership as well as other people in that area came. It was a warm late fall day, which was providential because the ball diamond was used as the meeting place. Many brought their own chairs, which, along with the ones supplied by the church, allowed most of the over three thousand people to sit. A huge plaque with the names engraved of those who had given of their time and money was presented. Those who had worked in the different crews were also honored. Joe Abercrombe asked the choir to form itself up front.

First came the three hundred white men and women of the regular church choir, which was still not integrated. Then Joe's worker choir gradually came forward with their sisters, brothers, mothers, and fathers—black, Indian, Mexican, and white. Then it happened. Those in the church choir grabbed the hands of the workers and those of their families and encouraged them forward. It took some time to get the sopranos, basses, tenors, and altos mixed into their ranks. Joe Abercrombe looked on as the mix evolved. His emotion was obvious as he raised his arms.

"We'll sing, 'In Christ There Is No East or West.'"

After a burst of noisy applause, the young Reverend Dan Altman stood before them.

"I've been asked to say a few words. We did get this project finished, but we can't sit back yet. The winters are long here as you well know. Some of us are thinking that we need a recreation building connected to or near the church itself, where the young and old can participate in indoor sports like basketball, volleyball, tennis, and swimming, to mention a few that come to mind. It's quite possible that many of those who come to play and compete may want to be a part of the church and the Christian love that made this happen. This will be one more way we can open our hearts in love to this community. I wonder if you know how beautiful a people you are becoming. Each day I thank God for allowing me to be a part of something that has put a smile on God's face. Christ is saying to you right now, 'I am proud of you.'"

Curtis Peabody took Zeb aside.

"I would like to ask you a question. You have been reluctant to join our church because of our attitude toward integration. But you've seen our integrated choir today, and many of them have expressed an interest in becoming members of our church. Do you feel we have come along far enough that you could also be a member? It would be a step in the right direction toward changing attitudes and the acceptance of all of God's people. You would be the first member to break the color barrier in our church, and I would be proud to have you do it. We want to be a church for all people."

Matt had been listening to this conversation, and as he came toward the pair, Curtis Peabody held out his hand. Matt drew him into a big hug.

"Some time ago, in hopeful anticipation of this time, I asked for and received Zeb's transfer of membership from our previous church. Zeb, will you please come up front with me so that we can do this properly." Zeb followed him up. The inner emotions showed in the wetness of his cheeks as tears kept pouring down his face. Someone stood and said, "We want Zeb," and in a second, the assembled people stood and took up the chant. Matt went through the procedure of transfer of membership as he had done quite often.

"This is a great day. Let us all continue to make this church a beacon of Christ's love to all. That will take work and constant rededication from each of us as we strive to be a church for all people."

The recreation building became a reality right next to the church. There was a lot of juvenile enthusiasm and a minimum of rowdiness because of the friendly but firm supervision by the Reverend Dan Altman and young Dr. Peabody.

Lorna, his very attractive wife, invited the young ladies of the church to form a few girls' basketball teams. The games they played were well attended by the young men as the girls dribbled and dodged up and down the floor in their blouse and bloomer uniforms. Matt especially enjoyed the swimming pool. Many received proper and friendly training under Matt's supervision.

The Community Center was seldom without activity, as the many rooms were built to hold classes in improving various skills for all ages. Mrs. Macklin was thrilled to be doing her magic with the little children sent by mothers who said they weren't doing well at school. The Reverend Allan Putnam, who was always impeccably dressed and a charmer, found that he had the ability to inspire young men who were dropouts from school to want to reach for their potentials again. It gave him a newly found respect for his own worth. Rev. Dan Altman would search out these young men, but Allan was the one who could inject a desire and tenacity for learning.

The church found many who liked to take part in plays, which they presented to an audience that filled the large hall of the Community Center. The large stage wasn't ample enough to hold the choir, and it often spread beyond its perimeters in front and to both sides. Popular songs, ballads, portions of opera, and spirituals soon filled its confines. There was a hard-core group in the church who looked askance at dancing, but Maude convinced many of them that the young people were going to dance anyway, and it would be best to provide a wholesome atmosphere for them. Zeb, with his violin and accordion, searched the church and neighborhood and came up with a group which included string, brass, woodwind, and percussion.

Once when Mike Doran and Marie came to visit, they attended one of these dances. Mike and his still queenly Marie danced well together. It was a tag dance and Mike tapped Maude. Those in attendance beheld another bright facet of that part of the rehabilitation crew. It was a waltz, and the two blended in the rhythmic execution of the dance. The floor began to clear as Mike and Maude went through the flawless maneuvers just as they had done numerous years ago. They finished with a whirl and the same sweeping backward bend they had executed years before. As they walked to the side, the onlookers applauded the one who was the sweetheart of all present, a person who had crept into all their lives with her love, giving, caring, and humanness.

41

Jessica

Matt took Zeb to the station. Zeb was going south to visit the area of the Sam Jackson plantation and foremost to visit Jessica's grave. Matt's last words were prophetic as they hugged good-bye.

"Zeb, the South won't treat you as well as Thorson's Bay. Hurry back."

Zeb sat in the rear of the last car with the others of his race. That didn't disturb him, because he knew the North and South still downgraded the Negro in all areas of interaction. As the locomotive puffed huge funnels of smoke that swept by his window, he seemed to hear the rails beat out a rhythmic tune. *Clickety-clack, you're going back.*

He looked around and saw the same signs of subservience of his slave days, and his heart bled for his people. It was evident that blacks were still on the lowest rung of the ladder. He was aware of a baby crying, just across the aisle. It might have been two months old. The young father and mother were shabbily dressed, and it was obvious they had missed too many meals. The mother looked with sad eyes at her baby, who tried to nurse and was getting little sustenance, which no doubt explained the baby's crying.

When a porter came down the aisle with his broom and dust pan, Zeb beckoned him with his finger.

"I don't know the rules around here. How do you get something to eat?"

"You pay the bill, and I'll get you most anything you want."

Zeb handed him a five-dollar bill.

"Here's your tip. I want three of your best meals and a bottle of warm milk with a nipple on it." He gave him a twenty. He had kept his voice low. "Will that cover it?"

"That's more than enough."

When the porter left, Zeb looked across the aisle.

"Where are you heading?"

The mother spoke. Zeb thought she seemed too young to be a mother.

"My husband's brother sent money for us to come to West Virginia for Ben to work in the coal mines. We're glad to get away from Chicago."

Zeb had read about a young black in Chicago who had swum too far from his beach. Totally exhausted, he tried to make shore by coming in on a beach for whites only. The whites threw rocks at him to prevent his entry. He drowned and Zeb knew no blame had been assessed. No doubt these two young blacks felt that hate and intolerance.

"When was the last time you had a meal?"

"I guess it's been about a day and a half ago, but we're used to that. We hope Ben gets his job."

In a short time, the porter came down the aisle with a cart carrying trays of food. He handed the mother a bottle with a nipple on it, then handed them two trays loaded with food.

"Compliments of this gentleman." He handed Zeb his tray.

Zeb grinned.

"I don't like to eat alone; let's eat this, and if it's not enough we'll get some more." He turned to the porter. "Make a large bag of sandwiches that won't spoil so this baby can get his milk from the real source."

Later that night, the young family had to change trains. The mother came to Zeb and kissed him on the cheek.

"You're an angel, I shall never forget you."

Zeb slipped three twenties into her hand along with his calling card. He had made his assessment of her. She was bright and had good command of her vocabulary. She could have been another Jessica, he thought.

"If things get too bad, write to me."

"Come on, Katie, we have to get off." Ben spoke for the first time. Katie kissed Zeb again.

"Thank you. God must have sent you." She hurried out.

Katie! That's her name, Zeb thought. *That fits.*

When the conductor called "Chattanooga," Zeb grabbed his bag and went to the rear door. Three white youths surrounded him as he stepped from the train.

"Oh, look at this dude," one of them confronted Zeb, "You look pretty fancy, Mose. What did you do, rob a bank?"

Zeb ignored him and tried to make his way through. One of them tripped him. When he fell, his hat came off.

"You lost your hat," another one said. He stomped it, picked it up, crushed it some more and handed it to Zeb as he got up.

Zeb took his hat and ran. He knew he had to stay out of trouble. Any retaliation would lead to incarceration or even death. The youths didn't chase him, so Zeb slowed to a walk.

As he stooped to drink from a fountain, he heard an angry voice.

"Hey, you black bastard, you can't drink here. What are you doing, looking for trouble?"

He was shoved off the sidewalk twice before he found a hotel that would give him lodging. As he paid in advance, he asked the clerk where he could rent a horse and buggy. He wanted to get away from Chattanooga as quickly as possible.

"There's a livery just down the street."

The next morning, Zeb rented a horse and buggy and headed in the direction of what once was Sam Jackson's plantation. As his horse trotted and walked, Zeb thought about his first meeting with Sam Jackson. One of the plantation owners had gone bankrupt and was selling everything, including his slaves. Zeb was six and he remembered no father. His mother had died a few months earlier. Since his mother's death, he had been ignored and looked unsaleable, half starved, dirty, and tattered.

The auctioneer looked at Zeb.

"Here's a scrubby little runt that might be good for something. Who'll give me five dollars?"

Jake Barnhill, a neighbor of Sam Jackson, spoke up.

"I'll give you three dollars." He had stuck his dirty finger in Zeb's mouth as though he were a horse and had cuffed him to get him to turn around.

"I'll give twenty dollars," Sam had said. The auctioneer looked back at Jake, who threw up his hands in the negative.

"Sold to Mr. Jackson."

Sam Jackson had smiled at Zeb.

"Come with me, we're going home." Sam untied his horse, which was hitched to his spring wagon. It had a seat up front and a place to haul things in back. Zeb started to crawl into the rear. "You're going to sit up front with me, I need some company." Zeb had told Sam about everything he knew by the time they reached Sam's plantation.

"My name is Zeb Hawkins. My mother died last winter. I never knew my dad."

"What can you do?"

"I can pick cotton and help in the kitchen, and I can read, but I guess I'm not supposed to do that. My mother taught our owner's children. She told me we're like hogs or cattle. If we knew anything, we might want something better."

"What do you think about that?" asked Sam.

"I know I want something better. Mother told me I knew more than their kids did. I like to learn."

185

"You'll get to learn all you can. Let's see what you can do," Zeb remembered Sam saying.

Sam's wife had died at childbirth, but the baby, their son, had survived and had lived for six years until he succumbed to scarlet fever.

Zeb was treated like a son from the first day. Sam gave Zeb his son's room, and he had the run of the house and access to the library, where they spent hours digesting history and the classics. Zeb's sponge-like mind voraciously absorbed the contents. Sam often played his violin and as Zeb looked on, he asked, "Do you want to try it?"

Zeb was no longer the half-starved waif. After a few months, he had started on a spurt of growth that made him unrecognizable to those who hadn't seen him for a while. His long arms and nimble fingers soon coaxed music from the strings, and Sam happily tutored his student. At one party, Sam wanted to show Zeb's virtuosity to some of his friends.

The audience had applauded, but instead of giving Zeb credit for his superior talent, they intimated that Sam had found a colored freak. He never exposed Zeb to his closed-minded audience again.

Early, Sam had filled Zeb in on his diversified business operations. Cotton was only one means of acquiring material wealth. Even at ten, Zeb showed signs of physical prowess beyond his age, and that was when Jessica came into the Jackson household, bringing joy and love to every corner of the house. As a six-year-old slave girl, Jessica had been orphaned when her mother died of smallpox. Sam immediately gave her the same privileges he had given Zeb. Zeb's job was to look after her and her education. Her willingness to learn made his job a pleasure. The piano intrigued her from the start, so a tutor was brought in to give her the proper introduction to the keyboard. Zeb adored his new little sister.

Sam Jackson knew that slavery was wrong. He often expressed this unpopular feeling, that no man had a right to subordinate another human being. Some who agreed realized they had a problem without a good solution. There was some truth in their argument, that releasing a flood of free people who had been trained to a bridled subservience wasn't the answer. They felt if all that ignorance and indirection were set free, the result would be chaos of such a magnitude that the South would be in anarchy. Sam argued that they should start preparing them for responsible citizenship. For the most part, that fell on deaf ears.

Those were happy years for Zeb. He never knew when his feelings for Jessica had crossed over into a consuming love. There had been times that they had danced around the room in delight over a new

186

learning experience. He became more careful of expressing his affection. Other young men on the plantation showed their desire to become more intimately acquainted, but Jessica kept them at bay by telling them she wasn't ready for that. When she was eighteen, Jake Barnhill's nephew, Clyde, came to live with Jake to learn about plantation management. One time when he had brought back a plow they had borrowed, he had taken a good look at Jessica. To him she was fair game, beautiful and all woman from every angle. He had asked to call on her. Zeb was in earshot when she refused Clyde.

"I'm engaged to Zeb," she said.

"You mean you prefer that black bastard to me?"

"Very much, and I don't care to discuss it with you." As she walked away Zeb heard his angry retort.

"You haven't heard the last of me."

Later, Zeb found her picking a bouquet of flowers.

"I heard what you told Clyde. Was it just a way to get him off your back, or am I supposed to assume it might indicate something that I have hoped for several years would happen?"

"Zeb, how could you be so blind as to not see I've loved you from the first day we met?"

That night at the dinner table, they told Sam Jackson.

"I've seen it in you two for a long time. Let's have the wedding in about two months. I want to build you a pretty cottage and give you your freedom as a wedding present. Zeb, you have been my plantation manager for several years, and from now on you will share in the profits. I don't need to tell you two to keep yourselves for your wedding night."

The spot for the cottage wasn't far from the big house. The guests invited included a few whites whose friendship transcended color. The night before the wedding, Zeb awoke, hearing Jessica calling his name. There was terror in her voice. Zeb knew he was too distant from her room, but he had heard her. He jumped into his dungarees and ran to the opposite end of the house and up one flight of stairs. As he neared her room, he heard her screams. He crashed the door and saw Clyde pull back from Jessica and turn to him with a large knife in his hand, The knife was no deterrent. Zeb grabbed the arm that held it, came down with the arm across his knee, and broke a bone in Clyde's forearm. The knife clattered to the floor. The crash of the door brought Sam with a lamp, and as he came in, he saw Zeb hit Clyde's jaw. Clyde crumpled to the floor, and Zeb knelt by Jessica's bed. Her voice was weak.

"Hold me," she said. Zeb took Jessica in his arms, and he realized her life blood was pouring from her. "We'll have to wait awhile," her voice was faint. "I'll be there when you come." Zeb heard her final sigh and realized she was gone. He held her, and in those moments of wrenching agony, he cried in uncontrollable grief. Sam was crying, too.

Zeb heard groans from the floor. Clyde was regaining consciousness. The distraction helped bring Zeb and Sam back to the present.

"He should be dead," said Sam, "but I'm glad you didn't kill him. The South would have made you pay."

The agony of Jessica's death would have been unbearable if her last words hadn't given him an undying hope that there would be a reunion of their lives. The certainty of her faith and his gave him a will to face the days ahead.

"She will be buried in the family cemetery. Zeb, I want you to dig her grave. I'll take Clyde to the sheriff and press charges, and I'll bring a coffin home for Jessica's body. Keeping busy will help some."

The sheriff had been reluctant to incarcerate Clyde, but Sam reminded him, in anger.

"He's a murderer of the lowest kind of depravity."

The doctor put a splint on Clyde's broken arm, and the sheriff locked him up. The funeral was held that afternoon, and Sam Jackson spoke.

"This is a testing time, a short interval in God's eternal plan for us. How we live here certainly must have a bearing on how we can appreciate His hereafter. Zeb and Jessica would have been married today. That joyous union of these two lives has not ended. It's just postponed. I also look forward to the time when her laughter and love will light my life again. We all loved her, and we can honor her memory by living this life so that we will be worthy of her love and of God's love."

In a few day, Sam brought Jessica's headstone home. On it were her final words:

"I'll be there when you come."

42

Going Back

The horse Zeb was driving stopped to spread its hind legs, and Zeb could see a puddle of urine finding its way to the roadside ditch before the horse proceeded on again. The stop temporarily awakened him to the present, but he was soon reliving again the agony and despair of Jessica's death. The faith which promised him a reunion with her asked him to forgive Clyde, but the seething anger and hatred couldn't be denied. He couldn't remember a white man ever having paid for his crimes against the black community, and this proved to be true again. In spite of the heinousness of his crime, Clyde was reprimanded lightly and released.

The callousness and unfairness helped Sam Jackson take up his long overdue stand against slavery and the South. He freed those of his slaves who had skills and desire and gave them money to make a start in the North. The remaining slaves were given to those he knew would be kind to them.

This disassociation took a year and a half. When Sam had finally liquidated his material ties with the South, he asked Zeb to go north with him.

"As far north as we can get," he had said.

Sam Jackson traveled extensively. He explained to Zeb that freedom for the blacks didn't mean acceptance. They still rode in the rear section of the trains and had to stay in the hotels that would accept them. They were on their way to Minneapolis, Minnesota, when Henry Thorson looked back at them and smiled. "Where are you headed for?"

"Somewhere, where people will accept us for what we are, not for what color we are."

"Come to Thorson's Bay with us," Henry Thorson had said.

Zeb's musings of what had transpired back when he was in his early twenties faded into the background as the reality of the present took over. He flicked the reins to get a little more speed, but the horse merely swished his tail, raised his head, and trotted a few feet before resuming his previous slow gait. Zeb began to recognize the familiar contours of the area he had once known so well. The borders of the old

Jackson plantation came into view. Nothing about the land was the same except those contours and creeks. Large fields of cotton spread across fertile areas, but the poorer hillsides were cluttered with share-cropper shacks and puny cotton on little plots of land. The land was feeling the poverty of its keepers, who were too poor to replace the fertility they robbed.

There was a house with a well-kept lawn near the place where the spacious old mansion had been. Looking in the direction of the old graveyard, Zeb saw a tree and some undergrowth. He couldn't see anyone around, so he knocked on the door of the house. A colored lady of middle age appeared. She looked at Zeb approvingly.

"Can I help you?" she asked.

"I hope you can. I once lived here as a slave, so I know there is a little cemetery over there. Someone very special to me is buried there, and I would like to visit her grave."

"No one is here right now." She smiled again and Zeb reflected that her smile was the first sign of caring he had received since he'd been in the South. "Hurry over there before he gets back."

Zeb felt her apprehension and wondered what it was that brought that sudden change. It was contagious and he felt an evil, fearful foreboding.

"I'll hurry." The rusty iron fence still enclosed the graveyard, and Zeb figured the position of Jessica's grave by the only stone left standing, that of Sam Jackson's wife. He scraped away the earth and underbrush, but couldn't find the stone slab that had been at the head of the grave. He became frantic, remembering the admonition to hurry. Just as he was about to give up, he stumbled over a piece of stone that stuck out slightly above the ground just beyond where he had been searching. Clawing with his hands and digging with a stick, he unearthed a part of Jessica's broken stone. As he cleaned away the dirt, the words began to reappear. "I'll be there when you come."

Zeb laid the stone above her earthly remains. still on his knees, he bowed, with tears rolling down his cheeks. "It won't be too long now, Jessica."

Shortly after Zeb was back on the road, he saw a fringed carriage coming fast with two spirited trotters stretching their strides in rhythmical pattern. This was probably the returning owner whom the lady of the house had some reason to fear. The driver stayed in the middle of the road, and Zeb had to swerve to the side with one wheel in the ditch as they passed. Then it hit him like a splash of ice water. That leering face was *Clyde Barnhill.*

43

Clyde

Until that moment when Clyde had forced him into the ditch, Zeb had planned to leave the South behind as fast as he could make connections to get on a train. Now, the image of Clyde's cruel expression, the certainty in his mind that this murderer was still venting his hatred on his race, left Zeb with a firm resolve to do whatever it took to rid society of Clyde's reign of brutality. During the long ride back to Chattanooga, he formulated his course of action.

In a long letter to Matt, Zeb gave Matt the complete story of his life. Close as they had been, Zeb hadn't talked about his years before Thorson's Bay.

> Dear Matt,
>
> Get me an undercover person to come and work with me, even if it takes an added bonus to inspire him. I'd rather have someone of my own race, but a black disguise will be authentic enough if he's a good actor. I plan to ask for a job as an ignorant transient by working for food only, and I hope my counterpart can work his way into Clyde's working crew. In the interim I'm going to try to find an old friend and fellow slave that I worked beside in my slave years. Will check in at this present address until I hear from you.
>
> Zeb

Zeb figured it would be a few days before someone would show up to help him. The next morning, he seemed drawn to the train station by an invisible magnetic influence. He noticed the same three young white youths standing by the tracks, no doubt waiting to cause some mayhem when the next train arrived. He went to the ticket window and saw a young man looking back at him with the obvious demeanor that being polite to a colored customer wasn't easy for him.

"Do you know the colored passengers are being harassed and brutalized as they get off the train?"

The man looked back at Zeb.

"I guess I just don't give a damn."

191

Zeb stuck a five-dollar bill under his nose.

"Do you know someone that does?"

The man looked greedily at the five spot.

"I'll get you the trainmaster." He went to a door behind him and reappeared with a burly-looking man almost as large as Zeb and certainly more polite than his ticket seller. He even managed a smile.

"What's your problem?" he asked.

Zeb saw the ticket seller pick up the five-dollar bill.

"There are three young men out there who tripped me and squashed my hat when I got off the train yesterday. I doubt that your company wants their customers harassed as they get off the train."

"We hire a policeman to see that that doesn't occur," the ticketmaster said. "Let's go take a look." A train had just arrived, and the passengers were unloading. The policeman was at the front of a car where people were getting off. The ticketmaster went to him. "Do you ever check the rear to see if they are having problems back there?"

"Naw, that's where the blacks get off."

"You're going to do it from now on, or we'll get someone who will," the trainmaster said. "This is railroad property. These passengers help pay our expenses and will be treated fairly." He looked again at the policeman. "Is that clear?"

As they made their way back to the rear, one of the same young whites hit an old, quite feeble black on the back of his neck so hard that his false teeth flew out of his mouth and landed in the dust. The trainmaster grabbed the youth and forced him to his knees.

"Pick up those teeth and take them into the lavatory and clean them good. Then bring them back and give them to this gentleman." He pointed to the black. The policeman went in with him, and they both soon came back with the scrubbed molars. The youth handed them to the their owner.

"Now, get lost, and don't come back here unless you have a legitimate excuse, or you'll be spending time on a rock pile." The three backed off and ran. The train master looked hard at the policeman. "This is the end of the car that needs your supervision. If you don't think you can do it, we'll get someone who can."

"I'll do it," he grinned. "I gotta eat."

The following morning, Zeb headed for the Asherton plantation. That was the name of the place where Sam Jackson had given the owner a slave whom Zeb knew as "Buck." It was a gamble. Buck would have to be about the same age as he. It surprised Zeb to suddenly be aware of his own age. Buck probably was either dead or elsewhere. The Asherton plantation wasn't too far from what was now Clyde's domain, so Zeb decided to play it out.

The Asherton place came into view. It hadn't changed much. The war must have passed it by, because the large house with a verandah on two of its sides sparkled with new paint. Two stately oaks shaded the lawn. As Zeb drove up to the hitching rack, a man came to him from the house.

Zeb spoke. "I see by the mailbox, this is still the Asherton place. Sam Jackson brought a slave here, named Buck, before he went north. I was wondering if you knew anything about it. My name is Zeb Hawkins, and Buck was my friend."

"My name is Bill Asherton. I was a little boy, but I remember that day distinctly. Buck is still with us. We stable horses for other owners and have some racing stock of our own. Buck manages our stable help, and no one can shoe a horse as well as he. Let's go find him."

Zeb followed Bill Asherton to the stables. He could see that they were well kept. A large number of stalls were full, and some of those who were grooming the spirited animals were white. *Here, at least was some integration*, he thought.

Bill Asherton stuck his head through a door and hollered.

"Buck, here's a gentleman to see you!"

A grizzled but still wiry black came out and looked at Zeb until recognition showed on his face.

"Zeb Hawkins?"

They embraced. Buck soon pulled back with a question mark showing on his leathered features.

"I came to visit Jessica's grave, but I discovered Clyde Barnhill now owns the plantation. I know those who work for him are in fear of their lives. I think murder is still a part of his method of operation. He's still the same vicious subhuman he's always been, and I've vowed to put a stop to his fiendish acts before I head north."

"You'll get it done," assured Buck. "I'll bet my money on you."

The next afternoon, Zeb heard a knock on his door. He opened it and saw a white male about middle age, well-proportioned, and neatly attired.

"I'm Art Bennett," he said. "I have been offered some monetary incentive to come and see you, so let's see what we can do."

They talked. Zeb filled him in on Clyde's vicious vendetta against his race.

"I'm going to get to work for him by posing as an ignorant transient who'll work for practically nothing except what I can eat. I would hope that you might get on in a similar manner, but first, you might want to get an idea of the kind of man we're dealing with. The closest town to his plantation is Trenton, about five miles east of his place. He may spend part of most days at the saloon in the afternoons." Art nodded in the affirmative. "I want to talk with the lady housekeeper to get her promise to keep silent and not let on that anything unusual is happening."

The next day, in the early afternoon, Art went to Trenton and entered the one saloon it supported. He ordered a beer and sat in a corner table and sipped and waited. There was little activity, but the names he overheard didn't mention the man he was seeking. When an hour had passed, the door to the saloon opened and in walked a man of surly countenance who Art immediately felt was Clyde Barnhill. He ordered a bottle and brought it to a table not far from Art. Clyde filled his glass and gulped it down hurriedly and poured another. The bartender came to his table.

"Mr. Barnhill," he said, "your bill is larger than I can handle."

Clyde gulped his second glass and sneered at the bartender.

"You've always got your money, haven't you?"

"I want it now," the bartender said. "And I don't want to take a lot of gaff every time I ask for it. The next town is up the way another five miles, and they're welcome to you after you pay this bill."

"Okay," Clyde said and attempted a smile. He opened his wallet and pulled out a few twenties from its overstuffed interior and handed them to the bartender. The bartender stayed with his hand still out. "Isn't that enough?" Clyde asked.

"Triple that, and you'll be close."

Clyde complied. There was no expression of appreciation on the bartender's face as he went back to his counter. An hour and a half later, Clyde finished the bottle and walked to the door stiffly but not unsteadily. Art watched him untie his trotters from the hitching rack. He had to struggle a little to get in the buggy. He jerked the reins to back them away from the rack, then took the whip from its socket and whacked them viciously as he yelled, "Git!" The bays bolted as they turned sharply toward the road, almost tipping the buggy as it careened perilously on the two wheels. Art formed some adverse opinions of Clyde Barnhill,

During this same time, Zeb again showed up at the Barnhill plantation. The housekeeper seemed surprised to see him again.

"I want to talk to you about Clyde Barnhill. There seems to be something very wrong here, and I need your cooperation to change it. I'm sending for a man to come and help me find out what's really wrong here. I'm hoping you won't say a word about this or act like you know anything about it."

She invited him in, and Zeb told her about Clyde's rape and murder of Jessica. "I think you are trapped here for similar reasons, and I know you are afraid. Can you tell me why?"

"He can be nice; he sweet-talked me into coming here about three years ago. He beats me when I don't respond fast enough to his whims or his love making. He says he'll kill me if I get any ideas about leaving, and I'm sure he means it. I haven't seen one of the field workers who was part of the crew lately. Maybe he spoke out of turn. Now that I've heard your story, I'm more sure than before that murder is just another alternative of Clyde's."

"You just pretend you know nothing about us. In a short time, you'll be able to go on with your life. I think I can promise you that." Zeb explained his plans to get a job, posing as an ignorant transient and about his helper who was to try to get on as a crew worker.

"May God watch over you," was her benediction.

Late the next afternoon, a large poorly clad Negro came through the Barnhill gate and trudged to the house where Clyde Barnhill was sitting on the porch. His manner was of timid subservience.

"Mistah boss man, ah needs a job, and ah'll work fo whatevah ya wan a gi me jis so ah kin eat."

"Can you handle horses?"

Zeb thought he saw some scheming glitter in Clyde's eyes.

"Yassuh, ah's purty gud wi hosses."

"We'll see, follow me to the barn." Clyde opened a barn door and entered with Zeb close behind. There were six horses in their stalls. Clyde pointed to the first horse. "Put a harness on old Baldy here." Then he pointed to the last horse on the other end, "and harness Spook. Hitch them to the manure wagon back of this barn, and haul out three loads of manure before you get anything to eat."

"Yassuh, boss, ah kin do it an ah tank ya."

Clyde went back to sit on the porch, and Zeb put the collar on Baldy and came back with the harness. He was doing what he had done in his early years, and he rather enjoyed being with horses again. He wondered about the name "Spook" as he went to the last stall. He took the collar from the peg in back of Spook, who spooked around wild-eyed at Zeb. When he slapped him lightly on the rear to get him to move over, Spook shot forward and hit the manger with his chest with a resounding crash and then pranced back and forth in the stall so that it sounded like six horses' hoof beats instead of one. Spook didn't kick, so Zeb worked his way to the front, talking soothing nothings all the way.

Soon Spook began to quiet somewhat with his ears going back and forth as though he couldn't fathom what was happening. Zeb had been

195

shoved against the side of the stall several times, but he acted as though it was normal procedure as he finally put the collar on Spook's neck. Zeb talked and patted Spook as he went back for the harness. Every part of Spook's smooth hide twitched at the touch of the harness, and his ears still went backward and forward. He stood still as Zeb fastened the straps with snaps and buckles. Zeb bridled Spook. As he led Spook and Baldy out, Clyde was still sitting on the porch. He took them around to the back where a large wagon used for hauling the overripe pile of manure showed evidence of its purpose.

Clyde saw Zeb bring the two horses out of the barn, and the look on Clyde's face was one of disappointment. He had been certain that he had given the transient an assignment that couldn't be carried out. He felt thwarted that Spook hadn't crippled or frightened the transient so badly that he couldn't work. Then he decided that no one could haul three loads of manure before dark, and, therefore, the transient wouldn't get to eat. That made him feel better.

It was dark when Zeb came in from hauling four loads of manure. He unharnessed and fed his team. Spook had given him little trouble, and he stroked his mane and gave him some friendly overtures and his oats before he left to go get his promised meal. Clyde had double-checked the size and number of loads Zeb had taken to the field and began to feel he had struck a bonanza. Actually, he didn't pay any of his workers, although they had been lured here by promise of good pay, food, and good working conditions. He knew how to squelch any signs of protest.

Most of the workers had nearly finished eating before Zeb came in to the cookhouse where they ate. An old peg-legged black brought him some rancid-smelling ham hocks and beans. The biscuits he served were burnt and hard, but they became palatable by soaking them in the soupy mixture of the barely edible ham hocks and beans.

Early the next morning, the rest of the workers went to the fields to hoe the corn and cotton. Zeb's job was that huge and smelly manure pile. That day, Clyde caught him giving Spook a little affection.

"Hey, you, what's your name?" Clyde asked.

"Jim," answered Zeb.

"Jim, if you want to eat, you keep that fork moving. Don't waste time on that horse. Now get back to work, or you won't be able to eat."

"Yassuh, boss."

Zeb never knew exactly how Art Bennett got onto the working crew. There he was the next evening quite authentically black and eating the burnt biscuits and cabbage that was served. To his working members he was "Josh." They ignored each other.

196

Nothing occurred in the next few days that could give Zeb any feeling that he was getting clues to cause Clyde's undoing until he was forking and scattering the manure close to the far corner of the field. It was there that he noticed a spot where a dog or wild animal had been digging. He drove his wagon in front of the displaced earth so that Clyde wouldn't see what was happening if he were looking, and Clyde looked a lot. Zeb noticed the hole was in a larger area where the ground had been disturbed recently. In minutes, he dug down far enough to feel something that resisted further digging. He lay on his stomach and scooped the dirt away until his fingers scraped on a piece of metal, which became a belt buckle. His hand explored around it and he knew there was a body beneath. He quickly replaced and leveled the soil and spread some manure over the spot to hide his discovery.

After the evening meal of mutton that smelled like dirty wet wool and which was too rank for Zeb to swallow, he nodded at Art to follow him outside. They sat on the steps as Zeb related his find. Clyde was sitting on the porch.

"Let's just sit here. Clyde won't be able to stand it for long. He jumped all over me the other day for giving Spook a hug and a pat."

Clyde was watching. He had just eaten a hearty meal and was feeling good about Zeb's inroads on that manure. He had never found another worker who could get so much done. The meat that he bought from the butcher shop for his workers was for the most part too ripe to sell to anyone else. The wormy corn meal and flour from the grocery store cost him very little also. *That's cheap labor*, he thought to himself. He had to keep an eye open for any disrupting influence in his crew, but that was the part of his job he liked. It was then that he became aware of Zeb and Art sitting on the cookhouse steps, and it soon began to disturb him, which was what Zeb had predicted. They stayed glued to the steps as Clyde came to them.

"What are you two doing out here?" His voice was belligerent.

Zeb spoke.

"Ah wus gis tay'in Josh bout a body ah foun berid in dat fa cornah. Ah was askin he if ah shed tay ya."

"Oh, that," said Clyde. He seemed flustered. "Spook kicked him in the head when he went back of him. He never mentioned any kin, so we just buried him."

Clyde suddenly changed his approach. He felt that he didn't need to explain any of his actions. "Now you two just let that lay and keep your mouths shut, or I'll shut them for you. Do you understand?"

Clyde reached inside his jacket and brought out a large knife, similar to the one he had used to murder Jessica. He came close to Zeb and waved it under his chin. In a second, all that transpired the night of Jessica's death stirred a seething anger in Zeb. He grabbed the arm holding the knife and brought it down across his knee. A bone broke again, and the knife clattered to the ground. In that moment Clyde looked into Zeb's face in recognition.

"Zeb Hawkins!" he screamed.

Art and Zeb pushed the cowering remnant of what had been Clyde through the door of the cookhouse, where the others saw their jailer and murderer whimpering and stripped of all his power over them. Zeb no longer had to use his hastily acquired vocabulary.

"Here's the one who killed one of you and threatened your lives if you talked. I found the grave you dug for him. Are you still afraid of him, or do you want to tell what happened? From this moment, you're free to go or do what you want to do. If you stay here, I'll see that you get paid. The hours will be shorter, and your free time will be yours to do what you want with it."

One of them spoke, maybe because he could use the language better.

"He killed Joe just because he asked for his money and better food, and the same thing happened to Jake last spring. I haven't been here as long as some of the men. I can't believe there hadn't been others."

"What is your name?" Zeb asked.

"Clem Peters. Mr. Barnhill promised me more money than I'd been getting because he needed me to be his field boss. He told me the food was good and that I'd have free time to go to town anytime, as long as I did a day's work. He acted like a good friend, and I believed him."

Some of the others nodded in agreement, and Zeb knew they were telling the truth, because the same approach had worked with the housekeeper. Art Bennett found a short piece of board and tied both of Clyde's arms together to give that broken bone some semblance of a splint. He used strips of a blanket from a bunk and bound his ankles together also. He finally stuffed a gag in Clyde's mouth from the same blanket to keep him quiet. The others had helped by tearing the strips, and Art could feel what was happening as the realization that they had a chance at freedom dawned on them.

"Stick him on a bunk for tonight," Art said. "We'll take him to Chattanooga tomorrow. He won't bother you or anyone else again."

Zeb had gone to the house and let the housekeeper in on what had transpired.

"When the trial is held, you will be well paid for the time you have been here, plus what is proper for the abuse and forced incarceration you have been through." The wheels were turning in Zeb's mind. "Do you like to cook? This place still needs to be kept in operation. If those men out in the bunkhouse eat better and are well paid they might consider staying. They'll need to work somewhere and if I buy this place, this may be better than what they will find elsewhere. You could get someone you'd like to work with to help you with the cooking, and you could buy decent food, which would be a change from the garbage Clyde gave them. There's better farm equipment. I know there's a manure spreader that unloads itself, and there are cultivators pulled by horses, which eliminates most of the hoeing. Work isn't the only thing. The men need time of their own to do what they want with it. I'd like to see a kind of model farm, where the workers would learn to have responsibilities, and if they learned to do it right, they might want to try it on their own. If I buy it, I'll call it the Sam Jackson Farm. You might like it here." Zeb looked at her to see her reaction. "I don't know your name," Zeb smiled.

"Maybelle Brown. I'd like to show them what good cooking is. Without Clyde, this might be as close to heaven as I'll get on this side."

"Good," said Zeb. He handed her five twenties.

"Until I buy this farm, Clyde will be paying the bill, although he doesn't know it. He may be bankrupt by the time he pays all his help their back pay, but I don't think he's going to get much sympathy. Get the men to hitch those trotters when you want to go to town to get groceries. One more thing, I'm afraid to ask. Do you know anything about keeping books on income and outgo?"

"I'm not exactly a dummy. My mom taught me the three Rs. I don't know who taught her. If you'd set it up like you wanted it, I see no reason I couldn't do it. For what you have done for us here, I can tell you, you would know where every penny went."

"Let me say it this way. You and I are going to make this a place where at least some of our people will have the opportunity to live as free people and be rewarded for their labors the same as anyone. I have a feeling that you are going to be one of the best persons I have discovered in the South. God works in strange ways to get something good to happen."

44

Going Home

The trip back to Thorson's Bay was uneventful. Zeb felt saddened to know that the South was even more violently subordinating his race. The case against Clyde didn't reach the courtroom. Clyde was found dead in his cell by hanging, perhaps by his own volition.

Zeb's home in Thorson's Bay wasn't far from the train station. As he disembarked, Jennifer came rushing into his arms, all fifteen years of her, beautiful, vibrant, gifted, and home from college. She kissed him.

"Oh, Zeb, I've met the train every day."

Zeb hugged this beautiful charmer and knew he was back where he was loved and wanted.

Thorson's Bay had taken Maude and Matt back into its arms, and because it was supposed to be a vacation for them, it sometimes seemed to have too many arms. Eva and Adam realized the demands on the couple's time.

"Come here when you need to catch your breath," Eva had said. Matt loved this woman who had given his dad so many years of happiness. She and Adam were both in excellent health, and the years had treated them gently. The thought occurred to Matt that even aging was a retarded process around Thorson's Bay, because those he knew seemed to have changed little over the years. Jim Beaver was still a striking specimen, and although he and Fawn had a family of four, they showed little wear and tear. Rosella, their oldest, was eleven, and went to school at the Mission and often stayed with Mike and Marie. She was pretty and smiled easily. Maude's parents hadn't changed much from when Matt had married Maude. Matt couldn't stay away from Jennifer, and Jennifer couldn't stay away from him, which made fair apportioning of his time a problem. Both Eva and Jennifer had satisfied a need in his life for family, but it was more than that. He knew that their love was reciprocal, and it gave him a warm feeling.

Doran and Marie had invited Matt and Maude to their lovely home near the Trading Post for dinner, along with Adam and Eva. Each seemed in the prime of their lives as they greeted their guests warmly.

200

Rosella was there, helping Marie with the dinner. One could see Mike liked being called "Grandpa." The ice cream, cranked to frozen perfection by Mike and Rosella, later topped the blueberry pie at dinner.

After dinner, they all went into the library to relax and reminisce. As Matt entered, he saw two pictures above the fireplace. One of them was of Marie that Star had painted, and the other was of Star that John Bannister had painted. Matt hadn't known that Doran had bought it, but he did know that John had given forty thousand dollars to the Hawkins-Berglund fund.

"I'm going to marry John Bannister some day," said Jennifer. "I've had a crush on him since I was six."

"Does he know it?" Matt asked.

"I met him at an art showing at college just recently," she bubbled. "He said he would wait fifty years if necessary."

As he gazed at the picture, Star seemed to walk out of the frame, and Matt felt the recurring agony of her loss. Maude was at his side. She knew what was happening, and Matt reached for her because he needed her to help him through this period of entangling loyalties.

Star's hold on Matt's spirits hadn't lifted when Matt decided to take a short jaunt up to the Mission to visit his dear friend Father O'Brien. He was old. Slowly getting up from his chair, he embraced Matt with a fervor of friendship that hadn't faded.

"I've followed your ministry; you have let God work through you."

"You have been my example. I hold no one in higher esteem than I do you. It's as though God sent me to you to apprentice under a skilled artisan. You have my deepest respect and love."

"My time here is short," said Father O'Brien, "and I'm looking forward to putting aside this body. Star will be there to help me with my next assignment. Heaven wouldn't be heaven unless we can extend our usefulness."

Matt told Father O'Brien of Star's reentry into his thoughts, giving him the same feeling of emptiness and loss.

"I can't explain it. For the most part, Star has allowed me to live a fulfilled life with Maude. I'm looking forward to my next assignment to do what God wants me to do here on earth, but I know that some day I'll reach and Star will be there."

"God meant for you and Star to be together, and you will be. Whatever lies ahead, God will compensate your reunion with fulfillment beyond imagination."

It took Matt some time to realize that the heavy pall of depression had lifted. He walked toward the Trading Post and felt at one with the sights about him. Not much had changed since he left, although the church had been renovated and enlarged. He walked on to see his own property. Some of the trees that had been left at the time of cutting were now quite large, and though they were not as majestic as the original ones, his property was well-forested and pleasing to survey. He soon saw the log cabin that the congregation had built for him. As he approached, a young man came out of the door with a bucket in his hand. He looked at Matt.

"You've got to be Matt Berglund. You're a big man in more ways than one."

"And you're Pastor Brightwell. I wondered if they were still using this for a parsonage." Matt had given the church permission to use it when he left. "Do you like it here?" he asked.

"Please, call me Bob. The word 'like' isn't strong enough. I'm welcomed in every home with obvious love and affection. I'm invited to dinners too often, and I feel more like an adopted member of their families. You may have seen the enlarged sanctuary, and it's often more than full. They mention you fondly and still give heavily to the Hawkins-Berglund Rehabilitation fund. It's not me. It's the people of this congregation who still thank God for what you made happen. I'm hoping you'll take the pulpit a week from next Sunday. As soon as they know you're here, they'll want to hear you, and tell you they still love you."

"I'll do it," said Matt, "but let me say that the young Reverend Bob Brightwell is doing a lot of the right things to keep Christ's love alive here in this area."

When Matt got off the train back at Thorson's Bay, it seemed like old times as he walked to the Thorson home to be with Maude, who was enjoying spending some time with her parents. When she let him in, she could see that Matt was a part of her world again.

"Let's you and I go canoeing tomorrow," he suggested.

They paddled along, pausing at times to enjoy the familiar views and remark about a few changes. A cottage with flowers in clusters and patterns indicated a woman's presence. A fenced-in pasture with a cow and calf helped to assure its permanence. For the most part, the tree-lined shores and marshes had escaped man's trespass. They were approaching the tree.

Maude pointed.

"Let's picnic here. It's here where you met Star, but it's also where Star gave you to me."

After the picnic lunch, they just sat on the blanket, happy to be alone together.

"I was thinking," Maude reflected, "about you, Star, and me.

According to this world's standards, we've had a better than average marriage. I love you, and I know you love me. We make a good team in the work we do. We also have an excellent relationship in our intimate moments. I know that you and Star had that ultimate and total relationship that only a few get a chance to experience. Although you are the ultimate in my life, I am the substitute. Star wanted you to have the best substitute and she chose me."

"You are not a substitute," said Matt. "I have been allowed to love two women, equally, but differently. I can't imagine what life would have been without you there, as a partner, a lover, and a daily companion. We both know that we've had a better than good marriage. I love you for all the reasons a man should love his wife. People look at you and consider me a very lucky man. You're beautiful, caring, sensitive, intelligent, and aware of my moods and fallacies and, most of all, you love me." Matt kissed her and she responded.

Her lips were an inch from Matt's.

"If we continue our present inclinations," she hinted coyly, "we could have a baby. I can't believe a little baby would interfere too much, do you?"

"It's time we found out."

The church was filling with many people Matt had never seen. Some, no doubt, were tourists, and the other unfamiliar faces were the result of his absence of seven years. Phil and Sadie Peterson were up front. Sadie waved her hand to Matt with her same open smile. Some who would normally be at the Mission were on hand, including Mike and Marie, Jim and Fawn, and their children. Adam, Eva, and Jennifer were in the same pew. Maude sat with her parents and Zeb. After the congregation had sung a hymn, Zeb, Jennifer, and Eva went up front. Zeb and Jennifer had their violins with them. Eva sang the first verse as the two violin virtuosos accompanied her on the hymn, "Children of the Heavenly Father."

Children of the heavenly Father,
safely in His bosom gather.
Nestling birds nor star in heaven,
such a refuge e'er was given.

Eva's contralto swept over the audience. Then the two violins played. Matt saw Mike Doran wipe tears from his eyes as he realized he was listening to the best. They all sang the next verse in perfect three-part harmony. Zeb sang the last verse with the fervor of his faith blending with the richness of his deep bass voice.

Matt went to the pulpit.

"This is the same pulpit from which I attempted my first sermon as a pastor. It was made by the gentleman who just sang to you. He is Zeb Hawkins, who many of you know is my friend and partner in our work for all these years. A pastor never forgets his first charge. The plaque by the door says that something happened here, and it wasn't just another church. It wasn't the preacher. It was you through whom God was working, with such a oneness of spirit that the whole north country felt its impact.

"I've asked around, and I'm told that this still isn't just another church. God must be very proud of you for your continuing example. You haven't forgotten Christ's simple instruction that we love one another as He loves us." Matt hesitated for a few seconds.

"I've checked Rev. Bob Brightwell's credentials. You are his first charge. He graduated at the top of his class. His teachers gave him high ratings in his desire to tell you and me about the One who walked among us and showed us the way. You here today are living examples by showing your loyalty to this love as the church grows and enriches the lives of this community and beyond. Do you really know what you are doing to your young pastor? God knows that he doesn't have all the answers and neither do I. According to his own testimony, you're giving him love and making him a part of your family circle. We, who attempt to explain God's love, wish we had the magic to reach each and every heart with God's message. We need encouragement from each of you to be able to make that message so clear that none evades it. Because of all the support he has from you, I predict that Rev. Bob Brightwell will be one of our best purveyors of God's message. His ministry will be more than successful. You have shown him love and caring when he's needed it. I know God wishes there were more churches like yours. God is proud of you. Our church conference is proud of you. I stand here, happy and proud to still be one of you. A poet states some of my feelings in this manner:

'Sometimes I try to ponder many things.
This love that's mine to feel, to share, that
lifts the fibers of my being to great heights,
to inner ecstasies that paint the world
with rainbow tints. This gift of love, it dwarfs
Aladdin's lamp and in its effervescence
Lends warmth and sparkle to the days like sun's first rays on
    morning dew,
Although there's much that doesn't seem too clear,
some salient answers softly filter through,

204

that somehow, just in loving, being loved,
I think I've walked with God a step or two.'"

Matt looked out at his audience. "The Hawkins-Berglund team
has recently been assigned to the Zion Church in Kongsberg. For those
of you not familiar with our Scandinavian heritage, Kongsberg means
'king's mountain' in Norwegian. The biblical city of Zion was a fortress
built on a hill and is also the name for the New Jerusalem, so it's a
great name for this church. We will begin our ministry there next
month. Maude and I are enjoying our respite back home, yet we are
anxious to see what challenges await us. Be assured, though, you'll
always be first in our hearts. As we sing our closing hymn, let's all raise
our right hand, which will mean that you will continue to be the great
church you are now."

Their hands went up as they rose to their feet singing:

Blest be the tie that binds
our hearts in Christian love.
The fellowship of kindred minds
is like to that above.

Matt stood by the door with Maude, and they shook many hands
as the people filed out. When Sadie Meeks Peterson came by, she
grabbed his hand and with the old twinkle in her eye, said. "Well, you're
still the biggest." She invited them to dinner.

"We'll come," came from Maude before Matt had a chance to open
his mouth.

As Maude explained later, "Sadie's one of the stars in my
crown."

Phil Peterson and Matt went for a walk before dinner. In the two
sections of land he now owned, no ax had ever felled a tree for commer-
cial gain. The tall pines, old monarchs of that virgin area, gave Matt a
feeling of awe. Here was a spot of Eden untouched. Matt saw many deer
that seemed unworried about their presence as they continued their
stroll. Phil surprised Matt with his question, "How could one look at
this and not love the God who put it here?"

As they sat down to dinner, Sadie looked at Matt.

"I hope you won't mind if I do the prayer today," she said.

"Please do."

"God, you know my prayers aren't fancy, but I just want to
thank You for the many blessings You have given me, especially for
letting Maude butt into my life and make me look good enough for

Phil. She gave me love and hope when I thought life had passed me by. Bless Matt and Maude. Bless the food we are about to eat, including my 'stupendous stew.' In the name of Your Son, Jesus, we pray. Amen."

Along with the stew, there were roast turkey and green beans from the garden. The wild turkey gravy on the mashed potatoes added another flavorful dimension, and the chocolate pie was the crowning finale for Matt.

The next day, as Zeb and Matt were walking along the edge of the lake, Matt thought of the many times they had walked here before.

"Zeb, do you remember when you picked me up and set me on your shoulder? You'd tell me to look at my beautiful world and then you'd say, 'Cub, you're going to help make it better some day.' Well, we've done some of that, you and I and Maude. It was as though God had appointed you to keep me on course. I love my dad, but I feel like I have two fathers, one for supplying my material needs and you for making me reach higher spiritually than I would have otherwise. I know your trip south left you with some scars. Since the time you sent me the letter with the story of your life, I have gained an even greater appreciation for the stature and depth of character you hung onto, in spite of the tragedy and hate that was all around you."

Zeb looked across the lake. As Zeb began to speak, Matt knew he was back in a different time and place.

"It's all the goodness and beauty God has allowed me to see and feel—my mother, Jessica, Sam Jackson, you, Star, Maude, Jennifer, Lorna, your dad, and Eva, and on and on, including those friends we have found along the way, like Hugh Summers. They all gave strength to me."

In that moment, Matt felt, more than at any time before, that he had been under the wing of an angelic presence that contained few foibles of average humanity. Zeb was an ever present strength, unobtrusive, but at hand.

"I don't know how God figures things out, but I guess He wanted you and me to get together. I didn't get to be with Jessica, but He gave me you to take her place for a while, like He gave Maude to you. I also know we've changed a lot of lives, and I'm trying hard to remember that after the experiences I had in the South. It's going to be good to be back doing what we do best."

Zeb was a genius, and his scope of accomplishments were many, and his grasp of finances was equal or better than those who spent their lives sorting out the right choices of investment. He could have toured the world as a violin virtuoso, or he might have been a public figure as a teller of stories, but he was where he wanted to be, Matt thought, *With me.*

"That's the way I feel, too. We are a team. It will be good to get back in harness."

45

Katie

It was six months after Zeb returned from the South when he received a letter from Katie, the young wife with hungry baby he had met on the train and had helped with food and money. The letter read:

Dear Zeb,

I had qualms about writing to you, but I'm in desperate need of help. My husband was killed in a mine cave-in four months ago. I have been staying at the Wilsons, who really can't afford to keep me. They have four children of their own, and Mr. Wilson's salary is hardly adequate for their proper care. I have tried to get a job, but this is a depressed area. I help a little as a cleaning lady for some of the more affluent homes, but I am a burden on this good family that allows me and little Ben to live with them. You told me to write if I needed help, so 1 kept your card. Maybe you can help me out of this hopeless situation. You were a miracle to us on the train and it seems I'm hoping you can be my miracle again. I can honestly say I hate to mail this letter, but I want something better for little Ben.

Catherine Radford
Alva, Kentucky
RR2

Zeb answered the letter immediately.

Dear Catherine,

Come right away. Am enclosing eight hundred dollars. Pay the Wilson's five hundred for your stay with them and use the rest for clothing and travel. We have a room for you. You can stay with us at the parsonage until you can make other arrangements.

Zeb

Ten days later, Katie and little Ben arrived. Katie looked neat, trim, and pretty in her tailored suit with shoes to match. Little Ben was toddling beside her. Katie came into Zeb's outstretched arms and knew she was loved and wanted. Zeb stooped, holding out his arms as little Ben shyly walked into them. He smiled back at Zeb's big grin as they danced around the room together. Matt and Maude made Katie feel at home with their warm welcome.

"Supper's almost ready. I'll show you your room while Zeb watches the meat loaf."

It was a large bedroom, with a crib for little Ben close to the bed. In the crib were a ball, a little harmonica, and a fluffy teddy bear. Maude and little Ben were friends at her first squeeze and smile.

"We'll holler when supper's ready." Maude put little Ben in the crib and left the room.

At supper, the conversation got around to Katie.

"Do you have any family?" Maude inquired.

"Not any more. My dad was a preacher, and my mother was a teacher. I had a sister and two brothers, all younger than I. The Klan set fire to our house. I escaped by breaking the bedroom window and climbing out onto the porch roof. It was slanted, and I rolled off into the trimmed evergreen border with just a few scratches. Our neighbors took me into their home. Their son was Ben, my husband. I had graduated, but Ben had quit school and was working at labor jobs. He was a year older than I and paid a lot of attention to me. I liked him, and after a few months, we got married. I have little Ben to show for it," Katie smiled.

Zeb held up a finger.

"I'm beginning to get an idea. I'm planning to build a combination church, school, and meeting place on the Sam Jackson farm in Tennessee. It's an experiment, and I'm hoping black, white, and other ethnic groups can work side by side without prejudice. There'll be work for training in woodworking and sewing, along with classes for those who want to increase their skills in reading, writing, and math for young children and older adults. I think I know now who'll be the teacher." Zeb looked across the table. "Katie, you can take a Normal Training course to get a license to teach in a few months. You'll be well paid and can work for a degree at your own pace."

Zeb got up and stood behind Katie, putting his hand on her shoulder. "I think God has picked you for this job. You'll be ready by Christmas, and so will our young Sam Jackson, who will complete his seminary courses to become the first minister to help those who work there find their potential."

Katie wiped a tear.

"I must be dreaming, A few days ago I thought my world had crumbled to where I could see no future. What has happened here has to be a miracle. I prayed that God would open a door for me and He has." Katie put little Ben in Maude's arms and ran to Zeb's outstretched arms. In her uncontrollable happiness, she kissed him and cried like a young child in the loving safety of Zeb's arms,

Christmas was coming to the parsonage. Katie had completed her Normal Training course and had received her teaching certificate. A tree was trimmed with strings of popcorn and baubles from previous Christmases, and a sprig of holly dangled from here and there. Candles, in fish shaped clips, were placed on the outer branches of the tree, to be lit when the presents were distributed. They needed to be watched carefully to prevent fire. Maude and Katie were filling the rooms with smells of pies, fudge, and taffy. Sam was coming home. He had graduated with honors, and there was a joyful feverishness in his anticipated arrival. Even Katie had caught some of the glow that emanated from Maude, Mat, and Zeb.

Sam didn't knock. Katie was dusting a chair when he barged in, eager to be home. They came face to face, almost colliding, and just stared at each other. Sam finally broke the silence.

"You're Katie?"

"You have to be Sam."

Sam stared at her in awe, realizing that he'd never seen a woman who shook him up this much. Katie was feeling the same way. No man had ever attracted her like this, not even Ben, her deceased husband. Maude came into the room, wiping her hands with a towel. She greeted Sam with outstretched arms and a hug. Matt was close behind, then came Zeb, and Katie knew that in that room, there was joy in pluperfect. It was the happiest of times. The Christmas program at the church showed the bulging membership that was the result of the Hawkins-Berglund threesome's tireless efforts at regeneration. The choir's angelic voices caroled the manger birth, and there was a gift for each child that had been specially selected. Then there was Katie and Sam, sitting side by side, in a euphoria of the discovery that they were in love.

Zeb was sitting in the parsonage parlor that was used as an office. He had invited Katie and Sam to discuss plans for their duties on the Sam Jackson farm. They knew they were to teach and minister to those within its perimeters.

"Maybe this seems too sudden," said Sam, "but Katie and I want to go there as husband and wife."

"I suspected as much," said Zeb, "and that just happens to be a perfect solution. We'll get Matt to tie the knot and go from there. Sam, you have shown good judgment in handling your investment portfolio. I'm going to add some more to include Katie. In a way, I feel you two are my family. I want you to continue to increase your worth, so that, like us, you give money as well as time to make things happen. The South, as you both know, is adamant to keep our race on the bottom rung, as is much of the North. You are going to have to find ways to anticipate trouble, and then do what it takes to thwart it temporarily, stay within your own perimeters and raise the economic, spiritual, and educational levels of the Sam Jackson plantation, of which you will be the overseers and eventually inherit. You will work with Maybelle Brown, who not only cooks for the crews, but keeps the books. From her reports to me, I'd say that she is thorough and accurate. Clem Peters also does a good job of keeping the crews busy and the farmland productive. Let them know they're appreciated. If you have some suggestions, be tactful. Use the house, for the present, to teach and minister. After you are more acquainted with its potential, I'm going to bring Hugh Summers down to supervise the building of an all-purpose structure to be used as a church and for recreation and education."

Maude and Katie had a talk.

"You and Sam might want to put off increasing the size of your family for a while," said Maude. "Some of the sharecroppers' wives need to know they don't have to have another baby each year, and you can be an example for them. The emphasis should be on the quality of life, not quantity. I'm quite sure God hopes that you will use good judgment."

Matt administered the marriage vows for Sam and Katie, and everyone cried at the parting. Zeb warned them to be watchful for outside interference, especially from that cesspool of hate called the Klan.

"I think you know what you're up against. A successful integration will be like waving a red flag before a bull. It will only increase the blind hatred so deeply ingrained in their stubborn, closed minds. Many of them go to church and plan their next killing or fire. It's a Satanic crusade against our race by so-called influential and responsible citizens. Many who don't sanction its practices just keep still, because they fear retaliation. You don't have to go if you feel you don't want any part of it, but so far it's succeeding better than I had imagined."

"Katie and I have considered these eventualities, and we want to help make it work," said Sam. "We are from the South, and that's where we're needed most. It wasn't meant to be any other way."

"I have something that might help," said Zeb. "Art Bennett, who helped me put away Clyde, has been keeping an eye on the plantation to see that the Klan and others don't interfere. I have given him an incentive to keep an eye on the Sam Jackson farm. We also are friends, and that may be one reason we are doing well." Zeb rose from his chair and stood behind Sam and Katie, with a hand on each shoulder. Tears poured down his cheeks.

"May God watch over my children."

46

Laura

A little baby came in early spring of the following year. All the doctor had to do was "catch." Maude named her "Laura," after her mother. They all adored and diapered her. Of course, Maude was center stage at feeding times, but Matt often watched and marveled at the miracle of love that was happening in their home. Zeb was in the midst of it, and often little Laura went to sleep with her head against his chest, listening to his heartbeat of total love. Maude and Matt had discovered that children solidified their rapport with the community they served and another baby came a little over two years after Laura's entrance.

Maude had quickly decided on the name "Mark" for her son. "I have a Matthew; I'd better stick to what works for me."

Laura learned to talk early, and Zeb couldn't think of a reason why she shouldn't increase her vocabulary and do some positive thinking. She learned her multiplication tables when she was three. At five, she read Shakespeare's "To be or not to be," with proper inflection and much understanding.

"Does that mean we're afraid to die because we don't know for sure what's coming next?"

Laura started school at five, and after one week, the teacher came to visit Maude.

"As near as I can tell, she ought to be in the fifth grade, and she would probably make them look bad by what she knows. All I can do is give her books to read and maybe let her try to help some of the others on a one-on-one basis."

"Let's try that for a while," Maude agreed. "We want her to have a normal growing up experience."

A few days later, Laura came home from school very upset. She told about her new friend Tommy who came to school with a cut lip and an ugly bruise on his cheek bone. Laura asked Tommy how it happened. "Dad hits me all the time, and sometimes he hits my mom. He hit me this time when I tried to stop him from hitting her."

This wasn't something new to Matt. In his work, it was necessary to be in touch with law enforcement agencies. Vagrants and drunks were a part of his rehabilitation routine. Not everyone changed for the better. Matt went to Laura's school and came to a door where he saw "Jasper Booth, Principal." He knocked and was invited in. Booth was middle-aged with a harried expression, probably caused by the mountain of paper work on his desk. Matt introduced himself.

"I'm Matt Berglund, pastor of the church closest to your school. You have a boy named Tommy Brown in the first grade. He came to school bruised and battered yesterday and confided to my daughter that his dad had done it many times before. Are you interested in looking into the matter, or do I have to look elsewhere?"

Booth leaned back in his chair.

"This is a deprived neighborhood. Hunger, booze, and broken homes are the norm. I'm not surprised you found a child abuser. I go home hating myself every night for not having the gumption to do something about it. I read an article in the paper about your past success in reshaping community life. You're here and you're concerned and you're serious." Booth got up out of his chair and ran his hand through his hair as he approached Matt. "You know what to do," he said. "Maybe I'll get some of my self-respect back if you show me the way."

Matt grasped his hand.

"The answers aren't easy, but if we work together you'll see a difference."

Booth studied Matt.

"I've encouraged the teachers to handle their own problems." He opened a door to another room where a lady was busy with some paper work. "Mary, go to Miss Findley's room, and tell her I want to see her now. You take over her class for a while."

Miss Findley came in soon with a worried expression. Booth introduced her to Matt.

"Let's get right to the point. What can you tell us about Tommy Johnson?"

"He's been absent five times already. His mother sent a note that he fell over the back of a chair one time and that he was beaten by a gang of kids another time. He's so disoriented that he can't concentrate. He's afraid to open his mouth and say what he knows, I think."

"Do you know anything about the family?" asked Matt.

"A little. When Mrs. Johnson brought Tommy to school, she said she worked as a seamstress, and her husband didn't have a steady job. She said he worked as a day laborer. She called him Bates."

"What can we do, pastor? There have been no complaints."

"You've been a lot of help already. I'm going to try something. If we don't, someone will get killed or maimed for life."

Matt gave Zeb the details and what he hoped, happened.

"Let me at him."

A man opened the door, finished the beer in the bottle he held, and looked at Zeb.

"What do you want?"

"I'm calling for the Zion Church. I'd like to invite you and your family to come and visit."

"We're not interested," Bates said, "and I don't need any black S.O.B. to stick his nose in here, so run along before I bash you with this bottle, too."

Zeb heard a moan from inside the house. He grabbed the hand that held the bottle and tore it from Bates's grasp. He shoved Bates through his own doorway. On the floor lay his wife in a semiconscious condition. Zeb shook Bates until his teeth rattled.

"Get the doctor who lives next door to the church and hurry, or I'll break every bone in your body."

Bates soon returned with Dr. Morgan. He had sobered and tried to be contrite.

"I hit her with the bottle!"

"She needs to be in the hospital fast." Dr. Morgan was urgent. "Let's get her into my carriage." Zeb carried Daisy Johnson out to the carriage.

"I'll get Johnson to the police station." Zeb grabbed Bates's arm. "Do you want to walk, or do I have to carry you?" They walked. "Let me ask you a question. If I'm a black son of a bitch, what does that make you who is a child abuser and maybe a murderer? For your information, your son will be staying with us until you're man enough to *act* like a man instead of a monster. Maybe God hasn't given up on you, but don't expect pity from this end."

Daisy's skull had been crushed. She remained in a coma until Dr. Morgan had relieved the pressure on her brain by drilling and prying the skull back to normal position. The healing process was slow, and it was two weeks before the doctor announced she would recover.

In the interim, Tommy began to shed some of his timidity. Laura made him laugh. They played games, and Tommy discovered it was fun to learn. He rapidly became a bright student, and Laura hoped out loud that he could stay with them always.

Zeb visited Bates Johnson while he was in jail.

"I guess your wife isn't going to press charges," he told Bates, "but if you don't stop acting like a mad dog, we have enough evidence to show your instability that will put you away for a long time."

Zeb visited Daisy at the hospital; he took Tommy with him. He had warned him to hug her carefully and the reunion was touching to watch as Tommy told her about Laura and his new outlook and rapport at school.

"I can learn, Mamma, and now I have lots of friends, but Laura is my best friend."

"Do you miss your dad?" Daisy asked him.

"No! I don't ever want to see him again."

Jasper Booth came in. Zeb introduced him to Daisy and then to Tommy. Jasper got on one knee where he could look at Tommy at the same level. He put a hand on Tommy's shoulder.

"Oh, you're the young man Miss Findley was telling me about. She says you're one of our best first graders. She says you're making a lot of friends." He held out his hand. "How about letting me be one of your friends."

Tommy held out his hand and Jasper clasped it and drew him in for a hug. Tommy decided he liked this man who held him. Jasper Booth had discovered something else. Daisy was pretty, very articulate and seemingly unaware what her open friendliness had done to him. He was a bachelor, suddenly wishing that he had a boy like Tommy and a wife like Daisy.

Daisy had no designs on Jasper, but the next time she talked to Zeb, she told him she wanted to divorce Bates.

"Even if he would change, I couldn't believe it would last, and I would be better off financially because he took more money from me than he made. All he wanted was a bed partner and someone to be his punching bag. He showed no affection for Tommy and resented his presence."

When Zeb told Bates of Daisy's desire for divorce, he suddenly allowed his base nature to assert itself with invectives and threats. Zeb knew that Bates was no better than Clyde who had killed his Jessica.

"You have just cooked your goose completely. Your sentence will be six years at hard labor with expulsion from this state at the end. I can't honestly say God help you."

Jasper Booth started a boys' club, which included Tommy and many others from poor and broken homes. They met in the church recreation room, went fishing, played games, and hiked, often overnight. A year later Jasper sat on the porch of Daisy's home.

"Tommy, your mother and I want to get married. Would you like to have me for a dad?"

"Oh, I hoped it would happen," said Tommy as he ran to him.

Jasper rose from his chair, caught Tommy and picked him up for a hug that was totally given from each participant.

The Hawkins-Berglund formula worked its magic for three obvious reasons, Matt, Maude, and Zeb, in any order of the names involved. One was the energy coming from all three participants. Another was the honest compassion of each one and the conviction that no problem was hopeless. The third, thanks to Zeb, was not only the giving of themselves, but also was the giving of money. It was always enough to do what was necessary to eliminate the despair of poverty. This produced a healthy, happy, and thankful community that in turn wanted to contribute to the church and the fund that remade their lives. One might say there was now a foursome, because little Laura was always bringing her friends to church to expose them to Zeb's stories and his contagious outpouring of love. The children in turn invited their parents to come, hear, and see the church that had caught the spirit of the Lord of life.

47

Mark

Mark never really had a chance to approach life in what one might call a normal childhood. Between Zeb and Laura, he absorbed language skills and facts and figures perhaps even faster than Laura had, due to his double exposure. Laura had him sitting in a desk like a student when he was still in diapers. He was more introverted than Laura or perhaps just more interested in facts and figures than the problems of humanity. He showed early signs of physical size, and he loved athletics with a dedicated seriousness that made him excel in sports. By the time he was nine, Zeb and he perused the financial page together, so much that Zeb gave him some money to invest and see if he could build his own portfolio.

Mark loved the idea of making money grow, and Zeb soon found that his little prodigy was expert at divining the ebb and flow of when to get in or out of the market. Zeb suggested he give a portion of his profits to the Rehabilitation fund, which he did cheerfully at a twenty-five percent tithe. He had inwardly decided that making money was more fun than spending it. That was his reason for being, to gather it and give it away. During these years of maturing, he was content to be a part of the Berglund family. He went to church, accepted its morality as good common sense, and was proud to be a part of something that reshaped and improved so many lives. He saw the conviction of faith in Zeb, his dad, and mother and hoped that same powerful compulsion could happen to him. He went to college at fourteen, not feeling any real necessity because he was doing well at what he liked to do, and he also knew he had the best teacher in Zeb.

Mark soon became a part of the swimming and wrestling teams. He was quickly acquiring his dad's proportions physically, and there were some news items which rated him as a young wizard in finance. Because of his size and his tendency to be a top student in the classroom, he seemed older than he was. The girls smiled at him a lot, although they were at least three years older. Maude hugged him when he left home for the first time to be on his own at college.

"You are our son. There will be times when its seems almost right to let go of what is right because of peer pressure and your own disturbing emotions. Some day I want you to be able to look the girl you marry straight in the eye with what God expects of all of us, just plain old-fashioned morality." Maude had held him as her tear fell on his cheek. "Now that I've said it, I'm certain I didn't need to."

Laura had taught Mark to dance. There was a tie between them that seemed stronger than most brothers and sisters have. While he enjoyed other girls in high school, Laura and he had a world of their own. They shared their dreams and opinions, and Mark participated in the youth activities of the church and school because it meant that they were doing things together. Laura was extremely popular in school and community, but when most girls were seeking relationships with one of the male sex, she was rooting for Mark and letting him know that so far nothing had superseded the sister-brother ties. Laura preceded Mark to college a year earlier in the same city where the Rehabilitation team had been sent and, therefore, still was part of the home circle. Mark, however, was wooed by Harvard. Thus, the admonition by Maude to her son, who was what any mother would have been very proud of, the son she had helped to nurture.

Inevitably, an attractive young lady invited Mark on a blind date to a sorority dance, and Mark didn't try to think of a reason to refuse. He was not yet fifteen, and as there was some time before the date the dance was held, he wrote Laura a letter, explaining the facts as he saw them.

Laura,

I've been asked to go to a sorority dance by a pretty young lady who is probably three years older than your rather oversized brother. You taught me to dance, so I'm not worried about that part. My age isn't a secret on campus, so I'm assuming it will be something like you and me dancing together. I really don't believe I want to get into much of this, but I don't want to give the impression that I'm just an intellectual freak.

Before I started college, I wondered how it would be without my sister close at hand. It isn't such a void as I imagined because some of you is a part of me here. Do you remember when we talked about when we were married to the one who will some day make that happen? We both laughed. You are not an intrusion, nor am I in your life, but I wouldn't trade places with any other brother. Wish me luck on the new happening for whatever.

Mark

219

On the night of the dance, Mark came to the sorority house bringing an orchid corsage for his date. All he knew about her was that he should ask for "Beth." Mark felt a few shock tremors as he viewed his partner dressed so prettily and smiling so sweetly as he handed the corsage to her. Her name was Elizabeth, but Mark was quickly informed she liked to be called Beth. She introduced him to some of her sorority sisters, and they evaporated any strangeness he felt. One of them said, "Wow, Beth, you did a lot better than I did with the one I'm stuck with."

The gymnasium had been decorated with streamers and Japanese lamps and a twelve-piece band was playing "By the Light of the Silvery Moon" when they arrived. Mark was a bit disturbed at his lack of indifference to his dancing partner. He could see surprise in Beth's eyes as they made the first circle.

"Where did you learn to dance like this?"

"My sister taught me what I know."

"I'll bet the girls like to dance with you," Mark was pleased to hear Beth say.

"I have to confess that I really don't know. You are my first real date. I guess you know I'm not quite fifteen, but I think you know I enjoy dancing with you, and right now, I wish I was old enough to ask you for another date some time."

"Why do you think I invited you to go to this dance?" Beth was looking right at Mark, and he was hypnotized into staring back at her, unable to shake the intensity of her attraction.

"I can't believe it," he said. "Am I falling in love with you?"

Beth steered him to the refreshment counter.

"Let's get a soda, and we'll talk about it."

As they walked to the counter, one of Mark's dormitory friends spoke to him.

"Look who's dancing with the dean's daughter."

They sat at a table as they sipped.

"I've seen you in class many times, but you never looked at me. Maybe it's a little school-girl crush, but I wanted to get to know you, and you know the rest. There's something else you might want to know. I'm only about a half-year older than you. I know what happens to people when they kiss, so let's hold hands and maybe have a small kiss about once a month until we let some more years come and go. It will also help us discover if this is the real thing. Is that all right with you?"

Mark felt a euphoria that he had never experienced. He knew they were both too young, but what he hoped would happen some day had happened, and there was no way he could run away from her hold on him. He clasped Beth's hands.

"What's happened to me is more than a crush. Of that I'm very sure. Should we seal the bargain with our first small kiss now?"

Beth raised her face to his, and their lips met for a brief moment and separated.

"How do you feel now?" Beth asked

"In love, and I know it's for the rest of my life."

"Let's dance," Beth suggested. "We'll get to hold each other without breaking our rules." As they danced, Beth said, "Look at me straight in the eye."

"That's no problem. You have my adoring, undivided attention."

"What do you see?"

"I see the most beautiful blue eyes, the sweetest expression, and a cute little nose that fans the fire each time you wrinkle it at me."

"That's our secret. Any time I do that when you're looking at me, wherever we are, it means 'I love you.'"

"There's one little thing that ought to be cleared up: I've been told you're the dean's daughter. You told me to ask for Beth when I came to pick you up for the dance. I was certain this would be a one-time event, so the last name was unimportant. It is now. So, Beth who?"

Beth wrinkled her nose at him.

"I'm Elizabeth Anne Thomas, much loved daughter of Dean Thomas of the College of Fine Arts. He and my mother will be a bit apprehensive of what has happened here tonight."

"I'm certain my parents will shake a little, too," said Mark.

48

One for the Road

The Thomas and the Berglund families soon adjusted to the fact of very young true love. The two participants explained their rules of extended courtship, which quieted the waters rapidly. When Beth came to visit that first summer vacation, she stayed a week. She wasn't a stranger after the first two minutes, when Mark brought her from the depot to the parsonage. It was total acceptance in a family where love was of unlimited quality and quantity. Beth instantly sensed the innate goodness of Matt as she came into his arms. It was the same with Maude, and she felt she had known Laura all her life by Mark's description of her.

Zeb soon appeared. Mark ran to him. They hugged and danced around the room, each exuberantly happy to see the other. Then he led Zeb over to where Beth stood.

"This is Beth,"

Zeb stood there.

"Look at you, look at you. Oh! You are beautiful."

Big tears rolled down his cheeks as he held out his hands. Beth came in close and wiped the tears with her fingers. She threw her arms around his neck and kissed him where a tear had been. Then she looked at him with her arms on his shoulders and smiled.

"Mark said I'd fall in love with you."

Music was Beth's major, the piano her forte. A tidal wave couldn't have kept them away from the well-tuned keyboard. Zeb sat in raptured appreciation as Beth brought the piano to life, and Beth knew she was listening to the best as Zeb brought his bow across the strings. They played separately and together. To Zeb, the touch and rendition were like Jessica's, his slave sweetheart whom Sam Jackson raised along with himself and allowed her to get the teaching and time to excel at the piano. No one in the room knew why tears rolled copiously down his cheeks. Jessica had been raped and murdered the day before they were to be married. The result was a feeling of incarnation as Beth's playing would have pleased Bach, Beethoven, and others with the same artistic excellence as Jessica. Mark informed Beth that Zeb had no peers. She listened to his total mastery of his violin, and wondered how so much love and talent could be in one person. As they finished, Beth and Zeb bowed and curtsied to each other as the limited audience applauded, and Maude listened, enrapt by excellence on the piano, not unlike her own.

Mark earned his bachelor of arts degree in three years, magna cum laude. He left a string of records in swimming, discus, wrestling, and javelin, along with the highest grade point average of college record, and it was time for Mark to decide the course of his future. Ross Tyler, whom young Sam Jackson had lured from his gang of cutthroats to become a part of the Berglund family with Maude as the one he loved with deep affection, was available to help when it was certain that the poor and the hopeless were getting the short end of the stick in courts of law. He was drawn to Ross as the answer to his inquiring mind, and Ross was equally enthusiastic with the possibility of a partnership. Money would be no problem because Mark's portfolio had increased beyond limitations. So it was law school and a degree of excellence, unsurpassed.

When Mark and Beth were twenty, they were married with the assurance by their families that they had waited long enough. Mark told his dad that they remained celibate. "It didn't lessen our love for each other."

The years sped by. Mark and Beth were caught up in the demands of their vocations. Beth was often a soloist in the Philharmonic and other orchestras of similar excellence. Mark and Ross detected a paid juror and exposed him and the criminal tactic of lawyers who, in turn, were jailed and discredited. Threats were unveiled by the same methods, by using the bribe to expose the bribed thugs.

A new problem arose. Mark and Beth had been so busy those first years, that they hadn't wondered seriously why no baby had arrived. Mark was almost twenty-eight. World War One came and Mark joined before he was drafted. Each knew there was a possibility that Mark could be a casualty. The last night they were together, Mark kissed Beth's tearful face. "Let's have one for the road."

Mark often wrote to Beth who lived with the Berglunds and shared the news. He was shot down twice, once parachuting to safety in friendly territory and, the other time, bringing his shattered Spad close to the earth, ejecting just before it exploded. Although he had received a bullet in the fleshy part of his left arm, he was up in the air again the next day, lightly bandaged. He and his squadron were cited for their bombing and strafing missions.

The Rehabilitation crew now consisted of Maude, Matt, and Zeb.

Their present church was in a blighted suburban area that had lost its energy because of the community outflow of its members to more prestigious and flourishing areas. Nevertheless, their formula of revitalization had worked without failure wherever they had gone. Beth stayed with Matt and Maude and was sought as a soloist often, but she began to show signs of pregnancy. She hadn't written about it to Mark. Maybe it was wrong to withhold the news, and she also asked the others to keep the secret. She had informed Mark of their present church and home with detailed instructions about its location.

They had been at this church six months when the war ended. About a month later a small two-winged plane flew over the parsonage, buzzed it, then circled upward and performed a series of loops and rolls. Beth came out of the house with a baby in her arms and waved a towel at the acrobatic plane. She was laughing and crying. The plane moved out beyond the suburbs and began to descend. Matt came running. He cranked the Model T, waved for Beth to get in, and started off in the direction of the descending plane. The street soon became a rural road. There in the center of a large pasture was the plane. Matt picked up Beth and the baby, lifted them over the fence, and watched Mark running full speed toward them. He bawled. It was he and Star going to their rendezvous, only this time, it was going to be Mark and Beth. Matt saw them come together, laughing and crying at the same time. To watch them seemed almost sacrilegious in this holiest of reunions.

They soon started toward Matt. Mark was carrying his son, John, and stopped every few seconds to kiss Beth. When they approached the fence, Mark hurtled over it into his dad's arms. As they looked at each other, there seemed to be no generation gap. Their similarity was more like twins than father and son.

Later, when Mark and Beth talked and tucked young John in his cradle, Mark wondered why there had been no mention of a middle name. Beth loosened Mark's necktie.

"I'm certain he's our 'one for the road' baby. I'm tossing the ball to you." Mark kissed Beth. "Lets make it John O. Berglund for J.O.B. The O. will be the beginning of 'One for the road.' It will be our secret. He'll probably get the nickname, 'Job.' It's still biblical."

Matt was in his study working on a sermon, when Mark knocked and entered.

"Dad, can we talk?" Mark pushed a chair close to where he sat.

"As long as you care to, son."

"You and Mom have never stated in strong terms the way I should think about religion, and I never felt forced to believe what was so evident and sincere in our home atmosphere. It has been a pleasure to

224

learn how to make money grow, but I guess I'm like Zeb and you. That isn't enough. I've seen a lot of death and dying, and in my squadron I was more like a chaplain than a commander. I've prayed for so many beautiful young lives before we went on our missions, and I've cried when they didn't come back. I've also been with some of them as they died with their hand in mine. I couldn't have endured it if I hadn't felt that God had something that was more fulfilling and lasting than what we have here."

Matt just listened. He saw the sensitivity and pain reenacted in the retelling and reliving the ordeal of death.

"I've talked to Beth," Mark went on. "I'm going to start seminary this next semester, which begins three weeks from now. Zeb has ballooned my investments during my time away, and now I'll continue to build them. You and I know change comes faster and with a more solid foundation in renewal if there is a return to a sense of self-worth by seeing evidences of rehabilitation in one's community. I will keep in touch with Ross, my friend and law partner. There will be injustice in that area, wherever we are. War has this one merit, you do what you have to do to get it done; that's what you and Zeb do. You don't wait for dribbles of aid from outside; you spend of your own to make change happen. I'll continue to build my finances for that same purpose. Laura, Beth, and I can be another Rehabilitation branch using the same approach. Maybe we could borrow Zeb once in a while if we need help."

Matt got up from his chair as Mark arose, and they hugged.

"Go to it, son," Matt said, "God gave your mom and me more than we could have been allowed to hope for in our son and daughter."

49

The Circle

This was the first time Matt, Maude, and Zeb hadn't taken the train back to Thorson's Bay. As Zeb bounced around in the rear seat of the Model T Ford, he wasn't certain it had been the right decision. The road varied from gravel to the fertile soils of the region. They had sloughed through miles of mud, which, when dry, would retain the zigzag ruts that made driving tricky and rough. On the intermittent graveled stretches, Matt drove faster, taking advantage of the downhill inclines to gain enough speed to help get up the inevitable next hill.

Zeb had finally decided his backseat worrying was useless and began to enjoy the rural scenes, with the croplands, cattle, barns, sheep, and horses. The farm houses were often quite large, showing the intentions for large families. Most barn lots had chickens by the hundreds, and some places, brood sows and their little pigs dotted the hog lots. Although he found all of this interesting, Zeb's mind was busy assessing what had transpired since their last visit to Thorson's Bay.

Four years ago, he and Hugh Summers had gone south to supervise the construction of an all-purpose building on the Sam Jackson plantation. It was located in an area where many sharecroppers, the "poor white trash," had been trying desperately to eke out an existence. Their homes were now renewed and refurbished. Their fields were fertilized into productive farmland. The hopelessness of malnutrition and poverty no longer existed, creating a thankful and contented people. Since Sam and Katie had been part of the scene for two years, much had already been accomplished in the schooling of the children and the adults who yearned to learn. Sam and Katie had discovered several adults who possessed skills and schooling, and they drafted them to teach the others. Hugh Summers didn't have to look far to find people who could hammer and saw.

The new structure was similar to those they had built in various other places, so it went up quickly. When it was nearly finished, those who lived on the plantation filled the large auditorium to hear Pastor Sam Jackson dedicate its purpose. The racial mixture seemed about equal. Sam's rapport with those present was obvious, judging by the boisterous applause as he approached the lectern. He blew a kiss to them and waited until they simmered down.

"This is a happy time, but there would have been no joyful dedication without the man who sits among you today. Many of you know him as the man who changed your lives from a living hell to the paradise it is today. But the climate around us is one of hate, murder, and a determination to deny true citizenship to others of my race and to those who accept us. In some ways, this may be worse than the shackles of slavery because of the evil ingrained in the attitudes of white supremacy. Here, on this plantation, we accept each other as children of God. We have discovered that intelligence and the capacity to use our minds has nothing to do with color. Zeb, this is all because of you and your dreams. Will you stand and let your people give you a sample of their appreciation?"

There was total pandemonium in the ensuing cheering and clapping. Someone said, "Thank you, Zeb," and it became an outpouring from everyone.

Tears flowed freely in the emotional display of their appreciation. Zeb was getting kissed and hugged, and he was enjoying it.

Sam finally pounded his fist on the lectern for some order.

"We want to be ready when the cooks are ready. I don't want to keep them waiting, so I'll wind this up quickly. What has happened here must happen beyond the borders of our plantation. We are like the starter that makes a loaf of bread become a food to sustain us and please the palate. God wants this light of love and faith we have to grow and shine so brightly that it reaches beyond our perimeters. There may be martyrdom and persecution, but that has been the history of those who seek Christ's will. That is the challenge of Christ's call to each person here today, that we'll lead others to a better tomorrow. Let's give God our best."

Remembering that day, Zeb felt good about what had transpired. He felt that Sam was his Moses. The plantation was a Promised Land for those within its borders. Art Bennett, Zeb's federal agent friend, was keeping a watchful eye on the Klan's activities, and God had been watching, too. Amazingly, there had been no maiming, killing, or destruction perpetrated. Zeb wondered how long it would take to change the thought pattern of the people. Would it be one hundred years, or one hundred fifty years, or would it be the cancer that tore the country apart again?

Zeb thought back to the letter he had just received from Katie. She and Sam now had a baby girl, a sister for little Ben. They named her Jessica. Zeb felt that Sam, Katie, Ben, and Jessica were his family. Not that he loved them more than the others, but it seemed to him that God was saying, "You've passed your torch along to two who'll give their all for Me when you are no longer running your race."

When Mark graduated from seminary, the bishop knew that Mark wanted to be a part of the Hawkins-Berglund effort to recharge anemic churches. Matt, Maude, and Zeb spent the past three weeks with Mark and Beth in assessing and planning the right medicine for their sick congregation. Laura came home for a few days, too. She was engaged to a young pastor, whose name was Scot McNeal. Zeb felt certain that this duo would be pursuing a similar approach in their ministry.

Zeb's thoughts shifted to Star. Time could not erase her impact on the lives of so many. Thoughts came. Did she have to be eliminated to bring Maude back into the picture? Without her, the rehabilitation churches may never have been so successful. Star had inspired Jennifer, whom he had nicknamed Buzz Saw. It's trite to say, "To know Star was to love her deeply." Her death must have broken God's heart. Jennifer's mother had ended her life to give her daughter a life. Love was evident in her final decision. To judge isn't our given right. Mark and Beth's son, John O. Berglund, was age three years, six months. Beth was pregnant again.

The Model T Ford crested a hill after much grinding in low gear. It was a long downhill stretch that curved to the right about halfway down so that one couldn't see the bottom. The car picked up speed, and as it rounded the slight curve, a bridge at the bottom came into view. At the same time, Matt saw a truck filled with young people approaching the bridge from the other side. The bridge was narrow, so Matt pressed the brake pedal to slow down to let the truck get across first. The brake suddenly lost its effectiveness. The fiber band that pressed against the braking drum had worn away. The car now began to accelerate faster. Matt grabbed the hand brake lever and pulled it back. It made little difference as the car continued to pick up speed.

"Those children!" Matt knew there was nothing else to do; as he headed for the roadside ditch, Zeb leaped out of the rear seat to land and roll on the bank between the ditch and the pasture fence. The car flipped over, tossing Maude against the bank. It came to an abrupt stop upside down, with Matt trapped beneath and the front wheels still spinning.

Maude and Zeb, bruised but able to move, rushed to the car. Matt was unconscious, and a little blood trickled from the corner of his mouth. The steering wheel was crushed against his chest. Zeb reached down and lifted the car. Maude attempted to pull Matt out from under

228

it, but couldn't budge him. The truck had stopped and five teenage boys came running. Zeb motioned for the boys to hold the car up. They showed signs of strain, but they held it while Zeb carefully picked up Matt's three hundred pounds, as if it were nothing, and carried him to the truck.

"I know the farmer at the top of this hill. We'll take him there and phone a doctor," said the driver of the truck.

Matt lay on the floor of the truck breathing shallowly. The young people were sobbing in each other's arms. They knew that Matt had prevented total tragedy. When they arrived at the farmhouse, Mrs. Greene, the farmer's wife, opened up her bedroom for them while she called a doctor.

Everyone had gone. Zeb and Maude stood alone at the bedside watching as Matt's life seemed to be ebbing away. Maude held Matt's hand as tears poured down her cheeks. Zeb could not stop his tears either. The doctor was on his way. Suddenly Matt raised his head slightly. His eyes showed a joy and radiance as he seemed to look beyond those present.

"Star!" he called. His head fell back on the pillow. Then came the stillness, the finality of death. Maude still held Matt's hand.

"Matt and Star are together again," she said, "and that's the way it should be. Star gave him to me to have during his time on earth. She was my best friend and I know there is room for me in each of their hearts when I join them."

Zeb moved over to Maude and held her like a child. She stopped trying to be brave and sobbed her grief.

"How are we supposed to handle this?" Zeb said. "It's like losing all reasons for living."

The funeral was held at the Trading Post Church, which still retained that name after all these years. Mark had said that he wanted to preside at the service. As Mark approached the pulpit, there seemed to be an audible gasp coming from the pews. Many of the congregation hadn't seen Mark for several years. What they saw before them appeared to be a reincarnation. Mark's height, overall proportions, and features all resembled Matt's.

"It probably isn't necessary to tell you that I'm proud to be my dad's son. I know you loved him too, not only as a pastor, but also as a friend. He left us still serving our Lord at full throttle. We have lost a valiant warrior who has left a legacy of serving that will be hard to emulate. Shakespeare says it this way: 'All nature might stand up and say, here was a man.' We can certainly apply that to my dad. God is asking each of us to serve our Master more fully, just as he did. We who believe know that Dad's spirit, his love and concern, are with us as we remember him this day." Mark looked out and above the assembly.

"Dad, you taught me that love was more than a warm feeling inside. It is an active caring, a sharing of loads that others find too heavy. Your multitude of friends and those who are your immediate family love you. The churches that you have helped to give new birth love you for your constant and unflagging example of Christ's love in action, for all to see."

Mark looked around the sanctuary as though he were addressing each person individually. "There must be a special joy in heaven today. We shed tears, but let us share in this celebration of love, fully given with joy. Let us renew our vow to live each day, so we all can be a part of God's community of love, here and hereafter."

Matt's body was buried beside Star. Her grave was on his right. On his left was a marker for Maude.

Maude went to Zeb and put her arm in his.

"I want to visit my parents for a few days, but I don't intend to stop now, because Mark and Beth can learn from us. I'm sure that Matt is telling us to give life what we always have, our best."

Zeb hugged Maude.

"When you're ready, I'm ready."